THE RAFT OF THE MEDUSA

The Raft of the Medusa by Théodore Géricault, 1819, Musée du Louvre, Paris

THE RAFT OF THE MEDUSA

A Novel

Robert M. Hertzberg

Copyright © 2002 by Howard R. Turner.

Cover/Jacket/Frontispiece illustration: *The Raft of the Medusa* by Théodore Géricault, Musée du Louvre, Paris, France; photo ©Erich Lessing/ Art Resource, NY

Library of Congress Number: 2002093919
ISBN: Hardcover   1-4010-7110-4
             Softcover   1-4010-7109-0

Back cover/jacket photo of author by Eleanor Sims

All rights reserved. No part of this book may be reproduced or transmitted in any form or by any means, electronic or mechanical, including photocopying, recording, or by any information storage and retrieval system, without permission in writing from the copyright owner.

This is a work of fiction. Names, characters, places and incidents either are the product of the author's imagination or are used fictitiously, and any resemblance to any actual persons, living or dead, events, or locales is entirely coincidental.

This book was printed in the United States of America.

To order additional copies of this book, contact:
Xlibris Corporation
1-888-795-4274
www.Xlibris.com
Orders@Xlibris.com

16209

"Personal causes," said Carl Jung, "have as much or as little to do with a work of art as the soil with the plant that springs from it." Emphasis on *as much*. Equal emphasis on *as little*.

And "How," asks Julian Barnes, "do you turn catastrophe into art?"

CONTENTS

FOREWORD 9
ACKNOWLEDGMENTS 13
AUTHOR'S NOTE 15
PROLOGUE: SUBJECT MATTER 17

1. ROUEN 43

2. PARIS AND MORTAIN—TWO UNCLES 52

3. VERNET AND GUÉRIN 68

4. CHASSEUR 122

5. CUIRASSIER 140

6. ONE HUNDRED DAYS 162

7. RUE DES MARTYRS 181

8. LA COURSE DE CHEVAUX LIBRES 201

9. FAITS DIVERS 217

10. CORRÉARD AND SAVIGNY:
    A VOYAGE TO SENEGAL 237

11. SCÈNE DE NAUFRAGE 276

Editor's AFTERWORD 301
BIBLIOGRAPHY 305

FOREWORD

Robert M. Hertzberg was born in New York City on October 22, 1922. He lived with his parents and his sister, attending Ethical Culture schools in Manhattan and Riverdale, the Bronx. He graduated from Olivet College in Michigan in 1943. Serving in the 104th Infantry Division during the Battle of the Bulge in World War II, he was awarded the Bronze Star for meritorious service. At the end of the war he worked as a film writer and editorial assistant for Twentieth Century-Fox Films and subsequently became a free-lance writer and coordinating producer of documentary, non-theatrical, and informational films, as well as special television programs, for a wide range of corporate sponsors and educational institutions.

Midway in his career he began focusing on writing fiction, finishing his first full-size novel in 1987, dealing with the trials and tribulations of a group of film-makers working feverishly to finish a film. His next novel told of the exploits, and the rise and fall, of the mythical inventor Daedalus, most famous for the wings that did not quite land Icarus on the sun. This work, finished about 1991, was written in a modern-age style, light-hearted and ironic.

His third novel probably took root in his imagination before 1990, and by 1992 it had occupied much of his thinking and study. Perhaps the best guide to this enterprise is revealed by excerpts drawn from his letters to close friends, dating from 1991 to 1997:

" . . . something that really excites me, Gericault and the painting of "The Raft of the Medusa . . . but to master the period and the Paris salon wars of the time (one must grasp David and Delacroix and Ingres and Gros as well), and the newspaper and court records of the Medusa scandal, (and my French is rather childish) . . . I don't know, I don't know . . . one can't play fast and loose with this period as one could with prehistoric myth . . . still, a large and exciting subject, the story of the shipwreck and the raft—genuine terror and 'extremity' . . . and the picture itself . . . the beginning of romantic painting, or modern painting."

He was also intrigued by the painter's turbulent, "Byronic" life: " . . . an affair with his aunt, illegitimate child, drinking and drugs, and falling off horses. And he was concerned about "finding a voice, a tone, an entrée . . . I have in mind a full length—well, not really a novel, but meta-fiction or quasi-fiction of some such pretentious term, lacking a better one . . . . "

"I am pretty much obsessed with, I circle around and around, the raft itself, and in fact the power of that picture to become obsessive may ('may,' understand) give me a contemporary (here and now) point of view to use as a frame." He had, of course, to study the painting itself in the Louvre. So, in October 1992, having announced himself as "absolutely into Géricault," he went to Paris to stand in front of the picture. Back home, he summed up his feelings: "Oh, yes, I'm hooked, and more certain than ever. The painting itself . . . the story of the shipwreck . . . Géricault's story . . . Oh my, yes."

There followed nearly seven years of research, more research, and his slow but sure method of writing, with constant revisions, interrupted by occasionally lengthy hang-ups which had to be unhooked. All his favorite interests and resources were brought into play: literary, art, social and political history—everything that shaped France and was shaped by France in return.

He took an occasional breather; in the autumn of 1999 he traveled to Florence and absorbed that community the way he had absorbed Géricault's painting. At that point he was about two-thirds through what he had planned for the book. He proceeded into the New Year—and then increasing illness (diabetes and emphysema) began to slow him down. In late April 2000, he was hospitalized, discharged after a couple of weeks, then readmitted when breathing became too difficult. Some time in late May he asked for his notebooks and tried to continue with his manuscript. His ebbing energy no longer enabled him to persevere. Pneumonia and increasing congestive heart failure took over. He died on June 10, 2000.

Two individuals have read Bob Hertzberg's manuscript of "The Raft of The Medusa." One of them, the author's agent Claudia Menza, feels that the work is of rare quality. The second individual is myself, the writer of this Foreword and the Afterword that follows the main text and comments on what the author's notes indicate he planned as the concluding sections of the book. Ms. Menza's opinion of the work confirms and strengthens what I came to feel after readings of the text. We both feel that what already exists is worth publishing as it stands.

A final note here about myself. Not long after the author and I met in 1947 in the course of our film work and got to know each other, we began to live together, and we remained together in devoted companionship that lasted until his death. I thus had the opportunity to observe the making of this book, from the trips to Paris that we made together to the many times when he would ask me to comment on this paragraph, that point, or another aspect of the work. Any use I might have been in these cases was perhaps due to my being more of a 'general reader' than a specially literary individual. Art history and creation we both were familiar with—but he was uniquely able to digest and profit from the exploration of art analysis and criticism, let alone his novelist's eye for character and plot. In sum, he has in the pages here, I feel, brought to life a creation, and its creator, within a dramatically alive and absorbing context of human affairs. And he has, in a vivid manner that is new at least to me, provided a new approach to revealing an individual genius of the past as if he could in many ways be living in our presence.

Howard R. Turner
Cambridge, MA
July 1, 2002

ACKNOWLEDGMENTS

No one has found any record of the author's intention as to dedication of this work. It is, however, appropriate for me, his legatee, to express special gratitude to two individuals: Sybille Bedford, OBE, and Claudia Menza; their devoted friendship and consideration extended generously to the author over many years not only helped him develop the manuscript as far and as fully as he did but also fortified my own decision to see it turned into a book that could be offered with confidence to the public.

H.R.T.

The italicized paragraphs in Chapter 10 consist of excerpts from the 1986 Marlboro Press edition of *Narrative of a Voyage to Senegal* by J.-B. Henry Savigny and Alexander Corréard, a report written in French, translated into English, and published in Paris and London between 1816 and 1818.

AUTHOR'S NOTE

"Fiction," André Gide suggested, "is history that *might* have taken place, and history is fiction that *has* taken place."

"The Raft of the Medusa" is a work of fiction based on the life of Théodore Gericault, the 19th Century French painter, and on the events surrounding one of the most scandalous naval disasters in French history. It is a novel, it is not history or biography, though I have made extensive use of historical and biographical sources; for these people did exist, quite a bit is known about their actual circumstances, the paintings were in fact painted (though their chronology is sometimes in doubt), and the survivors of the Medusa remembered and recorded the disaster as I have reported it. As a rule, then, I have remained faithful to the record, to the circumstantial facts in so far as they are known—but I have taken the novelist's liberty to interpret those facts, to provide motives and imagine states of mind, to inhabit the historical characters and think their thoughts; I have conflated certain less crucial characters and events or omitted them entirely; I have shifted certain locales and made minor alterations in chronology for narrative purposes; I have embroidered my own conjectural version of what is simply not known and speculated on alternate versions where the existing evidence is contradictory or ambiguous.

In light of all that, how close can this story be to 'the truth,' to 'how it really happened?' I can only say that, while I have taken liberties, I have not, in matters of substance, strayed from the realm of possibility. I have invented but I have not, to my knowledge, invented anything that might not plausibly have been the case. Where there are gaps and uncertainties in the evidence, a restrained leap of the imagination—fiction with scruples—may take us as close to 'the truth' as we can hope to come.

* * *

PROLOGUE: SUBJECT MATTER

PARIS, 1818: FAUBOURG DU ROULE

The scene is excessive, really, too full of the easy macabre that we associate with Romanticism. Picture this: two survivors of a shipwreck (who are known to have practiced cannibalism) are posing for an artist (who is seething with grief and anxiety) in a studio reeking of rotting human flesh. Altogether too much. Nevertheless, events had conspired; this happened.

Young Jamar, the painter's pupil and assistant, had done what he could to make the studio presentable. He had taken the severed head—a thief from the Bicêtre prison—up to the roof, wrapping it first in a wet cloth, and he had been glad to find that the day was cool and gray, the Lord only knew how they would manage when the weather turned warm.

With another wet cloth he had covered the limbs—two legs, an arm and shoulder, gifts from the medical students at Beaujon—but he was forbidden to move them, they had been carefully arranged for a still life. *Nature morte*! he thought, but without a smile now, it was no longer a joke, Monsieur Théodore's mania for research, for detail, for close observation. Jamar had never imagined that life in this studio would be the life of your ordinary student, he had understood from the start that he might be nothing more than Gericault's studio rat, but he had never bargained for the life of an abattoir attendant. And did Monsieur Théodore know that people went about saying *ce fou de*

Gericault—that madman? And did Monsieur care? It was painful. Jamar couldn't bear to see Gericault mocked. And these visitors they were expecting now, these gentlemen in whose honor he had removed the decomposing head . . . two more fellows to widen their eyes and exchange disturbed glances?

For they will certainly be disturbed, Jamar thought, hearing their step on the landing, their rattle at the door. And here are our cannibals now, he almost said. Oh yes, they will certainly be disturbed.

And so they were, so they had been from the moment the old porter had wrinkled her nose and said, Ce fou . . . yes, top of the stairs, you'll sniff it out.

Dr. Savigny recognized the odor at once and froze mid-step on the stairway. If I'm not mistaken . . . he said. M. Corréard turned and searched Savigny's face.

Auguste Brunet, who had brought them here, who had introduced them to Gericault to begin with, knew that he should have warned them in advance. Now he mumbled an explanation: From the hospital, you know . . . the anatomy theater . . . Gericault says that it puts him into the scene, you know . . . puts it into his head . . .

This smell? asked Corréard. He wants the smell of death? We must tell him that on the open sea one hardly notices . . .

Allow me to remind you, said Savigny, that I have already expressed doubts about the wisdom of this visit.

Corréard understood those doubts. At Brunet's urging, they had spent considerable time with Gericault, time enough to supply him with the details of their ordeal, to help him choose his scene, the moment he would portray, and Corréard's impression had not been entirely favorable. A fine painter, perhaps—there he had to agree with Brunet, he admired the man's charging Chasseur, his wounded Cuirassier—but he was a gentleman painter after all, one might almost say an amateur, and something of a dandy, altogether too fashionable for Corréard's taste. Still, one couldn't doubt the fellow's indignation at the story of their suffering. The painting would be seen at next year's Salon, Brunet had assured them of that. And how many others had come forward to support them in their struggle for justice?

I understand your reservations, Corréard said at last, but I cannot agree. He saw this as an opportunity that must be grasped. They would accustom themselves to the unpleasantness.

Yes, one does, said Brunet, one does. So, fumbling for their handkerchiefs, they went on up. Corréard generally got his way.

And they did in fact become accustomed to the odor, Brunet had been right, one did. The table-top arrangement of butchered limbs was another matter. They were covered, to be sure, but not really concealed. The wet cloth clung to the contours of the elbow, the fingers, the toes, forming a grotesque mass of implication that imposed its presence, drawing one's eye constantly against one's will. The eye, Dr. Savigny noted, is less easily inured to unpleasantness than the nose. Those limbs were an offense to the eye—and there was much else in that studio to keep doubt alive.

To begin with, Gericault seemed vague and distracted, almost as if he had forgotten that they were coming around. When they had arrived he was examining a small drawing tacked to the wall and seemed reluctant to tear himself away; they had stood there shuffling their feet for a long moment before he finally turned and told the gentlemen that it was kind of them to come. And over his shoulder they could see the subject of the drawing quite clearly: the severed head, sketched in four different views with a fine, precise line. So despite Jamar's efforts, the thief from Bicêtre made his presence felt after all.

Gericault had been clean-shaven and soigné when they had last met, but now he seemed to be attempting a beard—no more than a reddish fringe as yet, but distinctly untidy. As if to balance things out, he had cut off his hair—those golden curls with just a hint of red that caused such a stir among the ladies at the opera, not to mention the ladies in the arcades of the Palais Royal. He had let it be known that he would not be seen in public until this new work of his was finished—and then he'd had himself shorn. To hide the damage, he had knotted a scarf about his head, making his long face seem even longer, heightening the oriental effect of his almond eyes and the almost feminine fullness of his lips, and over the scarf he wore a little tasselled Greek fisherman's cap—an unpleasant sham, thought Corréard, affecting the dress of common folk; and besides, the fellow had certainly been seen in public, seen in the streets, wearing this outlandish masquerade.

Then there was the Turkish servant, Mustapha, who had appeared suddenly from the inner room in his turban and gown, silently passing a tray of Turkish Delight somewhat before they'd had time to get used to the general odor. Brunet and Jamar had each taken one of the sugared pastilles, and Mustapha had disappeared as suddenly as he had appeared. And à la Turque is à la mode just now, thought Corréard. More masquerade. More affectation.

More seriously offensive was the raft—or rather, the little wooden model that the ship's carpenter, Lavilette—another survivor—had made for Gericault. On this miniature raft—this replica of the stage on which their drama had been played—the artist had placed little wax figures, modeled on wire armatures, arranged in various attitudes of distress—and Corréard now counted the figures. We were only fifteen, he said, when he had arrived at a count of eighteen. At the end we were only fifteen.

Oh, the number, Gericault replied, still seeming preoccupied—he was fussing with the drawing materials that Jamar had laid out—I daresay the number will change, he said. The final composition might require more figures . . .

But how can the number change? Corréard wanted to know, looking to Brunet for support. Am I mistaken, Monsieur Brunet? If it is to be the final day, it must be fifteen.

Brunet knew what these fellows wanted, a graphic indictment of the Ministry of the Navy based on a factually accurate report (for they were certain that the facts favored their case), a pamphlet really. He knew also that Gericault had his own purposes and would give them nothing of the sort. Perhaps some of them are dead, he suggested weakly. The artist takes this liberty, you see, to show that there were many who died.

Yes, of course, Gericault agreed, eager to bring this to an end. Of course. Several of them have died.

But not on the final day, Dr. Savigny insisted.

Brunet tried to draw their attention to the other end of the studio. The very size of the canvas, he suggested, made certain demands.

Ah, the canvas! A great white expanse, nearly twenty four feet wide and sixteen high, newly stretched and glowing with possibility. It will be a monumental work, said Brunet.

It is certainly very large, said Corréard, and looked again at the little raft. This figure in the middle, he asked, the one with his arm extended . . . ?

Yourself, said Gericault. Yourself, drawing Dr. Savigny's attention to the horizon.

The two men raised their heads and stared intently at the great white canvas.

They see themselves in the middle, thought Jamar. They see themselves at the center of the scene. Their self-regard is beyond anything. And to what great cause had their suffering been dedicated? Like any animal, they had fought to survive. Anyone, he thought, might have done what they did to stay alive—but to see themselves as heroes . . . petitions to be forwarded in their favor . . . coveting the Legion of Honor, as if that could be awarded to cannibals!

Shall we begin? Gericault asked at last, one might almost have thought reluctantly. That particular pose, he said, Monsieur Corréard pointing toward the horizon . . . that is exactly what I wanted this afternoon. And then, if we have time, portrait sketches of you both . . .

Brunet was relieved. He had known Gericault for ages—known him since their days together at the Lycée Impérial—and he knew that, behind the impassive face, the rather forced smile, the man was in turmoil. In a few months Madame Caruel would bear Gericault's child. The Caruel family would keep them apart, of course, there was no question of their ever meeting again, and the child would be taken away, Brunet himself had been asked to make the arrangements. The man was certainly in turmoil—in Gericault, this cool, somewhat distant manner was a sure sign that he was struggling to contain himself—but the moment he took up his chalk, Brunet knew, he would be emptied, the turmoil would drain away, it would flow into the swift, sure line—*fil de fer*, Gericault called it, wire of iron. Yes indeed, thought Brunet, it is time to begin.

There they are, then, in that abattoir of a studio, the survivors and the artist, setting out on a work that would one day be said (with a grain of truth) to lie at the threshold of modern art. (Over the years many things would be said and most of them, in one sense or another, would contain a grain of truth: that the artist himself was 'a true harbinger of the modern spirit;' that he was the first of the Romantic masters; that no, his work heralded Realism instead—or perhaps both; that in fact he was a Romantic Realist; that, on the contrary, he had revised and extended Neoclassicism; that in any case he had put all France on that raft, the whole society.)

For the moment, in the studio, it is only Corréard who imagines himself on that raft, assuming a dramatic stance and pointing toward an imaginary horizon. With one swift stroke of his chalk, Gericault traces the line of Corréard's shoulder, and all at once he is in command.

Perhaps this is the way after all, Dr. Savigny thinks. The size of the thing! And fifteen . . . eighteen . . . did that really matter? This painting would be seen, it would speak louder than the words they had already written, it would show their suffering and their wounds, it would be their testimony.

But will we lose our story? Corréard wonders. Is he stealing our suffering, this dandy who seeks out dismembered bits for his 'art?' Can our suffering, our extremity, become this fellows art? Is that right? he wonders—but he holds his pose.

That's right, thinks Jamar, the turn of the collar, the fold in the sleeve . . . everything goes like lightning from his eye to his hand. He'll feel better tonight. We'll have a good dinner.

Gericault thinks nothing at all. Drawing obliterates the world, the chaos, that crowds in on him. He draws.

Much later, when the painting itself is finished, Corréard and Savigny will publish a description: "The principal group is composed of M. Savigny at the foot of the mast, and M. Corréard . . . " Failing to see that they have become supernumeraries in the scene, they will miss the point entirely.

PARIS, 1992: MUSÉE DU LOUVRE

And there they are, bang in the center of the picture but not the least bit central.

Central! The thing is so enormous that I must step back and back and back to find the center, and then the vagaries of gallery lighting defeat me, throwing a patch of light here, a patch of light there, glaring out entire sections.

How to see it whole, then? It happens that I have in my pocket a postcard of the painting from a friend who has doubts about this project of mine. Stay away from this picture, he writes, having sent it to me in the mail. It is dangerous, he says, people have been known to faint at the sight of it.

Yes, but that fainting was only in someone's novel. So too is my postcard, of course, but it is still very useful in front of the great work—a palm-sized map to guide one through the immense terrain, a view from a distance that reveals an intricately structured and coherent scene, not just a collection of striking Prominent Features.

A gallery-goer who, unlike myself, has been standing up close to the picture examining the Prominent Features, turns to her companion and says, Something terrible has happened here!

Indeed, the painting is suffused with suffering and terror, with that sense of awfulness and dread that the Italians call *terribilità*. It has been compared to a Last Judgment—man abandoned by God (the artist had looked long at Last Judgments by Rubens and Michelangelo)—but there is more than terrible despair here, there is also terrible hope. To see that, to see it whole, you will have to deal with the painting's sheer size and overcome the obstacle of bad lighting. You will need something like my postcard as an aid, but that may not be the only way, perhaps you can invent a better strategy. And having done that, what will you see?

Adrift amid turbulent waves, a makeshift raft much smaller than the actual one that the crew of the frigate Medusa cobbled together from the ship's masts and beams. That enormous raft—roughly sixty five feet long, twenty eight feet wide—had been put to sea carrying one hundred and fifty souls. Gericault's raft barely manages to hold the survivors of the thirteen day ordeal that ensued. There are twenty figures in all, but one of them is certainly dead and four of them almost certainly, no one would hesitate to count them as corpses. Of the living, two figures have been obscured as the painting has aged and darkened; some people miss them in their count, but a close examination will confirm their presence—so the survivors round out to Corréard's fifteen after all.

Allow your eye to enter the picture from the bottom and it confronts death immediately. A frieze of enormous livid corpses fills the foreground; four corpses watched over by a shadowy, impassive figure—no visible emotion—and a grief-stricken old man. One of the naked bodies lies across the old man's knee and these two have always been thought of (with no evidence) as father and son. The 'father' is the only figure in the picture who faces us directly, he turns his back on the pyramid of human distress that rises behind him—half-dead men struggling to lift their heads, to lift their bodies, clinging to each other to raise themselves up, some of them on their knees already, their arms flung out toward the horizon. The strong diagonal surge of their bodies pulls your eye up and across the entire canvas from the grieving old man to the apex of the pyramid—a black sailor struggling to keep his footing atop a barrel as he waves a cloth toward the horizon, signaling to a distant ship. Standing nearby, M. Corréard draws Dr. Savigny's attention to the ship on the horizon. It is a *very* distant ship—no more than a speck against the sky. From the ship, of course, this raft that fills your eyes would be less than a speck. The chance of a sighting seems very slight indeed—but there is hope.

Enter the picture from the top and that hope is the thing you encounter first, but the diagonal surge that pulled your eye up to the signaling sailor will now tug it down with equal force to the despairing elder among the corpses—all hope gone. Enter at the point of the raft's billowing sail—despite everything, we control the forces of nature!—and your eye will be drawn immediately to an enormous approaching wave behind it, or dragged down in the other direction to a cadaver half-submerged in the sea.

And there you have it. At least, there you have the 'subject'—not just the scene itself, but the meaning of the scene.

Subject and meaning, then; content, significance, representation; all those vaguely discredited terms that some of us, in our modern wisdom, have learned to be wary of in a painting—we cannot ignore them here. We are even tempted into 'story,' we begin to imagine a possible 'before,' we shudder to think of the possible 'after.' The artist, however, is in control of his forces, he won't let us escape into the past or the future, into narrative. As he worked on the canvas, the ship on the horizon—the embodiment of possibility—grew smaller and smaller, it is finally all but invisible. The painting insists on the present moment, *this* moment, an absolute moment: these human beings frozen forever between hope and despair.

These human beings . . . hope and despair . . . this picture is clearly something more than a masterful arrangement of paint on canvas. Still, like any other painting, it is that too—an arrangement of paint. There is a dialogue, a tension, a back-and-forth between the paint as paint, as brushstroke, and the paint as description. The meaning is not conveyed to us by description alone, by the skillful mimicking of water, timber, ragged clothes, flesh—any competent painter could have done that. Nor is it conveyed solely as thought, through symbol or incident or pathetic gesture. It is deeply imbedded in the formal arrangement, in the paint strokes themselves; in the sweeping, intersecting diagonals that surge through the picture, the conflicting forces that drag your eye from hope to despair and back again with no resolution. The form and the subject are finally inseparable, they are one and the same. You don't grasp this picture with your mind alone, deciphering the anecdote, understanding the event. You feel it physically. You enter into it.

The gallery-goer who had exclaimed, Something terrible has happened here! seems now to be trying literally to enter the picture. She pokes her head forward, as close as the barrier will allow, then she fumbles in her bag and pulls out a large round Sherlock Holmes magnifying glass! And now I understand: she hadn't been exclaiming about the naval calamity and its consequences, she had meant the calamity that has been visited on the painting itself. To achieve the deep, glossy black that he wanted for his shadows, Gericault had used pigment loaded with bitumen—a common trick at the time and a disastrous one. Bituminous pigment is chemically unstable, it never really dries. Over the years the surface of the painting has never been completely at rest. Expanding and contracting, it has become cracked and pimpled and pocked (the French call it 'peau de crapaud'—toad skin); the deeply shadowed areas have become doubly obscure; the painting is, in scattered patches, a slow, continuing wreck.

Something terrible! says the lady with the magnifying glass, stepping back at last and shivering a little and shaking her head. Has she finally torn her eye from the chemical corruption and been overwhelmed by the *terribilità*? Has she begun to tremble now at *that*?

But I am speaking for myself, of course, the painting overwhelms *me*; she or you or anyone may be less susceptible. Perhaps my postcard friend is right, perhaps I have become obsessed with this thing. Standing in front of it now, having planned and postponed this visit for so long, I do indeed half expect to find myself trembling. Time to turn away then (no one in *my* novel is going to faint in a picture gallery). Because a prologue should tell us what has gone before and what we will need to know, it is time to see what else these galleries have to offer.

* * *

There is nothing like the arrangement of pictures in a museum for making the past seem neat and orderly, for creating the illusion of logical progression from one thing to another. If we are presented with too much disjunction and contradiction, too much blurring and overlapping and looping back, if we are shown an imprecise world in which things may happen simultaneously or out of order—if, in short, we are shown the real world unmediated—we call it a jumble. We come here to discover 'schools' and 'periods,' influences and reactions, affinities and contrasts, movements and counter-movements and breakthroughs. Perhaps we know that it can never be as simple as that, but we still insist on making connections, we insist on making sense out of things, putting them in order and giving them shape. Distortion may be inevitable but, alas, we seem to have no choice. If we can't give a shape to things, how are we to see them?

What, then, is the shape—oversimplified, perhaps, but nevertheless a shape—that emerges in these badly lit rooms? It is 'Before and After,' with Gericault's great painting as the centerpiece, the hinge that joins the past and future.

The past, in this case, is the legacy of the eighteenth century, the Enlightenment and the French Revolution: the imagined triumph of logic and reason; a belief in the universe as a well-regulated machine and the dubious assurance of man's dominion over nature through a rational understanding of its laws; a belief in man's natural goodness and perfectibility, coupled with the belief that in the classical world of Greece and Rome one could find the model for all moral and physical and artistic perfection.

That legacy is embodied in the smooth, cool, porcelain-like surfaces of the classical scenes painted by Jacques-Louis David—that fierce Jacobin who had supported Robespierre to the very end, and then recanted. David held his beliefs passionately, while he held them, but he wanted 'neither movement nor passionate expression' in these paintings, nor was the artist's hand to leave the slightest trace on the highly polished surfaces. There must be nothing to disturb the sedate grandeur of his antique scenes, nothing to mar the noble simplicity, nothing to distort the formal perfection, the ideal harmony that the artist sought beneath the face of nature. Not things as they are, you see, not nature as it presents itself, but nature flawless and idealized, the 'beau idéal.' Not ordinary men, but physically perfect men—men as they *ought* to be, men as they *might* be—engaged in noble actions for the edification and moral elevation of the public.

The Oath of the Horatii, Leonidas at Thermopylae, The Intervention of the Sabine Women—we all know these pictures, whether we know it or not, from illustrations in history books and dictionaries. Composed in the manner of a Greek frieze, the scenes are from classical myth or history, from an imagined Golden Age, and the stoical heroes of these paintings often displayed their perfection by going about their noble business wearing nothing but skimpy bits of drapery, their sword belts and their helmets. Because the helmets resemble those of French firemen, these fellows are often mocked as 'pompiers,' and yes, it is easy, too easy, to make fun of these pictures. Except in the hands of a master, the style degenerates rapidly into the ludicrous and the academic. Still, it was the style of a revolutionary generation, and David *was* a master; the paintings are very beautiful. Beautiful but not welcoming ('paint the way the Spartans spoke' was David's motto). They keep us at a distance. We see them as if through a glass barrier.

Gericault shattered that barrier—one is tempted to say single-handed and in one blow. That isn't true of course (it never is), many forces had been at work, but Gericault's 'Raft' is what the young painters would remember. Eugene Delacroix—seven years Gericault's junior—would call this painting a 'sublime model.'

It's not that Gericault didn't admire David and his procedures. He had no quarrel with the Classical method and took from it what he could use—the careful anatomical study, the statuesque grouping of figures. But for those who had reduced that method to a formula, his painting of the raft was full of heresies. To begin with, there were no idealized classical heroes here, serene and brave, doing famous deeds and dominating their world. These were ordinary modern men trapped in a contemporary disaster— the makings of a sordid political scandal that everyone had read about in the papers. Far from dominating their world heroically, these men were helpless, they were at the mercy of nature's forces and they were racked with passionate and violent emotions. What is more, those emotions weren't conveyed discreetly through formal gestures and allegorical cues, they weren't restrained beneath a static and ordered surface; they were presented directly in their full force, they were imposed on the viewer through visual shock and a turbulent canvas.

Here was another way, then. The Classical style, the 'School' under David, was moribund, it had become cramped and airless, but a door had been opened, a path had been indicated that would lead eventually from the classic ideal to modern reality, from stoic restraint to emotional extremes, from precepts and conventions to spontaneity and natural feeling, from public declamation to private sensibility and self-expression. Before long the painters would be calling themselves Romantics.

Delacroix, who we think of as the great Romantic painter, disavowed the term. But Delacroix had begun his career just as David was ending his, and look—he is hanging here next to Gericault—look at the vivid color streaming through his paintings, the surging movement, the tempestuous drama, the swirling brushstrokes that sometimes threaten to *become* the picture. Indeed, something had fallen like a boulder into the stream of French painting and altered its course. Delacroix put it differently: Gericault, he said, 'had opened infinite horizons . . .'

* * *

And that is enough Art History. Here comes a giggle of schoolchildren with a befuddled teacher.

She doesn't have to tell them to stop in front of this picture. Like everyone else, they stop. Even the giggling stops—but then it bubbles up again, for one of the painted corpses displays his sex quite openly, and children know the truth: it is always, more or less, a comical sight.

A rescue at sea, says the teacher, trying to ignore the barely suppressed mirth. A very famous rescue, she says. A *glorious* rescue.

The children crane their necks, looking for a rescue. One of the brasher little boys raises his hand and is recognized. Who, he asks, did they rescue?

They were rescued, Pierre. By the French navy. A glorious rescue.

For the glory of France? Well, nothing can be done about it, the painting has been co-opted from the very start. It has been a banner for the Romantics, then a banner for the Realists. It has been a political poster for revolutionaries, a social document for historians, and when there is a French cabinet crisis the political cartoonists always manage to put the whole cabinet on that raft. Most recently, it has become a metaphor for AIDS. When a painting becomes an icon, you see, the iconic image slips its moorings, escapes from the painting itself and begins to lead a (usually disreputable) life of its own. It becomes available, convertible to any use. Do you think that you can still see the Mona Lisa or the Last Supper as paintings?

* * *

In 1984 the French magazine Paris-Match ran a popularity poll to determine the public's favorite paintings at the Louvre. The Mona Lisa, of course, came in first. Gericault's 'Raft' came in ninth.

* * *

In 1823, bedridden and near death, Gericault himself dismissed the painting as 'a vignette.' If only I had painted five pictures! he moaned, but I have done nothing . . . absolutely nothing!

Jamar and Mustapha and the other friends who crowded around his bed all exclaimed, But surely the Raft! The Medusa!

Bah! he said. A vignette. He wanted great walls . . . buckets of paint . . . brooms for brushes . . . but for the moment, he said, a pen and some paper would do.

Yes, drawing will help him now, thought Jamar. But no, what he had in mind was to draft a short will; he'd been thinking of Georges-Hippolyte, the son he'd never known.

BAYEUX, 1883

Sixty years have passed.

For his trip to Bayeux, Antoine Etex has allowed himself the luxury of first-class. Finding that he will be alone in the compartment, he settles himself in comfortably, inhales the reassuring scent compounded of new leather, new upholstery, fresh varnish, and turns his thoughts to Georges-Hippolyte—to the puzzle that he is setting out to solve.

Being a sculptor (just look at the west side, the *wrong* side, of the Arc de Triomphe and you will see), Etex finds himself imagining Georges-Hippolyte as an unfinished figure, still rough and ill-defined, just beginning to emerge from the sculptor's block of stone. And faceless, he thinks. He has only seen the fellow once, to be sure, and that was many years ago, but he prides himself on his memory for shape and contour, and now he is quite unable to summon up a single feature of that face. Undistinguished, he thinks, insignificant—and indeed, that had been his impression forty years earlier when the short, sallow young man had walked unannounced into his studio.

Monsieur Etex, he had blurted out with no preamble, no introduction, Monsieur Etex, I have come to express my gratitude in person.

Gratitude. But for what?

For what, the young man repeated awkwardly, for what . . . why, for my father's beautiful tomb . . .

If it was a question of a tomb, there was only one that Etex had worked on recently. It hardly seemed likely, but he had to ask: Your father?

Why, Théodore Gericault, of course.

The sculptor was astonished. He had been an admirer of Gericault's—he had completed the man's tomb at his own expense when the subscription had failed—but he had never been an intimate, he had never heard of a son. Indeed, he said. I was not aware . . .

At that the young man produced from his jacket an elaborately inscribed document, all calligraphic whorls and flourishes. You see, he said, pressing it into Etex' hand. You see.

Etex saw: a royal order—quite recent—granting Georges-Hippolyte the right to add Gericault to his name. I'm sorry, I was not aware, he said again, handing the document back to Georges-Hippolyte and searching his face for some slight trace of resemblance. Perhaps the eyes . . . the eyebrows? You must excuse me, he said. I don't believe it was generally known?

Several of my father's friends . . . and *he* knew. Georges-Hippolyte was pointing to the name inscribed at the top of the document: Louis-Philippe, Roi des Français. *He* knew. He knew my father at one time, you see . . .

I daresay, said Etex. When the King was Monsieur Valmy. Very likely.

Georges Hippolyte rushed on: I had thought that you too might have known, but you say not. I had thought that you might have known my mother . . . who she is . . . where I might find her—Etex shook his head—but of course . . . I see that I must abandon that hope . . . those who might help me cannot speak . . . I understand . . . you must excuse me, Monsieur, and I thank you again . . .

And with that, he was gone. Etex would never see him again, never hear of him again until (forty years later) a letter arrived from a Bayeux notary named Lefèvre informing him that Monsieur Georges-Hippolyte Gericault, a longtime resident of Bayeux, now deceased, had left Antoine Etex 2000 francs—and there was another matter, a larger sum, something to do with the further embellishment of a certain tomb . . .

So Etex has allowed himself first-class for the trip to Bayeux. To see Monsieur Lefèvre, of course, but first, to solve the puzzle of Georges-Hippolyte. What the devil had Gericault's son, of all people, been doing during all these years in Bayeux, of all places?

* * *

Monsieur Gericault? says the fellow in the station jitney (who would spell it Jéricho if he were asked). But he's dead, Monsieur.

So he is, says Etex. Georges-Hippolyte Gericault. You knew him?

Right, Georges-Hippolyte, says his informant. But we never called him that to his face, you know; you would have thought 'Monsieur Georges' at least, but no, it always had to be 'Monsieur *Gericault*.' As though he amounted to something— a shabby sort of fellow living in a shabby sort of place for as long as I can remember. The old Lion d'or. They can tell you about him there if there's anything to tell, but it can't be much. Strange fellow.

* * *

The cattle merchants who dine regularly at the Lion d'or all agree. Strange fellow, they say and shake their heads. Monsieur Gericault had taken his meals at their table for . . . how many years? Ten? Fifteen? Since before my time, says one. And never once had the fellow opened his mouth, except to fill it with food. Never said a word. Not a friend in the world. Went for coffee sometimes to a little shop down the street . . . alone. Went for long walks by himself . . . down to the sea. Always down to the sea. People would see him at the shore, staring out to sea as if he expected his fortune to come in on the waves. And he *had* a fortune, you know. At least, he owned good Norman land . . . must have had a tidy little income, though he was said to be tight-fisted with his farmer. And didn't they find a fortune in gold pieces in his room? Ask Madame . . .

* * *

35,000 francs in gold, according to Madame Lecontour. And this is how he lived, she says. I have better rooms, Monsieur. I have fine rooms. But no, this attic was all that he wanted. For twenty years, Monsieur . . . more than that . . . a strange man.

The little room under the eaves smells of mildew—perhaps from the streaked and peeling wallpaper, perhaps from the stained mattress rolled up on the narrow bed. Aside from the bed there is only a washstand, a table, a chair . . . and that is all he would have, says Madame. These things, and the trunk where they found the gold coins and the will. And did he leave a sou to any of us who cared for him and gave him his meals and washed his dirty linen? Not a sou, Monsieur, not a sou . . .

* * *

Well no, says Monsieur Lefèvre. He was only five when his father died, you know, and there were guardians . . . trustees . . . friends of his father's . . . most of it went to them, Monsieur . . . and the small bequest to you . . . and then this business of his father's tomb . . .

And you're certain of the date? Etex asks.

Quite certain. The will had been made on the 22nd of September, 1841—no more than a day or two after Georges-Hippolyte had paid his awkward visit to Etex in his studio. Aside from the instructions about his father's tomb, the young man had expressed his wish to be buried as close to that tomb as possible. The young man who had concluded that he must abandon the hope of finding his mother . . .

How old would he have been? asks Etex.

Twenty two . . . twenty three . . . Lefèvre understands what Etex is driving at. Too young to be thinking of such matters, to be making bequests, unless . . . can he have thought that he hadn't long to live? A strange man, says Lefèvre. Does Etex know that the fellow had been studying architecture in Paris? And then suddenly dropped his studies to come to Bayeux—to be near his farm, he had said—and to spend the rest of his days in that dreary attic room, doing nothing?

Perhaps intending that every day would be his last, thinks Etex; perhaps intending it and never daring it . . . day after day . . . year after year . . .

Thinking always, I suppose, of his father, says Lefèvre.

And of his mother, thinks Etex.

And now, says Lefèvre, his father's tomb . . .

In great disrepair, says Etex. The original monument didn't last . . . insufficient funds, inferior stone . . . it has had to be replaced with a simple marker. Now something proper can be done . . . in bronze, I should think . . .

PARIS, 1992: PÈRE LACHAISE

Yes, bronze. Bronze streaked with verdigris and, on this October afternoon, with golden autumn sunlight, thick with motes, that comes slanting through the trees. The sculptor's figure of Gericault—a copy of the one that hadn't lasted—wears a loose, flowing robe and his little Greek cap sits atilt on his head; in one hand he holds a palette, in the other a brush—but this is a sickbed, the figure is reclining, his palette arm is resting on a pillow, bedclothes cover him to the waist. It is said that the artist did in fact prop himself up in his bed to paint; but that would have taken a gathering of energy, and Etex' monument displays no energy at all. The hand holding the brush seems, like the expressionless, enervated face, like the flaccid body, entirely ineffectual. It will not paint.

The high base on which the body rests is decorated with replicas, in relief, of the artist's best known works—paintings turned into sculpture, an effect that infuriated Charles Baudelaire when the original monument was erected. Why, he wondered, should a stone-carver want to play the violin? Well, that is how he put it. Surprisingly, he had nothing to say about the bit of cloth that was added for modesty's sake to the naked cadaver in the sculpted replica of The Raft.

The monument is certainly well intended. But if you are pursuing Gericault—and that is, of course, what I am doing, though I keep telling myself that the paintings should be enough—if you are looking for the man, you will not find him here. The monument is almost touching in its inadequacy—like every other tribute paid to Gericault by those who knew him and admired him: kindness of expression, they said . . . warmth and affection . . . irresistible charm . . . brilliant and caressing eyes . . . animated and gentle . . . a good friend and comrade . . . but a man of the world . . . remarkably well built . . . above all, his legs were superb. Not a clue. This may be the sociable fellow they knew from day to day; it is not the man in Etex' monument, nor is it the man whose death mask was once hung worshipfully in every artist's studio.

That man was a fiery, erratic genius, producing masterpieces in passionate bursts of inspiration; defiant, melancholy, self-destructive, he was thwarted in love and despised by the critics; he died young (and of course unappreciated) of a painful disease—in short, the hero of a romantic myth.

But that is not the painstaking, patient artist revealed to us in his sketches and studies, choosing and rejecting, weighing, adjusting and readjusting, moving forward step by step, decision by decision, discovery by discovery, not in glorious bursts.

Well of course, the man himself is bound to be more complicated than the romantic legend—but how to find him? There are so many contradictory faces, each one presented to the world as 'Gericault.' Even the simple facts have been partially obscured by the reticence and discretion of friends and family, by a concern for reputation, a fear of scandal. Evidence was withheld or destroyed. Papers were burned. The things we want to know were whispered or left unspoken.

And why should we want to know? What right do we have? Aren't the paintings, after all, enough?

Yes and no. To begin with, the painting—very well, let us say Gericault's Raft—the painting is everything. Its meaning, its truth, its power to move us are all inherent, we surrender to the painting itself—and then the itch begins for another kind of truth. How was this done, how was it possible? What kind of man makes a picture like this? What forces came together in his life, in the world around him, to create this astonishing image?

And when we know, what will we know? Something *more* than the painting? Something *else*? Or is it all irrelevant—the political upheaval, the personal turmoil, the bellyache, the weather?

Perhaps . . . perhaps . . . come back to the picture. But the itch persists, we still want to know. The greater the painting, the more self-sufficient it is, the more we want to know: how did it happen? How was it done? Who did it?

My unkind friend has sent another postcard—a youthful self-portrait, the artist as a young smart-ass. If you want to know him, writes my friend, you will have to invent him first. Are you prepared for that? And am I? For in a way he is right, there are so many lacunae in the evidence, there is such a tangle of fact and legend, ambiguous documentation, unreliable testimony, conjecture, surmise, speculation—what might have happened, what must have happened, what we (or someone) would like to think happened—the story, I suppose, of anyone's life examined in retrospect, but am I prepared to add my own invention to the tangle?

When he disinters another man's life, the novelist is expected to flesh out the skeleton, to imagine the life, to say with conviction: this happened, this was so. He is not supposed to say, like the biographer, it may have, it might have, it must have, perhaps and very likely. Above all he must never say that we don't know; to be convincing, he must write as if we do. He is expected, then, to tell a certain kind of lie—a 'true lie,' we call it, a superior truth that transcends mere fact. Faced with alternate possibilities, conflicting interpretations, he is expected, for the sake of shape and coherence, to choose. As long as he takes an authoritative tone he is free to choose as he likes, he is even free to invent, to create his own version—the 'might-have-been' that William Faulkner called 'more true than truth.' The reader will understand: to tease out the elusive truth, we say, the novelist must pretend and dissemble, that is his job, he is only exercising his craft.

Still . . . under the best of circumstances, our knowledge of anyone must be partial, provisional, uncertain. What if, from time to time, the novelist refuses to choose, refuses to know everything, to resolve every contradiction, to be definitive? What if he says, *I* am telling this story, and demands the right now and then to be uncertain, to question, to speculate—in short, to have it both ways?

Etex' feeble memorial at Père Lachaise does at least give us two certainties: Born, 1791—Died, 1824. Only 33 years. That helps, of course, to keep the romantic myth alive, and perhaps it accounts for the flowers. For there are flowers.

In front of the monument there is a little space surrounded by a metal grill on which the repeated motif of the letter 'G' is intertwined with arrow-pierced hearts. On the ground inside this grill there are flowers—paper flowers, street-vendor's bouquets, single blossoms picked no doubt in some public park. To tell the truth, I put flowers there myself—three red carnations bought at the entrance. But who else makes this pilgrimage? Are there still struggling artists in Paris garrets with the death mask on their walls? Are there sandaled, back-packing students who run their fingers through their tangled hair and think, Ah, Gericault . . . ? Or hopeful young rock musicians—the romantics of our time— paying their respects to an early death?

The only other person here, in fact, is a perfectly ordinary looking middle aged fellow in a tweed suit and felt hat, photographing— not the monument but the grillwork and the flowers. Another writer? Someone planning, perhaps, his novel about Gericault?

Yes indeed, it is time to begin.

My version.

1

ROUEN

He is born at his grandmother Caruel's house in Rouen on the 26th of September, and he is christened on the following day: Jean-Louis-André-Théodore.

On the 19th of October his father, Georges-Nicolas Gericault, finally writes to his cousin: a bouncing baby boy, he writes (that is his style), who promises to be a strapping big fellow like his father. Since the happy event, alas, Madame Gericault, has been dangerously ill. She is on the road to recovery now, taking dry bread and some veal or chicken broth, but she will have to be prudent for several more weeks. As for the little one, he was doing very well day before yesterday, when he was honored by a visit from his father. Changing the subject, Gericault wonders if Auntie has taken advantage of the fine weather to visit and assess the woods that the family is thinking of selling. Send me a line to let me know, he says, and signs himself Your Loving Nephew and Cousin, Gericault, writing the name without an accent as is the family's custom. Then he adds a postscript inquiring about his cousin's affairs of the heart, wishing him success in a certain matter—provided, of course, that the sentiments are mutual and in harmony.

Nothing out of the ordinary there—but it is 1791. In flight from the revolution, in total disarray, the Royal Family has been arrested at Varennes and is still under guard at the Tuileries Palace.

The National Assembly in Paris has just proclaimed a constitution, prefaced by a Declaration of the Rights of Man and Citizen. The world has turned upside down, but the burghers of Rouen, it would seem, are going about their business.

To be sure, there is business to be pursued. Anyone who knows the ropes can profit very nicely from the revolutionary turmoil—the confiscated estates, the enforced sales of property, the revocation of state franchises and monopolies. There is land to be bought and sold, there are promising business opportunities, you have only to be careful. If you are one of the odd risk-takers who see a future in the new politics, you had best learn to spin like a weathercock: Girondist, Cordelier, Feuillant, Jacobin—who knows which way the wind will blow tomorrow? If you are a monarchist at heart (like most of the better folk in Rouen—the landowners, the lawyers, the merchants), you avoid politics, you arrange your affairs with as little fuss as possible, you are discreet. Beneath that caution, of course, lies simple, cold fear; you live in fear—but still, you survive and go about your business (has Auntie taken a look at the woods?).

Above all, it is important not to draw attention to yourself. If Georges-Nicolas Gericault and Louise-Jeanne-Marie Caruel had married in more settled times, they might have been expected to establish themselves in a fairly grand manner. The newlyweds weren't children, after all (she was 37 and he was ten years older), both families were substantial landowners and the Caruel family had tobacco interests as well. But they had married in 1790, and the times were far from settled. Georges-Nicolas had been a lawyer at the Rouen bar, but the jurisdictions of the Ancien Régime no longer existed and he was devoting himself now to rather vague commercial interests. Living in her mother's house, Louise-Jeanne had shared the duties of hostess to a circle of judges and lawyers who favored the monarchy; men who generally opposed the 'new thinking,' though they cautiously accepted the need for a constitution of sorts. To continue a salon of that sort, to continue entertaining on any noticeable scale at all, now seemed risky and unwise. Setting up a fine new household seemed equally unwise, so Georges-Nicolas had given up his rooms and joined his new wife and his mother-in-law in their house in the rue de l'Avalasse.

Louise was the last of the Caruel children still living at home, and her mother had not expected her to marry. She was still beautiful, to be sure, but bookish and getting on in years, and Madame Caruel depended on her. Monsieur Caruel had died many years before, quite mad, in the 'maison de force' run by the brothers of charity at Pontorson. The Caruel's elder son, equally unstable, was still under the care of the good brothers. Their younger son, Jean-Baptiste, was pursuing business affairs in Paris, and Louise's two sisters had married long before and left the house. Madame Caruel did not intend to lose Louise as well, and she was not a woman to be crossed. We must draw together in times like these, she said in proposing their new living arrangement, and Georges-Nicolas agreed, so we must, so we must. It would be a great comfort to her, she said, it would be a comfort to them all, and Georges-Nicolas nodded. And besides, she added, it would be prudent.

* * *

Prudence. A great public celebration has been ordered for the 25th of September to honor the new constitution. Louise is just coming to term, but Madame Caruel nevertheless sends out for the prescribed bunting and the servants are still tacking it up, trying to mute their hammers, while Louise is in labor. So it happens that, on the day after the fête, baby Théodore is born under the new colors—blue, white and red.

Preposterous, says his father. We are not Siméon.

Before this is over, Madame Caruel replies, we may be glad of Siméon.

Siméon Bonnesoeur, that is; one of the three boyhood friends from Mortain, in Normandy, who had married the Caruel daughters. The three of them—Bonnesoeur, Gericault and Julien Clouard—had gone to law school together, they had gone on to set up law practices in Rouen, and they had been introduced into the Caruel salon by their fellow student, Jean-Baptiste Caruel.

Siméon's landholdings at Mortain had seemed excellent qualifications to Madame Caruel, guarantees of stability and respectability. To be sure, his arguments for reform sometimes seemed extreme, but the Caruel circle did concede that some degree of modest reform was perhaps in order, and Siméon's more radical thoughts were put down to the brashness and inexperience of youth. His old friends, Gericault and Clouard, smiled at his 'advanced' ideas and laughed them off. Our Free Thinker, they called him jokingly, Our Rebel—but that was before insurrection was a fact and the Bastille had fallen. Now Siméon's 'tendencies' are no longer a joke, only a fool would laugh at him.

Madame Caruel is not a fool. Before this is over, she suggests, they may all be glad of Siméon.

Glad indeed, Gericault huffs. Glad to see his son born in a house decorated with tricolor bunting . . . the colors of insurrection?

The King himself, Madame Caruel observes, is said to have worn the colors in his hat.

Prudence. That is how one gets along. Gericault's absolute loyalty to the monarchy is quite unreasoned and consequently quite unwavering; but like it or not, understand it or not, he has to admit that if worst should come to worst, they may be glad of his brother-in-law. Good old Siméon, after all.

And worst does come to worst. By 1792 Siméon is serving as a deputy to the National Convention in Paris, sitting with the Montagnards on the left and voting to abolish the monarchy . . . voting at last for the death of the King. He modifies his vote, to be sure, with the suggestion that the matter might be taken to the people, that clemency might be considered. Indeed, many of the deputies make that suggestion, but they are attacked as 'lukewarms' and nothing comes of it.

* * *

Standing in the nursery doorway, Gericault trembles with the news. Regicide, he says. Our brother . . .

Baby Théodore sits in his mother's lap, pretty in his afternoon dress—embroidered linen, as lace is thought to be excessive at the moment. He turns his head toward his father, he puts out his arm, but Gericault continues to tremble. The child turns back to his mother and buries his face in her bosom, seeking the scent of her cologne. It is a sea that engulfs him entirely, that scent, it is everything.

Siméon! says his father. A regicide . . .

Madame Caruel looks up from her needlework. Not in front of the child, she says.

* * *

Fear now turns into terror—and does the scent of *that* engulf the two-year-old?

The King is dead. Bourbon absolutism, unable to bend, has finally snapped and shattered, to be replaced by the unbending absolutism of utopia—the Reign of Virtue. 'Without Terror,' Robespierre proclaims, 'Virtue is helpless. A man is guilty against the republic if he does not believe in virtue; he is guilty if he is opposed to the Terror.' Guided by the Committee of Public Safety in Paris, the revolution sets out to eliminate every trace of royalist sympathy, every ideological impurity. The tyranny of the informer and the accuser may not be as great in Rouen as it is in Paris or Lyon or Nantes, but it is great enough; the guillotine in Rouen may not be as busy, but Georges-Nicolas has more than one occasion to exclaim in bewilderment, But I knew the fellow!

His mother-in-law suggests that there is no need to make a point of who one knows and who one doesn't know. Indeed, Georges-Nicolas has no desire to dwell on the worst possibilities and Madame Caruel is pleased to find that he is easily distracted by minor irritations. Are the servants now to call him Citizen and not Monsieur? he asks, though the servants have expressed no desire to do so. And is everything now to be re-named? The months of the year? The face cards in the piquet deck? But he must calm himself, says Madame Caruel, who has hidden one deck of old-style playing cards at the bottom of her sewing basket while surrendering the rest to the authorities according to edict. He must calm himself. One manages.

And so they do. Simple prudence? Brother-in-law Siméon? The Committee of Revolutionary Surveillance knocks at many doors, but not at the house in the rue de l'Avalasse. For whatever reason, that house remains a cocoon of safety for little Théodore. While the festivals of the revolution parade in the street below, he stands in the nursery window and smiles at the banners and bunting, he points and cries Horsie!, he claps his hands to the rhythm of the revolutionary drums.

Damned pagan spectacles, Georges-Nicolas calls these festivals, will they never end? For there is a Festival of the Federation, a Festival of Unity, A Festival of Reason, festivals devoted to the Martyrs of the Revolution, to the Goddess of Liberty, to the

Tree of Liberty, and on and on. The Reign of Virtue must have its rituals, and these processions are decked out in a style laid down by the painter David in Paris—the style of Heroic Antiquity. There are chanting choruses dressed in classical robes, troops of maidens bearing olive branches, wreathes of laurel and roses, sheaves of wheat and baskets of fruit. There are oxen with gilded horns pulling altars that display the new cult symbols: the Goddess and the Tree, the Sword of Justice, the Tables of the Law, Hercules triumphing over the forces of evil.

There are also, on one occasion, the mummified heads of the martyrs of '89. Suddenly little Théodore is silent, uncomprehending and transfixed, and then his mother snatches him away from the window. For once he will not be comforted by the cologne scent of her bosom, he tries to pull away, he wants to *see*.

* * *

The calendar of festivals grows longer—events designed to provide moral instruction and to channel revolutionary ardor, to ward off unrest and unsanctioned violence. The culminating event takes place in June of 1794: the Festival of the Supreme Being, the proclamation of a new religion. 'The true priest of the Supreme being,' Robespierre sermonizes, 'is Nature itself; its temple is the universe; its religion virtue.'

Almost at once, officially sanctioned violence—purification by guillotine—accelerates. The revolution, like Saturn, is devouring its own children, judging people without witnesses or counsel and beheading them in batches. No one is safe. During the month of July opposition begins to grow at the National Convention, an anti-Robespierre coalition begins to form—and then, so suddenly that the delegates are surprised at their own audacity, it is over. On the 27th of July Robespierre and his chief supporters are arrested and they are, quite simply, guillotined on the following day—10 Thermidor according to the revolutionary calendar.

* * *

No one, not even the most fervent monarchist, imagines that all will be as before. No one, at first, imagines anything at all. In the streets of Rouen friends greet each other with an uncertain smile and a shrug, their eyes do not meet. In the great houses, windows are not thrown open to a new day. Rather, curtains are drawn and, as at the end of a fever, torpor descends . . . lassitude . . . exhaustion.

And what now? asks Georges-Nicolas. Do we know what is happening? asks Louise. Wait and see, says Madame Caruel. She retrieves the old-style playing cards from the bottom of her sewing basket and they resume their customary three-handed game of piquet.

I understand, says Georges-Nicolas, that some fellows plan to torch all those Liberty Trees that were planted in the park. An event to remember, you know . . . perhaps something the child should see? Louise rolls her eyes to the heavens. It will not be safe, says Madame Caruel.

The streets, in fact, are less safe than before. The prisons of the Terror have been emptied, the prisoners have been freed into a world of scarcity, devalued currency, hoarding and rationing and black markets. There are sporadic food riots, looting—and there is no will to condemn the rioters and looters.

The word 'government,' says Madame Caruel, hardly seems to apply—and that is what she fears the most. She is a practical woman, she does not imagine that the irreversible can be reversed, but she is certain that the family will manage, will find its place—if only there is an order in which place can be found. She is pleased, then, when the National Convention in Paris drafts a new, more conservative constitution providing a governing executive of five 'Directors.' The details, the political implications, don't concern her. As long as there is a system—any system—she believes that things can be manipulated to the family's advantage, and her belief is confirmed quite promptly in a letter from her son, Jean-Baptiste, in Paris. He has joined Madame Caruel's brother-in-law—Pierre-Antoine Robillard—in acquiring a tobacco manufacturing firm, a former state franchise. Madame Caruel will have an interest in the firm, Jean-Baptiste will be a principal, a position can be found for Georges-Nicolas if he and Louise will consider moving to Paris. Or do his affairs demand his continued presence in Rouen?

My affairs . . . says Georges-Nicolas, looking puzzled. One can't just pick up and move at a moment's notice, you know . . . and what about you, Mama?

Paris, says Madame Caruel, who knows that his affairs are close to non-existent. A position with the firm, she insists. We have connections in Paris, we have family. There is nothing to keep any of us in Rouen.

And that settles that.

2

PARIS AND MORTAIN— TWO UNCLES

At first, Théodore—he was five now—did not understand the move as a rupture. He had never been away from the rue de l'Avalasse, 'away' was a notion beyond his grasp, he never doubted that he would wake up always in his own bed in his familiar room and Mama would be there. He didn't like to see things packed and moved about but, being assured that everything would soon be as before, he entered into the bustle of preparation, taking it to be a kind of game, and once he learned that there would be a carriage and horses he thought of nothing else.

Within an hour of leaving Rouen he had wheedled his way up to the coachman's seat, and when they reached the relay post he pestered until Uncle Jean (who had come from Paris to help with the move) was allowed to take him out to the stable to see the horses changed.

Jean-Baptiste was astonished at the boy's fearless approach to the horses. Up! he demanded, and his uncle lifted him and sat him astride one of the broad-backed coach horses, keeping one hand pressed firmly to his back, the other to his chest, much to Théodore's displeasure. You'd think he'd been raised on a farm! Jean-Baptiste reported later, to which Madame Caruel replied, To be sure, the child does smell of the stable.

To be sure, so he did, and he was delighted. They allowed him to ride outside all the way to Paris, where he sniffed the air excitedly and then saw to his astonishment that there were horses everywhere!

Peering out the carriage window, Madame Caruel remarked that there had clearly been more disorder here than at Rouen, and indeed, it was a shabby, unkempt town that they came to. For over five years Paris had ignored its usual occupation—the business of being Paris. It was now a city of broken street lamps and muddy streets running with rivulets of filth. Buildings that had not been destroyed or defaced by revolutionary zeal had simply been neglected and gone to seed. One thought of soiled and tattered second-hand clothing, and in fact second-hand dealers had become the busiest men in Paris. As in any city where careers can be made and destroyed overnight, possessions changed hands with feverish rapidity, one could buy another man's past at bargain prices and, if need be, sell it at a profit tomorrow. The arcades of the Palais Royal had become a great flea market, Sèvres dinner services from the Ancien Régime jumbled together in the stalls with souvenir paperweights made from the stones of the Bastille. A young man on the rise could find the furnishings for his rooms here, or outfit himself in last year's version of the bizarre fashion that was now à la mode with the 'Incroyables,' the young royalist fops who were suddenly strutting about everywhere wearing clothes of an eccentric cut and pattern and dropping their R's: 'Ma Paole, c'est incoyable!'

This sort of thing is frowned on by the old families—and the discreet new entrepreneurs hoping to become old families—of the faubourg Saint-Germain, and it is in Saint-Germain that Madame Caruel now settles her family in a large rented apartment.

*   *   *

While the others ignore him—they are busy giving orders and issuing the usual complaints of arrival—Théodore walks slowly from room to room, touching anything familiar that he can find in the jumble of wooden cases and randomly placed furniture. Everything from Rouen is there, of course—he runs his finger through the groove that just fits his fingertip in one of the ormolu acanthus leaves that encrusts Papa's desk, he brushes his palm over the satiny marquetry of Mama's little rosewood table—everything is there, but the rooms are not the same and nothing is in its place. The faint smell of beeswax is everywhere as always, but it is mixed now with the sour smell of packing crates and wood shavings. They told him that everything would be the same, but it is all wrong and he wonders if perhaps he doesn't feel well. Then they will have to put him to bed, and Mama will come to feel his forehead and talk to him, and he will stay in bed . . . he will stay in bed until all this is over and everything is the way it is supposed to be.

I blame myself, says Georges-Nicolas. Riding outside like that all day, he might have caught anything.

I think not, says Louise. There's no fever. It's the excitement.

In any case, says Madame Caruel, It may be more convenient not to have him underfoot just now.

* * *

The question of schooling arose.

Having been made treasurer of the Robillard tobacco firm, Georges-Nicolas had felt obliged to discover how people of a certain standing went about these things here in Paris, what they thought best, and the Pension Dubois-Loiseau had been highly recommended. Very sound, he had been told, by all means, take their advice.

In our experience, Monsieur Dubois had advised, they're never too young to begin the . . . great adventure, shall we say? The little fellows take to boarding school like . . . how shall I put it? . . . ducks to water?

But it can be difficult to explain at first, his colleague, Monsieur Loiseau, had said. It may be best just to bring him along, you know, without speaking of it. A little surprise, a few tears, perhaps, and then it's over . . .

It seems very hard, Louise protested, but Madame Caruel said nonsense, nonsense, and Georges-Nicolas suppressed his own doubts.

'A little surprise,' then—the moment when the ground tilts and the world slides into disorder and confusion. Standing puzzled in the Dubois-Loiseau courtyard, Théodore sees that his mother's eyes are searching his face, he sees that she is expecting him to weep, and all at once he understands that the others are to leave and he is to stay. It is not a slow dawning, it is a sudden blaze that stuns him, immobilizes him, leaves him unable to speak or to weep or do anything but stare blankly into his mother's eyes. If either of them thinks, How can you be so cruel? it is she, deprived of his tears. He thinks nothing, nothing at all, while he is kissed and patted on the shoulder and Georges-Nicolas murmurs, There's a brave fellow. Then, when their carriage is out of sight, he thinks: I will still be Théo; I will just do nothing, I will stand absolutely still and close my eyes and do nothing, and I will go on being Théo; whatever this is, it will not happen to *me*.

That is one way to ward off chaos—at least until someone claps you on the shoulder with a hearty Come along, young man! and then you have no choice. From the very start, the strategy of withdrawal is compromised by the quotidian, by the need to get along from moment to moment, from day to day. 'Just do nothing' is modified until it comes at last to be seen as nothing more than simple laziness.

Sixty years later, Madame de Pracomtal—a distant cousin—would remember being taken to play with Théodore on Thursdays, his 'free day' at home from school. I called him lazybones, she would write, he was exquisitely lazy and terribly spoiled by his grandmother. When it came time for him to go back to the Pension there was always a scene and tears, and then dear Madame Caruel would convince his parents to let him stay at home overnight and not go back to school until the following day.

When chaos is imminent and withdrawal fails, tears and a scene may serve one's purpose. One learns.

It is common enough, Monsieur Dubois assured his pupils parents, he is just your typical schoolboy (by which he meant stubborn, often sullen, often listless but subject to tantrums). Nevertheless, he added, underneath it all Théodore is a charming lad, and Monsieur Loiseau had to agree. Yes, charming. Everyone said so.

* * *

Except for Théodore's schoolboy misery (it will pass, Monsieur Dubois assured them), the move to Paris had been a success. The tobacco firm had flourished. Madame Caruel finally had an adequate supply of the snuff on which she doted. Georges-Nicolas had managed to double the small fortune that Louise had brought to their marriage, and he began to invest in real estate—country properties, farmland. When, in November of 1799, General Bonaparte overthrew the corrupt and inefficient government of the Directory and set himself up as First Consul, Georges-Nicolas had only one reaction: Consolidated Third, he said, has gone up nine points.

But what are we to make of this fellow? Louise asked.

The Runt? said Madame Caruel. Do we need to make anything of him? Wait and see. He can hardly be worse than what we've had.

Louise may have been wondering if allegiance might be possible. Madame Caruel, like Georges-Nicolas, was not concerned with allegiance. If they were loyal to anything, it was to the past. For the present, what mattered was getting along.

Nine points! Georges-Nicolas repeated, and Madame Caruel shrugged and said, There you are.

At first, all Paris—all France—seemed to shrug. The Directory was seen as rudderless and adrift, a government of dissension with nothing to its credit but military victories against the European coalitions that were harassing France, and those victories belonged to General Bonaparte. So why not? Wait and see.

Within a year the French were congratulating themselves on their prescience. Bonaparte had proved to be an efficient administrator, a semblance of order had taken the place of Directory confusion, the currency had been stabilized, the government's credit had been restored —everything that Madame Caruel and Georges-Nicolas could have wished, which is not to say that their allegiance had been won. No, the Bonaparte enthusiast in that family was little Théodore, inspired by the general's great victory at Marengo.

In June of 1800 Bonaparte had crossed the Alps through the St. Bernard pass to defeat the Austrian army at Marengo on the plains of Lombardy, putting Northern Italy under French control. When the news of this victory was announced at the Pension Dubois-Loiseau there was a burst of wild cheering, the boys all threw their caps in the air, they began to stomp their feet in marching rhythm, they were reprimanded unconvincingly and then they were given the rest of the day off.

At home, Théodore insisted on the geography lesson that Dubois-Loiseau had failed to provide. Georges-Nicolas found the boy and his mother sprawled on the drawing room carpet, looking for the St. Bernard pass in the atlas spread out before them.

Bonaparte indeed, said Georges-Nicolas. Impudent fellow.

Nevertheless . . . Louise ventured.

Delusions of grandeur, Georges-Nicolas continued, ignoring Louise's tentative interjection. Daresay the little man thinks he's Hannibal.

Théodore was astonished. Elephants? he asked.

Not exactly, my dear. Our generals uses horses nowadays.

I *thought* horses, said Théodore, who had been imagining Bonaparte galloping through the snowy pass, calm and determined but on a fiery horse (the very terms that the general himself would use when telling the painter David how to portray the event). Cavalry, Théodore assured his father, is the key to modern warfare.

* * *

According to Uncle Siméon it is nothing of the sort; that is a schoolmaster's notion, he tells Théodore, not a soldier's. The cavalry may be swift, he says, it may make a fine picture, but with our modern weapons it is the foot soldier who counts. It is always the foot soldier. Our general understands that.

Théodore has been sent to spend the summer with his Bonnesoeur cousins at Uncle Siméon's farm in Normandy. Another separation, but he's grown used to that, he knows by now that he will indeed go on being Théo and it gives him a certain bravado, he has decided not to sulk. Besides, his mind is still filled with the hoof beats and clamor of an imaginary Marengo; there are horses here at Mortain and Siméon has promised to let him ride. And if his uncle's thoughts on the importance of cavalry seem puzzling, Siméon's way of saying 'our general' (Papa and even Mama persist in 'runt' or, at best, 'little man') suggests a sympathetic ear, a fellow Bonapartist.

Well, yes . . . up to a point. The regicides of '93 have good reason to support a man who is determined to prevent the restoration of a vengeful monarchy. There may be doubts about the depths of the general's republicanism but he pays it lip service, he calls himself Citizen Bonaparte, he has sworn to protect the rights and privileges won by the revolution and he has forced Imperial Austria to recognize the French Republic . . . he is perhaps the best that one can hope for. So Siméon smiles at Théodore's enthusiasm for the hero's great victory. Your father, he says . . . but then he thinks better of it. Horses, he says. That is why you're here, young man. Shall we begin with the stables?

Théodore runs ahead and waits impatiently for his uncle at the stable door, making rapid circles in the dust with the toe of his boot. He will have to be reined in, thinks Siméon, he's far too eager, he knows nothing of horses, he will hurt himself. What Siméon cannot see is that Théodore himself has been frightened by his own churning state of excitement and anticipation. There is a buzzing in his ears, an agitation in his loins that he has never felt before. At any moment, he fears, the trembling inside him will burst out and he will begin to shake. Mama, he feels certain, would know how to calm him, but now he must do it for himself.

He stops circling his toe. He brings his legs together and he stands erect. He presents himself as he has learned to do for Monsieur Dubois's early morning inspections, and the posture itself, the simulation of containment, allows him to contain himself. Siméon is surprised, then, at the boys deliberate, methodical approach to their inspection of the stables. He sniffs the air like a connoisseur of stable odors and looks about as if to locate the various elements that contribute to the rich scent—the hay, the manure, the straw bedding damp with urine; he inquires about the feed; he asks what he takes to be appropriate questions about breed and lineage; he ascertains the proper nomenclature for the various items of horse tackle that hang on the stable wall. Then, with only the slightest hesitation—he feels the inner trembling returning, but this must be done—he puts out his hand and touches a muscular dapple-gray breast. The trembling dissolves at once and he moves closer, inhaling the horse's odor. This one, he says.

Siméon is caught off guard. A stallion, he protests. Not suitable.

Théodore digs his heels in. What do you call him?

Thunder, says Siméon. Do you understand? *Thunder*. But Thunder is already nibbling peacefully at a fistful of hay that Théodore has held out to him. Well then? The boy does seem to be quite fearless, the horses haven't shied from him, he's an exceptionally tall fellow for his nine years, he seems husky enough . . .

Thunder, says Théodore. He likes me, you see. He won't mind. If you'll show me how to saddle him, and everything?

Very well, says Siméon with a sigh. At least the boy doesn't propose to start out bareback. Thunder, says Siméon. Lord help me.

* * *

Something resembling a style begins to emerge:

While Thunder is being saddled he sniffs at Théodore's hair. After that he accepts his young rider (with indifference, to be sure, but without the slightest balk) and Théodore begins to learn, though his uncle (who believes in rational, methodical instruction), will not call it learning. Pay attention, Siméon keeps saying as he takes the boy patiently from walk to trot to canter. Pay attention. Do you think you know all this? But that is exactly what Théodore thinks, and Siméon is forced to the uncomfortable conclusion that in some odd way it may be true.

Having had all that he can stand of the fenced-in enclosure, Théodore finally insists, Let me ride, and in exasperation Siméon opens the gate. Mind what I told you about falling, he calls. Go limp. Roll. But Thunder has broken into a gallop and Théodore hears only his own heartbeat in his ears, Uncle Siméon is obliterated, everything is obliterated, it is only Théo and Thunder, Théo and Thunder, and he manages the gallop without a thought. (He will ride Thunder all summer long. Years later, Eugène Delacroix will note that Géricault never chose to ride anything but stallions.)

Among Siméon's books Théodore has found an old manual on horsemanship and he has read the words that explain everything: horse and rider must become as one. In the forest there is a high tree stump that he uses to dismount. He unsaddles Thunder, he takes off his own clothes and with a little leap from the stump he remounts. Afterwards, he has no distinct memory of anything about that ride, he has only the bruises to prove to himself that it actually happened. Before getting into bed that night he examines the insides of his thighs by candlelight, rubbing the bruises to sharpen their dull ache, and then he goes to sleep contentedly with his hands, palm to palm, pressed between his thighs.

Théodore discovers Bourglopin, the local blacksmith, and begins to pay him daily visits. Bourglopin, who is quite prepared to believe in the fascination of his own work, is pleased to answer the boy's endless questions (It doesn't hurt them, does it?—that sort of thing) but is disturbed to notice that on each visit Théodore draws closer and closer to the heat of the forge, as if testing himself. And one day, while Bourglopin is hammering out a shoe on his anvil, Théodore suddenly plunges his hand into the shower of sparks. What made you do that? asks the alarmed smith. To see if it would hurt, says Théodore. And now you know, says Bourglopin. And what am I to tell your uncle?

One of the mares is foaling and Théodore insists on being present. He wants to see, he wants to know what happens, but it is more than he had bargained for. He had never flinched from Bourglopin's furnace, but this . . . he wants to turn away . . . he wants to watch . . . he forces himself. Siméon observes his struggle and tells him gently that he needn't stay, but he shakes his head and refuses to leave. What is wrong? he whispers. Why, nothing at all, says Siméon, this is how it goes. This is how one comes into the world. Horses, says Théodore, and his uncle corrects him. All of us, says Siméon, and after a thoughtful pause Théodore nods without quite understanding.

* * *

Horses. They turned my head, he wrote many years later; he was sure that as a schoolboy he would have done better in Latin and Greek if only the masters had assigned some of the beautiful descriptions of horses and riders in which the classics abound. Unfortunately the Lycée Impérial, where he was enrolled in 1806 at the age of fifteen, didn't cater to individual whims.

The school was under the patronage of Napoléon himself ('Citizen Bonaparte' having been replaced by the more imperial sounding given name, just as 'First Consul' had become 'Consul for Life' and finally 'Emperor'—thus, Lycée Impérial). Down to the smallest detail, everything about that place was dictated by Imperial decree: the dark blue uniform jacket with sky blue collar and cuffs, the scarlet vest and knee-breeches, the bicorne hat; the limit of six handkerchiefs allotted to each boy (better not catch cold); the strict order that linen and stockings were to be changed every five days; the unvarying diet of boiled beef and beans; even the dancing lessons—for these boys were being trained to live in the great world of empire.

Despite Napoléon's hand in all this, Théodore hated it, as who would not. He did think the uniform rather splendid, though, and on free days he would strut his scarlet breeches about the faubourg Saint-Germain, sometimes alone, sometimes accompanied by two of the older boys—Brunet and Lebrun—who had taken him up as a kind of mascot, but also as a friend.

One would think that an age difference of three or four years would be a barrier to friendship between schoolboys, and Brunet and Lebrun did indeed find Théodore rather childish at times. They rolled their eyes at his habit of identifying in a loud voice the style of every carriage that passed them in the street: Calèche! Landau! Cabriolet! Coucou! When he suddenly took it into his head to run alongside one of the finer carriage horses until it had outpaced him, they simply turned their backs and refused to know him (though they rather admired his impulsiveness). And then he would come back to them with such an appealing, penitent smile, his beautiful eyes downcast; he would say, Friends? in the endearing way that he had and they would all laugh and lock arms and go off together. The boy could hardly say Bonjour! without making one feel cherished and indispensable. He was, in short, a charmer.

Also, he could draw—a talent that, to his own surprise, earned him respect from his fellow students. He had approached Monsieur Bouillon's drawing classes with the obligatory schoolboy groan; but set to making a charcoal drawing of a plaster cast of the Apollo Belvedere, the other boys were at a loss while Théodore just did it. His eye followed the statue's folds and contours, his hand followed his eye—and what, he wondered, was the problem? Years later Lebrun would write: he had an extraordinary talent for copying anything he saw. We were all astonished, and it was we, his earliest friends, who told him that he was destined to be a great artist.

Lebrun exaggerated. The other boys were respectful, but as for astonishment, they were more astonished by the vulgar grotesqueries that decorated the margins of Théodore's Latin grammar than they were by the Apollos and the Dying Gauls that he copied from Monsieur Bouillon's plasters. Bouillon, however, was impressed by these drawing class exercises and so, in fact, was Théodore. Life for any fifteen year old boy tends to be disordered, a chaos of mistakes and accidents and warring impulses, always wanting something, always missing something, always waiting for something, but Théodore found that when he was drawing all that stopped. When he was drawing there was only the concentrated moment itself, he was Théo, he was drawing, and that was all—like riding, he thought. It was like riding.

* * *

Before long, Uncle Jean was made aware of this new development. After some hesitation, Théodore had brought a drawing home—an Antinous with a chipped nose. Georges-Nicolas had dismissed it with a joke about the nose, but Louise had seen at once that this was no schoolboy scribble and she had put it aside to show to her brother. She looked to him as a connoisseur and a man of the world.

The tobacco firm having continued to prosper, Jean-Baptiste had not been modest in displaying his growing fortune. He had set himself up in a rather grand house in the faubourg; he had acquired a small chateau at Chesnay, near Versailles; he had begun to buy pictures (mostly Dutch and Flemish) to adorn all the paneled boiserie that he now owned; he had begun to buy horses to fill the stables at Chesnay.

Théodore had been invited to ride at Chesnay from time to time but, given his choice, he preferred to spend his summers with the horses at Mortain. He'd rather ride Siméon's wild beasts, Jean-Baptiste had complained to Louise, and she had simply nodded, suspecting that her son could give her brother lessons in horsemanship. If she hoped that Jean-Baptiste would become a mentor to the boy, it was not as a sportsman. She was concerned with matters of taste and style and she knew that Georges-Nicolas could not be relied on to provide what a young Parisian gentleman would need along those lines, though she could hardly put the case so candidly, even to her brother. She hoped now that Théodore's drawing would speak for itself, would indicate a seed that might be cultivated, and so it did. Jean-Baptiste was delighted at the chance to display his connoisseurship and his savoir-vivre.

He held up the drawing at arms length, turning his head this way and that and squinting. Well, well, he said. Well, well, well. What have we here? The child has a talent.

Perhaps you have noticed, said Louise, that he is no longer a child? Unpolished, perhaps, but not a child. *Unpolished* . . . but in any case, this is not a child's drawing.

Polish, Jean-Baptiste murmured, grasping her intention. Polish. He gave it some thought. If it's polish you want . . . does the boy look at pictures?

In this house?

Then he must come to me. And he must come with me to the Luxembourg.

* * *

Too many things happening all at once, everything confused and jumbled together—he hated that. His afternoon with Uncle Jean at the Luxembourg Palace (whose picture galleries were now opened for public viewing on certain days) left Théodore in turmoil.

To begin with, Jean (who had been too occupied with business affairs and acquiring property to think of marriage before he was fifty) had brought along his young fiancée—his latest acquisition. Only twenty-two but orphaned and possessing a considerable fortune as well as an aristocratic family name, Alexandrine de Saint-Martin had inherited a collection of paintings far superior to Jean's: a Saint Catherine by Parmigianino, a Ruisdael landscape, a handful of minor Dutchmen. She was interested in pictures, she was well informed, and Jean thought that she might help him with Théodore's introduction to the masters of the Luxembourg.

Alexandrine and Théodore had met, of course, but it was at a large family gathering to celebrate the betrothal. Théodore, whose mind, as usual, was on other things, hadn't taken her in as someone to be noticed; she had simply been the fiancée who must be passed around the room politely and greeted in a certain way. Mama had said that she was rather plain, and that is how Théodore had seen her. But seeing her now in Uncle Jean's landau—they are waiting for him in the courtyard of the lycée, she recognizes him with a widening of her dark, deep-set eyes, she acknowledges him with a slight nod and a half-smile—seeing her now, Théodore suddenly finds her very beautiful.

He stumbles his way through a greeting: Madame . . . Mademoiselle . . .

Surely, Aunt Alexandrine is permissible, says Uncle Jean. It will be the case soon enough.

Aunt Alex, she insists. Come, sit here beside me.

And so the turmoil begins, to be compounded at the Luxembourg where the paintings of Rubens burst upon him. The wild-eyed leaping horses, their manes streaming like flames from their impossibly arched necks (More in the line of Siméon's horses, says Uncle Jean. We go for something tamer at Chesnay). The writhing tumults of pink and pearly female flesh (Perhaps we should move on, says Uncle Jean, while Théodore stares and Alex talks rapidly of loose brushwork: Not at all like our Monsieur David). The intense pleasure in surfaces, the shimmering silks, the lustrous velvets (He does make rather a show of his fabric effects, says Alex. As if you could reach out and touch them, says Uncle Jean). Above all, the famously gleaming jewel-like colors, the luscious swirls of the paint itself—Théodore does indeed put out his hand to touch, but then he doesn't dare.

Go ahead, it won't burn your fingers, says Uncle Jean, though Théodore can almost believe that it might.

Better not, says Alex.

As they return to their carriage Théodore is trembling inside, his ears are abuzz. Monsieur Bouillon's drawing classes have not prepared him for the shock of Rubens. During the ride back he holds himself stiff and erect, struggling to control his agitation, struggling to keep his body calm and still, while Alex and Jean exchange glances. Then, when the carriage has finally come to a halt in the lycée courtyard, Alex leans toward him and kisses him on the cheek. As if I were a child! he thinks. And she is wearing Mama's cologne! Everything is confused and jumbled together . . .

Dear Théo, says Alex.

He leaps from the carriage and flees.

3

VERNET AND GUÉRIN

* * *

By the time of their next outing (for Louise had got her wish, they had taken him on) he had managed to compose himself. They visited the picture galleries at the Louvre (now renamed Musée Napoléon and filled with loot from the Emperor's conquests) where he made a deliberate effort at restraint, expressing polite enthusiasm for what in fact astonished him: the soft, glowing light that suffused the world in Titian's paintings; the hard, glaring light in Caravaggio that presented the world in violent relief. And how do they put the light there? he wondered, though all he said was Very fine, very fine.

He chatted politely about the fine spring weather as they drove up the Champs Élysées to the Étoile where they admired the work of Monsieur Chalgrin and his construction crew, laying the foundations for the enormous triumphal arch that the Emperor had ordered to honor the fighting men of France.

Standing up in the carriage for a better view of the groundworks, Théodore reeled off the proposed dimensions that every schoolboy in Paris now knew by heart: Fifty meters high! Forty five meters wide! The size of it! Have they got anything as big as that in Rome? he wanted to know.

On the whole, theirs are smaller, said Jean. No half measures here. But I don't suppose your father approves? The Emperor is . . . not his style?

Oh, Papa . . . you know Papa . . .

The tone of that made Jean smile. The boy may have inherited stubbornness from his father and his grandmother, but not that particular stubbornness: the resolute opposition, no matter how the family had prospered, to anything that was not 'before.' Théo, of course, had never known 'before.' If, in due course, he were to enter the tobacco firm, he would be the first family member to do so with a clean slate, so to speak; a clear eye to the future, no regretful backward glances. Jean would be delighted to report to his sister that the boy did indeed have possibilities.

* * *

Having cultivated Théodore's artistic leanings and his taste for Imperial Glory, they turned their attention next to his passion for horses. All Paris was flocking just then to the equine spectacles being mounted by Signor Franconi at the Cirque Olympique, and Théodore wondered if Jean and Alex had been to Franconi's yet? He had not, but he understood it to be very fine if one enjoyed that sort of thing. They took the hint and made arrangements at the Lycée for Théodore, in his best jacket and breeches, to accompany them to an evening performance—one up on his school chums who had only been to a matinée.

The Franconi family of equestrians, while originally Italian, had made its career in France. The 'Signor' had been retained for its cachet, the Emperor's recent conquests having made all things Italian the fashion of the moment (even the ices sold at Franconi's were produced by Signor Tortoni). On the tanbark at the Olympique the Franconis specialized in elaborate dressage displays and school exercises, daredevil riding, bareback acrobatics and—what really drew the crowds—dramatic recreations of great Napoleonic victories: Austerlitz, Ulm, Marengo... massed riders in bright scarlet and blue and gleaming brass, performing military maneuvers; wounded heros leading thundering cavalry charges; mock saber battles on horseback; deafening artillery barrages that were all drumrolls and flash-powder and colored smoke. Théodore was, once again, beside himself.

Going back after the performance to compliment Franconi (it was the thing to do), they found themselves in a perfumed crush of brocaded waistcoats and high-waisted gowns with half-bared bosoms—fashionable Paris in evening clothes—and Théodore for the first time in his life created a slight murmur among the ladies (and some of the gentlemen as well): the charming almond-shaped eyes... the charming golden curls... the charming smile... the scarlet breeches! Signor Franconi took notice of him too—perhaps it was the breeches, the look of a child-cavalier—and he broke precedent by motioning the boy to come forward. Théodore did not enjoy being patted on the head, but he forgave it in this man who had in an instant become his idol. A young horseman? Franconi inquired.

I ride a little, Signor, Théodore stammered. Not like this...

Alex whispered something to Jean, who produced a card from his waistcoat pocket and handed it to Franconi. The boy is a great admirer of yours, he said. At the moment he is training at the Lycée Impérial, but perhaps, on his free days, he could come to you and learn a thing or two?

Théodore stared with astonishment and gratitude at Uncle Jean. Franconi stared at Jean's card. He had no wish to run a riding academy, but he understood that the Caruel name was not without significance. The family would make suitable arrangements, of course. And the boy . . . well, the boy was certainly charming. Perhaps he could ride. What do we call you? he asked.

Théo, Signor, said Théodore—a greater compliment than Franconi could have understood.

Very well, Monsieur Théo. Come around next week—Thursday, is it?—and we'll see what you can do.

* * *

In later years, it sometimes seemed to him that his entire life had been shaped, that his true education had begun and ended, that the man, Gericault, had been formed in the boy, Théodore, at Franconi's.

First Principles:
He arrived on the first Thursday with a lump in his throat, of course, and a pounding heart. The horse-circus aroma—sweat and manure, urine and leather—had an instant calming effect, and he was almost swaggering, even a bit contemptuous, by the time he approached the pretty little mare—Tortoni, of all names!—that they had given him to ride. Then, when he was mounted, he discovered that Tortoni refused any gait but a walk. He coaxed, he prodded, he kicked her in the flank, but round and round the ring she went, walking with dainty little steps and nodding her head from time to time as if to acknowledge some applause that only she could hear. Pounding across the countryside on Thunder at Mortain, he had always felt perfectly at ease, certain that he and the horse were in complete agreement. Mincing about the ring on Tortoni with no agreement at all, he felt chaos descending.

The horse wants to walk, said Franconi. The boy wants to ride off like a Turk. Who is to be master?

Théodore brought Tortoni to a halt—at least he could manage that. I am, he said, surprising himself, for with Thunder he had never thought of himself as master.

Monsieur Théo, have you consulted Tortoni on the matter? Our horses are not fools, you know. They are not farm animals, they have minds of their own.

Théodore was nonplused. Consult Tortoni? He sat there looking puzzled, and Franconi finally took pity. Listen, he said. You will decide to change gait when *she* is ready. Once you have grasped that, you will discover that she will decide to change when *you* are ready. It is really very simple.

Théodore was not so sure, but Franconi said Go! and he went. And all at once he discovered that he and Tortoni had decided to trot . . . to canter . . . to gallop! He and Tortoni. It was not that different from riding Thunder after all, it was only more complicated; one couldn't just ride, one had to pay attention. It was like drawing in Monsieur Bouillon's class, the line following the charcoal in his hand; the line leading the charcoal on . . .

So you see, said Franconi when they were finished. You ride like a bumpkin, but you ride. Come again next week.

Perseverance and Mortification:
Like Franconi himself, the Franconi boys held themselves very straight and rolled like sailors when they walked. Whenever Théodore thought that he was unobserved, he followed behind Franconi and tried to imitate the bearing and the gait, but he found the roll impossible.

He found also that he had in fact been observed, and that he looked ridiculous. Passing him in the ring, the other boys would suddenly exagerate their gait, breaking into an imitation of his own hopeless imitation. Born on horseback, they would boast, pointing proudly to their bowed knees. It can't be learned, Monsieur.

Théodore thought otherwise, and he devised a method. In bed at night he forced himself to sleep on his back with his dictionaries, his histories, his Greek and Latin grammars pressed all in a row between his knees. Uncomfortable, to be sure, but he managed to sleep that way night after night, week after week, adding another volume to the nocturnal library from time to time. And for his pains he got nothing but bruises—bruises that he examined with pride each morning, caressing them and savoring the ache, but only bruises. His legs—the shapely legs that would one day be called 'superb' in the memoirs of a friend—remained unbowed. Perhaps barrel hoops, he thought, they might do the trick, but that would have to wait until he went to Mortain for the summer.

Hand and Eye:
Carle Vernet, that fashionable painter of elegant, slim-legged, swan-necked horses, came around to do preliminary sketches for a set of Franconi prints. Vernet's horses—prancing delicately, flaring their nostrils haughtily, staring coquettishly at the viewer—were not the sort of horses that Théodore admired, but they were all the rage and Théodore made plans to watch the master at work. Franconi would not, in any case, allow him to ride while the company was rehearsing. He was to sit in one of the boxes and observe, and he chose a box in the second tier just behind Monsieur Vernet, looking over his shoulder.

At first, he couldn't understand what the man was doing. Vernet had given firm instructions that there was to be no posing; the rehearsing equestrians—this morning it was mounted balancing acts, tumblers and jugglers—were to go about their business as usual. 'As usual' meant all of them at once, riding criss-cross and round about the ring, avoiding each other skillfully but creating a scene of great confusion. And with swift, light pencil strokes,

Vernet seemed to be creating equal confusion on his drawing paper: a welter of curls and swirls and feathery hatchings that Théodore's puzzled eye took some time to sort out. Bit by bit, however, there emerged under Vernet's pencil a random gallery of gestures and attitudes: a flexed elbow here, an outstretched leg there, a horse's arched tail, clasped acrobat's hands, a startled eye, a twisted, straining torso—fragmentary notations, nothing that Théodore had been taught to think of as 'drawing;' but as he shifted his glance from Vernet's rapid scribbling to the observing eye, flicking this way, that way, he thought that he understood. Unlike Monsieur Bouillon's plasters, the world would not sit still. To capture it, one had somehow to catch it on the run, catch it in one's eye and, at almost the same instant, catch it at the tip of one's pencil. One had to pay attention.

I can do that, he murmured without thinking.

Monsieur Vernet turned around and glared. For a moment Théodore feared that he was about to be challenged, but Vernet was not interested in encouraging the young (his own son had taught himself to paint without a word of comment from Papa).

What you can do, said Vernet, is be silent, and he went back to his sketching.

Experience:
A trio of bareback riders—handsome boys, hardly older than Théodore himself—invited him to join them in a secret pastime that, they insisted, would greatly improve his riding. He knew better, of course; his friends at the Lycée had assured him that such predictions, and odder ones that he had heard, were all nonsense. He had always refused any friendly offers of further enlightenment, but now he was becoming increasingly conscious of his own inexperience and he was determined to end it. He admired the skill of those three riders, skipping rope in unison on the back of a cantering horse; he admired their bulging calves

and thighs, their muscular buttocks straining at their tights; and after all, as the trio said with a wink, what harm was there in it and who would be the wiser?

Indeed, no harm was done—there was some awkwardness, perhaps, and a little disappointment—but before long Franconi did in fact appear to be the wiser. Stay away from those boys, he said quite firmly—and was it true, Théodore wondered, that someone could tell just by looking at your face? In any case, he had begun to find those fellows slightly unpleasant—they seemed to feel that coarse comments and lewd smirks were called for—and he obeyed Franconi's injunction without protest.

But then there was Franconi's young wife. She too was not much older than Théodore, and she was rumored in the company to be restless in her marriage to the older man. To tell the truth, much more than that was rumored, and little wonder, given the provocative glances that she scattered in every direction and the deliberately careless way in which she adjusted the little fringed skirt that she wore for her balancing act. The vulgarity of this behavior escaped Théodore entirely, but the provocation had its effect. He thought that Signora Franconi was marvelously beautiful—more beautiful even than the rope-skipping boys—and he was flattered indeed when she offered to show him how to balance on horseback.

In his innocence, it took him a while to understand that he had mistaken her meaning. He was puzzled, to be sure, to find that the lesson was to take place in her horse's dark and narrow stall. He was puzzled to find himself sitting astride her horse's broad back, facing the Signora. He was puzzled when she took his hand and drew it toward her. Then, as she moved closer to him, throwing one leg across his thigh, he was no longer puzzled. At first, however, he was alarmed. I'm hurting you! he said, and she said, No . . . Then she said, Yes . . . do . . . and in later years the sharp odor of horses' bedding would always bring that moment to his mind.

Afterwards, he was in despair. How could he face Franconi? How could the man fail to guess? He was certain that he had ruined everything, but then Franconi never said a word, and that too was a lesson.

Taken all in all, Franconi's riding circus was an education.

* * *

Jean-Baptiste and Alexandrine were married in the spring. The contract was quite specific about the paintings that she would bring to the union.

Before they had returned from their wedding trip, Louise had taken to her bed with a vague weakness and a long, slow decline had set in. The doctors could not agree on a diagnosis; they arrived, in fact, at no diagnosis at all, though they were precise enough about the various barbaric therapies that they prescribed and Louise adamantly refused. Madame Caruel busied herself with increasingly elaborate broths and infusions, all to no avail. Georges-Nicolas dithered. Louise grew weaker, and Théodore began to spend his free days at home, reading to his mother at her bedside.

You should be riding at Franconi's, she said, and he shook his head. When you're feeling better, Mama. Théo my dear, she said, but then she didn't have the heart to go on.

You're still drawing? she asked. Yes indeed, Monsieur Bouillon saw to that. And would he show her how he was progressing? Of course, he would bring his drawings around next time (after he had restored the fig leaves that he had removed one day after class to amuse the other boys).

When Jean-Baptiste and Alexandrine returned to Paris, Madame Caruel urged them to put off their plans to establish themselves at Chesnay; she needed them here in Paris, she said, to support her through this crisis. Jean had never known his mother to need support in a crisis, but of course they stayed on. They called on the invalid nearly every day, and Louise confided her anxieties about Théodore.

You know his father, she said to Jean. You knew him before I did. You know that he is a good man . . . a kind man . . . but Théo just puzzles him, he throws up his hands. The boy will need guidance . . .

We have always enjoyed Théo's company, said Alex with a smile. Our young chaperon, you know. He will always be welcome . . .

Yes, always, said Jean. The boy has youthful enthusiasms, of course, that may puzzle his father. We understand that these interests are not be discouraged . . . he is young . . . but in time, I thought, the firm . . . ?

Perhaps, said Louise. Perhaps not. It may not suit him. Will you bear that in mind?

It may not suit him, Jean repeated. We will bear that in mind. Perhaps something else, he said (though he couldn't imagine what that might be).

Partly, Théodore understands what is happening, partly he refuses to understand. 'When Mama is feeling better' is his formula, and his father and grandmother encourage it. Much improved today, they say. A turn for the better, don't you think? The worst is past. He is prepared, then, and he is not prepared when someone comes to his classroom at the Lycée and announces that he is wanted at home. He shrugs his shoulders to show the other boys that he has no idea what this is all about, and all the way home in the carriage that has been sent for him he sits there thinking . . . nothing at all. He observes the passing carriages. He fiddles with his brass sleeve buttons, breathing on them and polishing them.

They have already hung crepe on the doorway, they have changed into the proper clothes, but no one has prepared words for Théodore. They say what people say in the circumstances.

Papa embraces him weakly and murmurs, My poor boy, my poor boy. Then he sits down abruptly and stares off into the distance. What are we to do? he murmurs.

God's will, says Madame Caruel, accepting Théodore's kiss. Her suffering is over, it is a blessing.

You must be strong now, says Uncle Jean, for your grandmother and your father.

Would you like to see your mama? Alex asks. Everyone stares at her, but Théodore says Yes, please, and she leads him upstairs.

The air in the room assaults him, it is heavy with Mama's cologne, though for a moment he thinks that it might be Aunt Alex's. But the scent grows more intense as he approaches the bed, it must be Mama's. Mama's cologne still lingering in the air, and Mama . . . now at last the words form silently in his mouth . . . Mama is dead. I must look now, he thinks. He leans closer, and all at once he feels as he felt on that morning when they had abandoned him in the courtyard at Dubois-Loiseau—the world tilting and sliding into disorder and confusion. This time, however, he can't squeeze his eyes shut and say that it won't happen. It has happened. No sense, no reason, no meaning at all, it is intolerable, but it has happened. He steadies himself, he will not allow himself to fall over in front of Aunt Alex. But he had better leave the room now before he starts to tremble.

Nothing at all, Alex says when she returns to the others downstairs. He just stood there for a while and looked, and then he went to his room. I don't think he realizes yet . . . not fully. I think he's afraid to take it in.

He would not have used the word, but chaos is what he is afraid of, what he has always feared: confusion, disorder, jumble; things happening for no reason; things scattered and out of control. He had fled to his room so that Aunt Alex would not see him trembling, and now he finds that he cannot stop it. He is sure that they are waiting for him downstairs, but he won't go down like this. Mama would know how to stop it, riding Thunder or even Tortoni would stop it, but now he must find a way to stop it himself. It seems foolish at a time like this—he knows that he must be serious—but he thinks of drawing.

He has no drawing paper at home. He opens an old exercise book to a blank page, and for the first time that blankness seems threatening, a kind of chaos—emptiness sprawling formlessly across the paper, a confusion of nothingness. But he can change that. He takes up his pencil and makes a mark on the page, and instantly the emptiness gathers itself into a kind of order around that mark. The mark orders the blank page.

He doesn't know what he will draw now, but he begins to draw.

* * *

When they told him what he had inherited from Mama it sounded like a great fortune. It was in fact only a small fortune, but it was enough. He was independent before he knew what independence meant.

Papa and Uncle Jean, as trustees, might have kept him short, of course, but Madame Caruel advised against it. If he was to be a young gentleman of means, he must learn how to spend and not to spend, that was surely what Louise had intended. A few mistakes could be afforded, after all, and he would learn the value of things.

There were no protests, then, when he gave himself a very generous allowance, and with money in his pocket he set out for the first time to buy something for himself that wasn't an ice cream or an omnibus ticket: paper, pencils, charcoal, a box of paints, brushes—everything that was needed to set up a young artist's atelier. Not at home, for Papa would only be puzzled and demand an explanation that Théodore couldn't really provide. The artist's supplies stayed in their wrappings, waiting for summer vacation and his trip to Mortain. Uncle Siméon would understand. Uncle Siméon might even tell him how to explain to Papa that he had now gone as far as he intended to go at the Lycée Impérial.

Trying to find himself—that was how almost everyone would choose to misunderstand what he was doing. Before long Uncle Jean would say it. Even Uncle Siméon would say it. Searching for himself. As if each of us contained some pre-existing essence, the thing that we have always been, waiting to be discovered. As if we did not, act by act as we go along, create what we are becoming—the sum of our own acts.

Georges-Nicolas would see him only as stubborn and willful. Too simple and ungenerous a judgement perhaps, the man had no imagination, but in its way it came closer to the truth.

* * *

Just before leaving for Mortain, he went to ride Tortoni one last time. He hadn't been to Franconi's for months and he thought that perhaps, with his mourning band, he shouldn't ride for pleasure, but everyone assured him that he needn't mourn forever and encouraged him to go. It would be good for him.

The need to ride had been growing in him, and while he was saddling Tortoni he was surprised by a sudden surge of anticipation, a sort of tingling in his breast that made him think for a moment of his encounter with Signora Franconi. He fumbled clumsily with the cinch and Tortoni shied away, he had to whisper her back into place before he could finish the job.

Watching from his ringside seat, Franconi saw that they were both nervous as they began their exercise. Tortoni would lead, then Théodore, then Tortoni again, they were not together. By the time they had reached a gallop it was clear that Théodore was urging Tortoni on, driving her to go faster, faster than she cared to go, and Franconi became alarmed. He stood up and blew his whistle, and Tortoni clattered instantly to a halt.

As he rose from his saddle and stirrups, as he somersaulted over Tortoni's ears and onto the tanbark, Théodore thought, For no reason at all!

You see, Monsieur Théo, said Franconi. That too is a possibility.

So he went to Mortain with a sore shoulder, a skinned nose and hurt feelings. Tortoni had not been honest, she had been subject to Franconi's command all along.

* * *

From the very start, Siméon had thought that Théodore was headed for trouble. He was fond of the boy; when the time came he would try to warn him against the pitfalls that lay ahead, he would try to keep him within bounds. Still, he rather liked the idea that someone in the family would kick up some dust.

I understand that you've been riding at Franconi's, he said. Perhaps you will try to teach Thunder some manners?

Thunder won't behave for anyone but me, Théodore boasted.

You must try to rectify that, said Siméon, by the end of summer. One day soon, he thought, this young man will overstep himself.

In the enclosure Théodore did as he was told. He rode Thunder as he had been taught to ride at Franconi's—the patient dialogue between horse and rider, the paying attention. He was showing off and, trusting him, Thunder took to it very well. Before long they were performing polite school exercises to the delight and amazement of Siméon and all the cousins. But what, Siméon asked, are you two getting up to when our backs are turned?

That was another matter. Alone together in the open fields, Théodore and Thunder agreed to revert to the old ways; the instant communion, each of them surrendering his will to the other; the reckless cross-country gallops, because that was what both of them willed.

I am reluctant to forbid it, said Siméon, that is not my way. But if you two are determined to break each other's necks . . .

There is a wildness in Thunder, it is in his nature, said Théodore, feeling certain that this sounded like some fine Roman poet and was bound to impress. He warmed to it. There is a tempest within him that must break out, he said, there is a turbulence . . . a fire . . .

That is very grand, said Siméon with a smile. But I wonder if the wildness isn't in yourself, Théo? You have shown us that you can ride like a gentleman, but you choose to ride like a madman.

He had never thought of it that way, but Wild Théo! certainly had a nice ring to it. That madman Gericault! was even better. He was delighted.

Siméon was relieved when he began to draw, though it brought him home late for supper just as often as when he was riding. They would have to send someone to fetch him, and more often than not they would find him in the stable or at the enclosure, sketching Thunder. After several unsatisfactory attempts out in the fields, Théodore had settled for poses at rest, frustrated by his inability to draw Thunder in motion.

The great artists of antiquity, Monsieur Bouillon had told him, always chose a moment of calm, the moment before action or the moment after. When he was sketching Monsieur Bouillon's plaster casts it had never occurred to him to question that dubious Davidian pronouncement; but now, with Thunder, what he wanted was to capture the moment of action—he had seen Monsieur Vernet do it at Franconi's, he knew that it could be done—and he found that he did not know how.

He turned instead to a close inspection of the animal's anatomy. With his eyes and with his hands (for Thunder allowed him every kind of liberty) he studied how the horse's motion was constructed, how the body parts fit together, how they were articulated by the joints, how the muscles tightened and stretched with every movement, where the skin hung loose and where it grew taut. Autodidact that he was, he could not avoid the occasional false analogy to his own body, but in the end he did construct for himself a fair understanding of how things worked and he began to test that understanding in his drawing.

Make your line, Monsieur Bouillon would always say, don't scribble, but that was easier when the subject was a plaster cast, not a living thing. What Théodore meant to be firm and solid in his drawings of Thunder seemed always, when he was finished, to be a little tentative, a little fussy, a little flat. He would not show his drawings, then, and he was mortified one afternoon to find that Uncle Siméon had come up behind him silently and had been observing him at work.

That is very fine, said Siméon when he saw that his presence had been noticed. Théodore turned the drawing paper over at once. That was not a schoolboy's drawing, said Siméon.

Perhaps not, said Théodore. I hope that I am no longer a schoolboy. Then it all came out: he could not return to that prison, the Lycée Impériale; he had no interest in preparing for the university; *this*—drawing, painting—was what he meant to do; he understood that he still had everything to learn, but he could take himself to the Luxembourg or the Emperor's galleries at the Louvre and learn more in an afternoon than he would ever learn at the Lycée; perhaps he could study in some artist's studio . . .

It was a novel idea, a shocking idea, even to that renegade Siméon. Artists, it was understood, were born into their métier. Painting was a family trade like any other, passed on from father to son. That a young man of good family should *choose* it as a career was all but unheard of. If *that* was the kind of dust this young man meant to kick up—oh Lord! Still, Siméon enjoyed the prospect.

Your Papa . . . he said.

Théodore shook his head. Uncle Siméon knew Papa. Papa was on old dear, but he would never understand. It was Mama who would have understood.

Perhaps your Uncle Jean . . . said Siméon.

Perhaps. But Uncle Jean had already begun to speak of the tobacco firm.

Well, that may be the way, said Siméon. Like your Papa.

Théodore took that in. Everyone knew that Papa spent most of his time on his own affairs, his investments in property; he hardly ever went to the firm's offices.

As for the rest, Siméon continued, I understand that Jean has an eye for pictures, he and his new young wife. No one will listen to me, you know, but if you had *their* support your Papa would have to agree to it. You must tell them that your Mama would have wished it.

Théodore thought about that and nodded. Then he said that he wanted to buy Thunder and take him home to Paris.

One shocker after another, Siméon thought. What next? And what the devil would Thunder do in Paris? he asked. And how would he get there? And just how do you propose to pay for him?

I will ride him to Paris myself, said Théodore. Everyone keeps horses in Paris, you know. And as for paying for him . . .

Yes, said Siméon, I had forgotten. Still, the price would be pretty steep. The lost stud fees . . . and do you really think that he would take to Paris?

If he's with me, said Théodore. As far as he was concerned that clinched it, and Siméon saw his point. Except when he was with Théodore in the summer, Thunder was moody and unmanageable, he was nothing but trouble for the stable boy. Only Théodore knew how to handle him.

I'll tell you what, Siméon said. I will not take money from you. You let me have that drawing you've just made, and you do one of yourself, if you think you can manage it with a mirror. That will be your payment, and that way the two of you will not be forgotten here at Mortain.

In the event, Théodore unwrapped some of the supplies that he had brought with him and produced not a drawing but a painting, oil on paper. A self-possessed young man stares haughtily out of the picture, looking off to his left, avoiding the viewer's gaze. A clutch of soiled paint-brushes sticks up into the bottom of the picture, though we cannot see the hand that holds them. Théodore declares himself to be a painter here, but in fact he has handled the medium unevenly and without much skill. The flesh tones of the face are muddy and overworked; there are a few hopeful highlights here and there, but the face remains a flat mess of paint, somewhat redeemed by the arrogant glance of the eyes. The ruffles at the young man's throat are more successful, suggested by nothing more than a few smart strokes and squiggles of bright white paint; future art historians would call it Brio. One imagines the young painter saying to himself (perhaps for the first time), That's right, that's all that's needed, let it be.

So Siméon's family has its souvenir (and its heirloom), and Théodore has Thunder. Half apologetically, Siméon writes to his brother-in-law Georges-Nicolas to explain about the horse and to make sure that stabling can be as easily arranged as Théodore assumes. He writes to his brother-in-law Jean-Baptiste to suggest that the boy is trying to find himself; that he seems to have a gift and should perhaps be set free to explore it—at least for the time being; that dear Louise would surely have wanted it that way. Théodore writes to Aunt Alex (he had promised to write but so far hasn't done so) to enlist her as an ally. He tells her that he is working to improve his drawing; that he has begun to paint; that he is eager to show her how much progress he has made and to have her opinion; that he looks forward to going with her again to see the work of Monsieur Rubens and Monsieur Titian and all the rest.

His trunk is to be sent back to Paris by coach. Siméon has given him a fine new saddle as a gift and a little sketch map of the roads he must take. Siméon has also made him promise to allow at least two days for the journey—three would be better—not riding like a madman and not riding at night. His saddle bag is filled with apples and cider, bread and cheese—and before he is quite ready, before it is all completely settled and plotted in his mind, he and Thunder are on the road and Thunder, for the first time since they have known each other, seems uncertain.

Well of course, says Théodore, you don't know where we're going, do you? Trust me. And Thunder does.

Like an idle passenger on a long sea voyage, Théodore suddenly tastes absolute freedom—the exhilarating sense that the world and its jumble cannot touch him, that he can do as he pleases. The world may lie behind him, the world may lie ahead (and there is certainly some unpleasantness awaiting him in Paris), but for the moment he is out of it and there is only the moment. He does not intend to savor it at a slow trot.

Thunder assumes that Théodore knows what he is doing, and before long they are tearing along the road in a way that alarms the farmers at the roadside and gives rise to rumors of imminent danger: a boy fleeing . . . from brigands, perhaps . . . British soldiers . . .

Théodore is beyond noticing, he is beyond thinking. He has emptied himself of everything except riding in harmony with Thunder and he gallops on unaware of anything else, not counting the passing milestones, not observing the landmarks that Siméon has told him to watch for, not seeing that night has fallen. He doesn't come to his senses until foam from Thunder's muzzle begins to fly back into his face, and that finally brings him to a halt.

By the time he has dismounted he has come out of his daze sufficiently to know that his body is sore and aching, and he knows that Thunder too must be in pain. They have been riding at a gallop, riding without pause all day and into the night. Any other horse—certainly Tortoni—would have protested long ago, but Thunder has trusted him and kept on going. Now, to Théodore's shame, the horse is covered with sweat and caked with mud, his shanks are bleeding from roadside brambles, his hide shivers when he is touched, his breath is coming in short, coarse snorts. Not paying attention, Théodore whispers to himself. Not paying attention. The words—they are, of course, Franconi's words—fill him with chagrin.

He is afraid to remount. After they have rested a while he starts down the road again on foot, leading Thunder and speaking to him gently: It's all right, you see . . . we're just at the edge of a town . . . we'll find someplace . . . an inn . . . we'll stop for the night.

He finds that they have reached Saint-Germain-en-Laye—so close to Paris in only a day!—but that gives him no joy, it is only a measure of how much he has overdone it. There is no joy, either, in commanding food and lodging for Thunder and himself, though it is the first time that he has spent his own money in this way. He can think only of having Thunder cleaned up and cared for, watered and fed. He hurries through his own meal, and then decides against the bed that he has engaged. He goes out to spend the night on stable straw, to be near Thunder.

By morning Thunder is himself again and Théodore's aches have subsided. They go on with their journey at a dignified trot— Like gentlemen! Théodore tells Thunder. Still, Georges-Nicolas is greeted by a disheveled, sorry sight when they finally reach Paris.

In later years it would be said of Georges-Nicolas that he was a chicken who had hatched an eagle. His demeanor, when Théodore finally broached his dissatisfactions and his desires, was just exactly the demeanor of that alarmed and puzzled fowl.

His puzzlement was quite simple. He could not understand the career that Théodore proposed for himself, he could not grasp the notion. To the best of his knowledge, no such career existed—not in the sense that he understood the word 'career.'

His alarm had more complicated causes. Georges-Nicolas may not have been a passionate man, but in his way he had loved his wife. The simple fact of having Louise there to care for him, to listen to him, to talk to him, to *be* there—that had been his bliss. He had never imagined living without her, living on alone. Madame Caruel, to be sure, continued to manage the household, he could not complain about his comfort, but Madame Caruel had always dealt with her son-in-law dismissively, they were not a pair. No; since Louise's death, Georges-Nicolas had begun to think of himself and Théodore as 'the household.' He had begun to think of Théodore as all that was left to him of Louise. The boy might be boarding at the Lycée, he might be staying at Mortain, but he would always return to this domain that he shared with his father. He might be headstrong, one expected that of the young; but now this 'career' that he spoke of so seriously, this 'vocation'—it suggested another way of living altogether (though Georges-Nicolas could not think what it might be) and that was threatening.

Madame Caruel, who was often accused of spoiling the boy, misunderstood in her own way. She imagined that Théodore, with a purse of his own now, was proposing to become a young man about town—so many of them nowadays were amateurs of the arts. He was perhaps a bit young for that way of life, but times had changed and she would not judge. It was probably as instructive a way as a university education, and in any case, how did it preclude the boy from entering the tobacco firm—if not at once, eventually?

Théodore said, You don't understand, and went to his room to sulk. Madame Caruel raised her eyes to the heavens. Georges-

Nicolas said, Oh dear, oh dear. All three were happy to accept Alex's invitation to spend a few days at Chesnay.

* * *

Uncle Jean liked to boast that the Chateau de Grand-Chesnay had been designed by the great Mansart. It did indeed have the usual mansard roof, but it was a builder's house, not an architect's—a small, quite ordinary middle-class chateau with outside shutters at the windows.

Georges-Nicolas and Madame Caruel went down to Chesnay in the landau. Théodore rode down on Thunder, who was beginning to learn the courtesies of Paris streets and busy highways. Théodore got there before the others and wasted no time in making his case.

He produced his summer's-worth of drawings, guessing rightly that Uncle Jean and Aunt Alex would think better of them than he did. Then he said flatly that he intended to learn how to paint (Monsieur Rubens and Monsieur Titian came up again) and that he would under no circumstances return to the Lycée.

Had he asked for advice and support Jean might have given him an argument, but the flat declaration left his uncle floundering. Jean didn't care that much about the Lycée in any case. But surely, he said, one may take an interest in painting and still have an occupation? You do know that there is always a place for you in the firm?

Théodore took the risk that Siméon had suggested. Like Papa? he asked in a pointed way.

Like your Papa? Jean knew perfectly well what the boy was suggesting. If the father could have a sinecure, how could the son be denied?

Why, of course, said Alex, answering for Jean with a tone of finality. It is what Louise would have wanted.

Jean was learning that Alex possessed a mind of her own and a determination to have her own way. And he did remember his sister's words about Théodore and the firm: it may not suit him. Perhaps not yet, he thought. Perhaps in time. Wait and see. Yes of course, he said, like your Papa, he said, and Alex smiled.

And whose studio, she asked, do you propose to enter?

Théodore hadn't got that far. He remembered the drawing lesson he'd had at Franconi's and, for want of anything better, he said, Monsieur Vernet's.

Horses! said Alex.

A gentleman, said Jean. That would be satisfactory.

But alas, said Alex, I don't believe that Monsieur Vernet is known to take students.

Jean bristled. The student in question, he said, is a young man of good family, not some studio rat from the Beaux Arts. We will speak to Monsieur Vernet. He is a gentleman. He will understand.

Théodore was amazed. By the time Georges-Nicolas and Madame Caruel arrived it was settled. Théodore would be given a suitable starting position at the firm (a wink from Aunt Alex here), and Uncle Jean would speak to Monsieur Vernet about lessons. Georges-Nicolas could only say, Yes, I see, yes, I see. Quite. Shall we set up a little room, then, for your hobby?

First you must send him to your tailor, said Alex. As you can see, he's grown out of his clothes during the summer, his ankles and wrists stick out like a scarecrow's. Besides, she continued, he must stop dressing like a schoolboy. Why not send him to Jean's man? He's very good at the English cut that all the young men are wearing.

Théodore blushed. He knew all about the English cut. Its skin-tight fit showed a man off immodestly while pretending to cover him. Still, if one had good legs . . .

Come and look at my pictures, said Alex, taking him by the arm—and he was instantly aware of Mama's cologne, Alex's cologne. That, and Alex's bosom, which was barely hidden by the low-cut, high-waisted mode of the moment. All at once he thought of the licentious scribbles he had made, and then destroyed, in odd fits of frustration during the summer. He blushed again and suppressed the thought. You are no longer a schoolboy, he said to himself.

Do you admire Parmigianino? Alex asked.

Oh yes, he said, never having heard of the fellow. Nor did he admire the painting of Saint Catherine when he saw it. The colors were . . . well, pale and weepy. And if they're going to torture the poor lady, he thought, she should do something more than simper. But he said, Very fine, very fine, and they went on to the Ruisdael.

* * *

Vernet recognized him at once, this half awkward, half self-possessed young man with the charming smile and the beautiful almond eyes. Franconi's? Vernet asked, and Théodore nodded his head. You announced that you could draw? Vernet asked, and Théodore blushed. I meant that I could learn, Monsieur. That I hope to learn.

And what, the art historians ask, can young Gericault have hoped to learn from the brittle stylishness, the facile mannerisms of Carle Vernet? It is a fair question. The choice had been arbitrary and unconsidered, and before long Gericault himself would say (quite rightly) that one of his horses could eat six of Vernet's. Yet he stayed with the man for two years. Why?

To begin with, the Vernet name carried some weight and reputation. Painting had been the family's trade since the seventeenth century. Carle's father, Joseph (known for his seascapes and his views of the major French harbors), had been one of those ancien régime artists granted the royal favor of an apartment in the Louvre palace—a building more or less abandoned at that time by kings who preferred Versailles.

Brought up in that ramshackle palace, the precocious young Carle was known among the artists of the Louvre as a talented draughtsman and a clever talker. It was rumored that his father paid him six francs apiece for word-plays and witticisms to be used when dining out. Perhaps. That may have been only a family joke, but it would not have been out of character. By the time Carle won the Prix de Rome he had achieved a reputation as a man about town and a sartorial dandy 'à l'anglais,' avoiding the excesses of the Parisian Incroyables, but not without ostentation. His fellow students at Rome reported a wardrobe of eleven suits, fifteen breeches, thirty-five embroidered waistcoats, and no one ever forgot those waistcoats. Mention his name, and someone was bound to laugh and say, Thirty-five waistcoats!

Here was a man of fashion, then, at a moment when the possibility of elegance was just presenting itself to young Gericault. Here was a man who loved horses, a painter of horses and a horseman himself—a sportsman in the English style with a passion for hunting and racing. Here, above all, was a man who refused to be a teacher—at least, not a schoolmaster of the sort that Gericault was trying to escape.

Vernet made that clear to him at the outset. My understanding with your uncle, he said, is that you will hang about and observe and not get underfoot. If you should wish to copy any work that you may find in the studio, you may ask for permission, but you must not expect to have your efforts corrected. And if you should wish to copy at the Louvre—the Musée Napoléon, I should say—a card can be arranged.

He referred to his former home with a note of bitterness. Someone had finally taken an interest in the Louvre palace—the Emperor himself—and the painters had all been evicted. The Emperor had been offended by their housekeeping habits. If we don't get them out of there, he was reported to have said, those buggers will end up burning down my museum.

Carle's young son, Horace, had been delighted to get out of that place. He had his own ideas about how a fellow should live, and he didn't share his father's pride in the family's rooms at the Louvre. You can't imagine the awfulness, he said to Gericault. Damp, dark, dirty, freezing in the winter, horrid cooking smells at every hour of the day . . . you can't imagine!

An easy-going, uncomplicated young man, Horace was not the least bit put out by Gericault's presence in the Vernet's new studio; he welcomed the companionship, and he welcomed the chance to play the man of experience, taking the young novice under his wing. Keep your eyes open, he advised. Monsieur my father won't tell you anything. He has never told *me* anything. Just watch what he does. And copy. Copy here in the studio, copy at the museum, copy drawings, copy paintings, copy anything at all and you'll find out how its done. If you'd like, we can copy together and I can give you some pointers . . .

Horace had inherited his father's self-confidence as well as his skill. At nineteen, only two years older than Gericault, he was already launched on a career whose shallow brilliance would raise him to enormous popularity in his own time and leave him all but forgotten in ours. He had a sharper eye and even greater fluency than his father, but clever observation and skillful execution would be the outer limits of his achievement, and he would never recognize the limitations. He was quite content to model himself after his father; he was not a man to quarrel with success, he desired nothing more.

Horace always carried a little sketchbook with him, saying that one never knew when one might want to jot down an attitude, a gesture, an expression for future reference. He advised Gericault to carry a sketchbook of his own, and by chance Uncle Jean had provided the very thing—one of the firm's blank account books, the best quality paper, just the right size and shape. The book had been meant to suggest that the young man was in fact doing something useful for the firm—a kind of camouflage—and now it served that purpose very well. Georges-Nicolas was delighted to see what he took to be the firm's business carried home diligently every evening and out again the next morning.

* * *

One imagines the two young men sketching together, and one wonders. Horace, for all his limitations, had an eye. Would he have seen through the awkward inexperience of Gericault's drawing to the underlying strength, the 'iron wire' of his line? Would he have sensed an emerging talent, still tentative and clumsy but larger than his own? And would that have troubled a man of Horace's unreflective temperament? Would he have shrugged and said, Well, that is his way, not mine? If Gericault in his uncertainty attempted now and then to imitate the wispy, feathery Vernet line, would Horace, out of simple friendship, have said, No, leave that to us . . . do it your way . . . make your own style?

* * *

In any case, they found that they shared a fervent admiration for the Emperor—a great relief to two boys who had been brought up in royalist households. They embraced on that and swore loyalty to Him and to each other. They became friends.

Advised by Carle (for their were some matters on which he was prepared to give advice), they bought themselves tall hats and walking sticks, they rehearsed the easy, negligent manner that was thought to be 'English gentleman,' and they launched themselves on Paris as dashing young boulevardiers.

They did all the things that were expected of such young men. They went to the opera, they went to concerts at Notre Dame, they went to see the Spanish dancers who had taken Paris by storm. They went to performances at Franconi's, and Gericault made a great show of familiarity when he took Horace back afterwards to meet the performers. They dined at Frascati's. They watched the couples dancing at the Tivoli gardens but hung back when they were encouraged to join in. They ogled the whores in the arcades and streets around the Palais Royal and they frequented the political cafés in that neighborhood—royalist, Jacobin, Bonapartist, they were quite impartial. They drank too much cheap wine and, true friends, they supported each other while they threw up in the gutter.

To Carle's great distress, they also rode together. Ce fou de Gericault, Carle complained; that madman is teaching my son to ride like a madman.

Indeed, there was a great deal of showing off and reckless competition in their riding. Horace might be his superior in the studio, but Gericault knew himself to be the better horseman and he made a point of it. To that big oak across the fields, he would say, take all the fences, last one there buys dinner, and Horace always bought.

When they rode down to Chesnay (Gericault thinking that Aunt Alex would be pleased to meet Vernet fils) they turned the journey into a series of road races and cross-country dashes that left them in a sorry state when they finally arrived.

And is it your custom to call on people unannounced in the middle of the day? Alex asked, trying to sound severe but unable to suppress a smile. If you've come to see your Uncle Jean, he's in Paris attending to affairs, she said, while you and your friend are riding about the countryside like two ruffians. You will clean yourselves up at the horse trough, please, before you come tracking mud into the house. And then, I suppose, you'll want something to eat?

While they were washing up Horace said, I think she likes you.

Of course she likes me. She's my aunt.

Well no, Horace said, she's not *really* your aunt, it's not the same.

Of course it is, said Gericault, and he shook his head in puzzlement.

Alex gave them a cold lunch. She showed them her pictures, and Gericault noted that Horace seemed genuinely enthusiastic about the vapid Parmigianino. She took them out to the stables to admire the horses that Jean had been buying, but she declined to join them on a ride to see the Emperor's stables at Versailles. I can't ride just now, she said. You understand, the doctors forbid it. And has Jean spoken to you about that, Théo? We hope that you will agree to be godfather . . .

Afterwards Horace said, But she does like you, and again Gericault said, Of course she does.

That's not what I meant, said Horace, but once more Gericault only looked puzzled and they both let the matter drop.

* * *

Two years with the Vernets—and what, in the end, does he have to show for it? To be sure, he has an admirable friend, a riding companion and a fellow bon vivant. He has a stylish wardrobe that shows off his slim figure, though the clothes do seem to require constant editing and updating. He has his sketchbook, and he has the beginning of an ability to lay paint on canvas convincingly, he has kept his eyes open and seen how it is done. He has stacks of copies of Carle's delicate and mannered horse paintings, and he suspects (quite rightly) that his own versions show more energy, if less elegance, than the originals. He has a card that permits him to copy at the Musée Napoléon, but that work remains to be done, he has hardly made a start at it, he has procrastinated, he has spent too much time going about with Horace. If he is to be a painter, a great deal remains to be done.

At some point the balance tips. At the breakfast table Papa inquires politely, as usual, about the progress of his son's hobby, and all at once enough is enough. The word 'hobby' has struck home. In a rush of regret, Gericault understands that his time at Vernet's has not been entirely serious.

And how will leaving us make you serious? Horace asks. What will you do? Bury your nose in the classics? Paint scenes from Homer and Plutarch in some freezing attic with twenty other *serious* students? The Death of Hector? Romans and Sabines?

I don't know, says Gericault. Perhaps. Don't be angry.

Horace isn't angry, it isn't in his nature, but he isn't far wrong in his guess about the direction that his friend will take.

* * *

No art historian has failed to mention Scylla and Charybidis, the frying pan and the fire, in writing about the choice that Gericault made. At a time when wide cracks were opening in the decorous facade of the Classical style, he went from Vernet to the most doctrinaire and formula-ridden of the Neoclassicists, Pierre-Narcisse Guérin. Not a pupil of mine, said David of Guérin, but I think he's been listening at my studio door.

He had certainly been listening to, and taking to heart, the doctrine of the Beau Idéal as it was summed up by Quatremère de Quincy: 'Realism (de Quincy called it Le Vrai) is low and trivial, it most often reflects a spiritual shabbiness, while beauty is everything sublime and pure, the visible synthesis of fitness and truth and harmony.' Painting, then, was not to portray nature, the compromised matter of life, but an ideal world—truth, purity, sublimity; one did not paint real men but abstract, eternal types embodying lessons in honor and morality. The proper setting for all this was, of course, Greek and Roman antiquity.

As a reaction to the elegant frivolities of the Rococo, this classicist doctrine had once seemed very powerful; as an expression of the ideals of the Enlightenment, of the Revolution itself, it had carried great conviction—but the power and conviction were gone now. Except in the hands of David himself, the formula had become stale, it was sterile and exhausted. To fulfill the Emperor's commissions, even David had reluctantly abandoned antiquity to paint modern scenes of Imperial glory (just as he had once turned from antiquity to paint scenes of the Revolution—the Tennis Court Oath, the deaths of heroes).

To supplement the accepted genre of classical history, a new category of modern history painting had to be invented for the Decennial Competition of 1810: 'tableaux représentant un sujet honorable pour le caractère national'—painting to please the

Emperor. David showed a scene of the Emperor's coronation. David's closest follower, Antoine-Jean Gros, showed scenes of Napoleonic warfare—the Battle of Aboukir, the Battle of Eylau—and a shockingly realistic scene of the Emperor visiting the dead and dying in a plague hospital at Jaffa; modern reality, the turmoil and carnage of battle, the horror of disease and death, painted with a feeling for color and drama that went against everything in the classical formula, everything that Gros himself had once professed to believe.

When Gericault saw these paintings he got out his sketchbook at once and paid tribute, not by copying but by translating Gros's dramatic, painterly language into his own language: bold, inky pen strokes and jagged splashes of sepia shadow. He himself was startled by the sudden confidence with which he worked, the certainty, the lack of hesitation—the sudden appearance, in fact, of a personal style. He had never heard Gros's somewhat scandalous advice to young painters—'Posez, Laissez,' put it down and let it be—but that is exactly what he had done.

He had formed an instant allegiance to Gros's modernist dictum—in effect, 'let it be fresh'—yet, having decided that he needed a teacher after all, he turned instead to Guérin—a rigid classicist whose work was labored, methodical, driven by theory and dogma and, on the whole, devoid of life. In expressing their surprise at this choice, the art historians invariably roll their eyes and quote Molière: Que diable allait-il faire dans cette galère?

In fact, it made a certain amount of sense. Gros might be free with his advice, but he did not take pupils. David took them in immoderate quantities, but Gericault's family remembered David as a Jacobin regicide, there would have been arguments, unpleasant scenes, resistance. Guérin, on the other hand, was thought to have vaguely royalist sympathies, and his students were a new breed of painters-in-training—young men of good family who prided themselves on avoiding the coarse manners and unkempt dress affected by students at the École des Beaux-Arts. Quite acceptable.

Beyond that, Guérin was, after David, the most eagerly sought teacher in Paris and he was, despite his limitations as a painter, a very good teacher. His pupils followed a rigid, unvarying course: they copied from plaster casts to begin with, then they advanced to drawing from the live model, and finally—when they were thought to have acquired enough discipline to resist the more seductive qualities of color—they were allowed to move on to life studies in oil. A strictly regulated course of study, yet Guérin had a reputation for tolerance and, within limits, laisser-faire. He insisted that his students master his own 'scientific principles' of figure construction and composition, but once those principles were mastered he encouraged each of his students to develop his own manner according to his individual gifts. He did not turn out many students who painted like Guérin.

Above all, Guérin was a patient man, and it was perhaps inevitable that Gericault would try that patience to its limits. Fourteen years later, bedridden, near death, unable to sleep, it comforted him to reminisce about his days as a gadfly in Guérin's studio. I was impossible, he told Alphonse Montfort, a loyal assistant who sometimes, to keep the invalid company, slept over on the little couch in his bedroom. I was hopeless, Gericault said. If it wasn't one thing it was another . . . whatever came into my head . . . always something absurd . . .

* * *

The naked model is seated on a small wooden plinth, his back is turned toward the students to display his bulging muscles, his left arm is raised and pointed firmly to the left (he prides himself on holding this pose endlessly with no support). In Gericault's drawing it is the right arm that is raised, pointing to the right; all the other body contours and muscular tensions have been adjusted accordingly, and correctly.

What the devil are you doing, Monsieur? asks Guérin, who has come up behind Gericault's shoulder. Do you understand that you've reversed the position?

Gericault turns to look up at Guérin with a puzzled face. Then he turns back to stare at the model. Fancy that, he says. Why, so I have.

Guérin will not take the bait. In fact, he rather admires the skill with which this little trick has been pulled off, but he will not say so in front of the other students. Take care, Monsieur, he says, not quite knowing what he means by this, and he leaves the studio.

Gericault stands up, he takes his drawing block and his pencils, he crosses the studio and he seats himself on an unoccupied bench on the other side.

What the devil are you doing, Monsieur? asks the little fellow seated next to him, speaking in the flat, uninflected tone that the students use to mimic Guérin behind his back.

Why, reversing the position, of course, says Gericault. Then he bows very slightly from the waist and says, Gericault, Monsieur.

Dorcy, Monsieur, the little fellow replies, trying with no great success to suppress a grin. Tell me, Monsieur, he goes on. This 'reversing the position' . . . do you always wear your tall hat to do it?

Always, says Gericault. Among gentlemen.

Ah well, we're all gentlemen here, says Dorcy. Reaching under his bench he produces his own tall hat and puts it on his head.

With considerable effort, they both keep a straight face. Gericault begins to turn the page on his drawing block, but Dorcy says, No, let me see. After a while he nods his head, Gericault flips to a clean sheet, and they both turn their attention to the model—both still wearing their tall hats.

* * *

Dorcy—Pierre-Joseph Dedreux-Dorcy—is a young man whose circumstances are much the same as Gericault's. He comes from a good family with property in Versailles. He has an independent income and Paris is teaching him how to spend it. At twenty-one, only two years older than Gericault, he is too young, really, to learn what he has just learned. In an instant, Gericault's drawing has made him understand that while certain things may lie within his own grasp, there are things that do not lie there and in all likelihood never will. In an instant he has learned the difference between skill (he knows that he has that) and . . . what shall he call it? The real thing, he says to himself.

One might expect a young man to mount a fierce defense against this kind of self-knowledge, finding much to criticize in the other fellow's drawing, seeing him, perhaps, as an unworthy rival, discovering in one's own work fine qualities that only need a little polishing. Dorcy, however, mounts no such defense. In an instant he has decided to make a friend of the real thing.

* * *

Guérin takes Dorcy aside.

It's that fellow Gericault, he says. He sits in front of his easel dressed for the boulevard, and you must copy him, and suddenly there is a fashion for tall hats in the studio. He chooses to decorate a simple figure study with a background of columns à la Veronese . . . it just came into my head, he says . . . it is nothing but a childish prank, Dorcy, the man is a prankster . . . yet all of you feel that you are obliged to dream up something equally fanciful. And why should you want to follow him? Let him go his own way, Dorcy. All this unnatural color . . . the paint laid on thick as pastry cream . . . that is not your way.

Dorcy is silent and Guérin, in all fairness, retreats a little. Alas, he says, the fellow's got the stuff of three or four painters in him, I don't deny that. Perhaps he'll get it sorted out one day. But his way can never be yours, Dorcy. Leave it alone. It's not for you.

Perhaps not, says Dorcy, stopping short of Alas.

* * *

Guérin takes Gericault aside.

Monsieur, he says, your color isn't true. And all this chiaroscuro . . . all these contrasts of light and shadow . . . one would think that you paint only by moonlight. (Which is to say that Gericault has tried to paint atmosphere, not the clear, toneless, light in which Guérin's figures are frozen.)

As for your figure studies, Guérin continues, I would say that they are to the human body what a violin case is to the violin. (Which is to say that, instead of attempting Guérin's exaggerated purity and perfection, Gericault has exaggerated and distorted for the sake of liveliness.)

Gericault replies to these criticisms by requesting an extraordinary favor—permission to copy one of Guérin's most admired paintings, the Offering to Aesculapius. Perhaps it will help me to correct my faults, he says—meaning to be impudent, of course, but keeping a straight face.

You are enormously presumptuous as well, says Guérin. No one else in this studio has been granted that. I doubt that I will find anything favorable to say about the results, but . . . well, we shall see . . .

I have your permission? Gericault asks in astonishment.

The painting is not to be moved, says Guérin. You will bring your things up to my studio and work there.

* * *

Bedridden and reminiscing, Gericault told the story to Montfort:

Always something absurd, he said. Monsieur Guérin's studio was up above, you understand, and the other fellows were maddened by the thought of me, the chosen one, working alone up there on my Aesculapius while they all slaved away at their académies down below. Dorcy, of course, defended my right, and one thing led to another, which always meant a water fight in that studio when Monsieur was absent. There were buckets of water all about the place for safety's sake, you know . . . the models always insisted on overheating our stoves. Well, when the fellows tired of sprinkling poor Dorcy they turned their attention to the true object of their wrath. They came tiptoeing up the stairs and took me by surprise with a full bucketful and scampered back down again before I could retaliate. You can imagine that I didn't mean to be surprised a second time. I stood ready with a bucket of my own, waiting for their next assault, waiting for the first creak of footsteps on the stairs . . . and as luck would have it, it wasn't the fellows at all but Monsieur Guérin returning from his business! By the time the poor man reached the top of the stairs, dripping with water and stony-faced, I was seated at my easel again, the picture of innocence—but it can't have been very convincing. Monsieur Gericault, he said in that maddening, quiet little voice of his, you will now take your easel and your paintbox and return to the studio downstairs. And then, of course, he had to say something about my painting. The work of a madman, he called it, and don't smile, Montfort, he was quite right. I had copied his Aesculapius quite accurately, you see, but it had occurred to me to liven it up, to give it some energy, and you can imagine how well that went down. It was absurd.

* * *

Always something absurd, says Dorcy, taking the measure of his new friend. Sit down, Gericault, he says. Stop pacing.

I can't, says Gericault. I can't bear the thought of being hated, Dorcy, what am I to do?

A fellow student—Monsieur Lafond—has taken offense at some careless remark of Gericault's; he has demanded satisfaction.

I can't bear the thought of this fellow's enmity, says Gericault. I can't imagine what I said to him . . . one wants only to be loved, you know . . . it never entered my head . . .

Precisely, says Dorcy. It never entered your head. You want only to be loved, you say, yet you *will* put on airs, you *will* speak without thinking, you *do* manage to sound cheeky and insolent most of the time, and I doubt that you're even aware of it. Perhaps a little humility, Gericault . . .

Gericault sits down at once and addresses Dorcy with the full force of his beautiful eyes, his beautiful, vulnerable smile. I am humble, he says. I will make myself humble. Help me, Dorcy.

You can easily help yourself, says Dorcy, if you will only think before you speak . . . before you do something rash. Meanwhile, I happen to know that Monsieur Lafond will be satisfied with an apology. A carefully worded letter should do the trick.

In this way Dorcy begins to take care of his friend, chastising him freely yet shielding him from the chastisement of others. You do need a keeper, he says with a laugh, you are dangerous to know. And, rather liking this picture of himself, Gericault agrees.

* * *

Before long they come to be thought of by their fellow students as inseparable—'the long and the short of it' is the studio joke, for Gericault is a good head taller—but there are some things in which Dorcy will not follow Gericault. He will not ride with him. Self preservation, he says (and he means it), go and ride with your friend Vernet. He will not accompany Gericault more than once to those dubious arenas on the outskirts of town where gentlemen and riff-raff mingle to watch bizarrely mis-matched combinations of animals tear each other apart—a goat and a bear in the ring with a pack of bulldogs, a donkey together with a wild boar and a tiger, that sort of thing.

Gericault had proposed it as a sketching adventure—a challenge, he had said. Ever since his first efforts with Thunder in the fields at Mortain he had puzzled over strategies for capturing a moment of action, and now he had got it into his head that the animal fights would provide the perfect exercise. Everything will be swift and unpredictable, he told Dorcy. We'll have to keep our eyes open.

To see what I don't care to see, thought Dorcy, but he went along. And indeed, he didn't care for what he saw. He didn't care for the bloody spectacle, nor did he care for the peculiar hush, the indrawn breath and intense silence with which the audience greeted the cruelest moments. Finally he closed his sketchbook and turned his back, and he didn't care for the impassive way in which Gericault kept right on as if it were nothing more than a circus performance, flicking his eyes this way, that way, covering page after page with swirling pencil strokes that did in fact capture the fierce leaps and terrified cringes of the animals.

I can't think that you actually enjoy these disembowelings? Dorcy said afterwards, and he didn't care for the answer.

Enjoy? said Gericault. But it has nothing to do with that. Just see how useful this has been, see what it has produced—and he riffled the pages of his sketchbook. After all, these things will take place, Dorcy. They will take place with us or without us.

Without me, said Dorcy. I will not go again.

He went gladly, however, to the Grenelle barracks and parade grounds where the two of them filled their sketchbooks with military attitudes and detailed notations on the splendid new uniforms that the Emperor had ordered up for his conquering armies. He went gladly to the Musée Napoléon galleries at the Louvre whenever Gericault went there to work at copying the great Van Dycks and Rubenses, the Titians and Raphaels and Caravaggios that the Emperor's armies had stripped from the churches and palaces of Europe.

On five mornings out of every ten the galleries of the Musée Napoléon were reserved for the use of students. The fruits of empire, you see: on the one hand, the richest collection of paintings the world has ever known; on the other hand, the sons of a rich and rising middle class, a generation of art students who were, for the most part, young men of independent means and, just possibly, independent thought. Their teachers were of two minds about setting them loose among the foreign masterpieces. There was much to be admired in these paintings, to be sure, one could learn much from them—but one could learn too much. The austere practices of the French School were in danger of being corrupted by the fruits of empire.

Nevertheless, the galleries were turned over to students on five mornings out of every ten, and Gericault, shadowed by Dorcy, never missed a morning. Monsieur Guérin was all very well, he told Dorcy at the outset, but the masterpieces at the Louvre had something else to teach. Just look, he said. There are other ways . . .

Did you know, asked Dorcy, that Monsieur David disapproves of this display—all these paintings from Flanders and Italy? A fellow who paints in his studio told me this. Monsieur David calls them a bad influence, and he argues that in any case we can never see the paintings rightly, that they lose much of their beauty when they are torn from the walls they were intended for. He says that studying them here may produce scholars but will never produce painters. Did you know that?

Gericault, finding himself unwilling to suggest that the great Monsieur David might be wrong, replied with an irrelevance. I am told, he said, that some of Monsieur David's students think nothing of batting their tennis balls against canvases that don't meet with their approval. (Alas, it was probably true.) Perhaps this friend of yours, he said, is one of those athletic critics? Now stop it, Dorcy, and just *look* . . .

Dorcy understood what Gericault was seeking here: the strong movement, the sensuous brushwork, the intensities of light and color that one didn't encounter at Guérin's; the force and vigor that were absent from Guérin's frozen pantomimes. Dorcy doubted that this was his own quest, but he looked, he understood what was wanted and he began to copy diligently.

Copying. It is a way to understand what is happening in a painting and how it was made to happen; a way to follow the painter's process, to learn his ruses and stratagems, to examine not only his decisions and his choices but (if you are clever) his indecisions and his rejections, the ideas that were discarded along the way, the intentions that could not be realized, the unintentional strokes, the accidents, that suddenly seemed just right and were allowed to stand. A musician can do something like this when he translates the composers notations into sound. A poet can read and reread another man's work until he gets it—the whole process—by heart. A painter can copy.

Before long Dorcy understands that Gericault, working at his side, isn't really copying at all. He is reading the pictures in his own way, he is translating them into his own language, exaggerating here, muting there, changing proportions and perspective and palette. He is not reproducing, he is reinterpreting, appropriating these pictures for his own use.

Do you intend to learn from these masters, Dorcy asks, or do you mean to teach them a lesson?

As no one else seems able to do it, Gericault replies, I mean to teach myself.

* * *

In the end, even Dorcy's presence at these museum copying sessions cannot prevent them from turning into something absurd.

The other fellows from Guérin's studio take to strolling past the two copyists at work, feigning only a casual interest but winking and laughing silently at the odd couple—Dorcy with his neat and careful imitations, Gericault with his loosely brushed interpretations. Gericault ignores this surreptitious audience but Dorcy is uneasy, he fears that sooner or later someone is going to make a remark—and sooner or later, of course, someone does.

Oh Lord, says Dorcy, here he comes.

Monsieur Lafond, that is. Monsieur Lafond, who had challenged

Gericault over an imagined insult and then accepted his letter of apology rather grudgingly. Monsieur Lafond, who now stops and stares as Gericault lifts his brush, loaded and dripping with thick pigment, from his palette. Ah, says Lafond. Monsieur Rubens's pastry cook, he says (for that is the joke going around the studio).

Before Dorcy can intervene Gericault drops his brush and wheels around and punches the man in the nose. No great harm done, really, but there is blood on Lafond's jacket, blood on Gericault's palette, blood and paint spattered on the Grande Galerie parquet.

Oh Lord, says Dorcy.

* * *

Vivant Denon, the museum's director, writes to Monsieur Guérin: It is with great regret, Monsieur, that I inform you of the decision that I am forced to take regarding one of your students, Mr. Jerico [sic], who is now permanently forbidden entry to the museum. In the past, this young man's privileges have been suspended temporarily for his scandalous conduct [there had been some mix-up over his entry card and there was a to-do with the guards] and it was only your interest in this student that led me to permit his re-entry. Your recommendation and my indulgence gave me the right to expect some consideration, but Mr. Jericho's [sic] unseemly behavior proves him unworthy of our kindness. Several days ago, in the Grande Galerie of the museum, he permitted himself to strike and revile another student who, out of respect for the museum and fearing his own expulsion, behaved with moderation and restraint and demanded only an explanation. These are the facts according to the testimony of the guards, and Mr. Jericho [sic] has not denied them. I am very angry, Monsieur . . .

*   *   *

Guérin, needless to say, was furious, but it was he who sorted things out—to his own satisfaction, at least, if not to anyone else's. Lafond was to refrain from a challenge; Guérin would not have such a scandal in his studio, and Lafond must understood that his position in the studio was at risk if he was unable to swallow his pride. As for Gericault, he must understand that his continued presence in the studio on a regular basis would be generally disruptive and particularly offensive to Monsieur Lafond. Nevertheless, Guérin knew how to value his students: if Gericault wished, he might still come around from time to time—not too often—to work from the model and be criticized; if he intended to enroll himself at the École des Beaux-Arts—who else would have him now?—he might present himself as a student of Guérin's.

And how was Gericault to regain entry to the museum? Perhaps you can paint your way in, said Guérin. Present something at the next Salon. I daresay you think yourself ready for that?

No, I hadn't thought . . . said Gericault. He hadn't thought.

*   *   *

He had in fact been writing out strict agendas for himself in a deliberate effort to conquer his own thoughtlessness—the impulsiveness that always lurked at the edge of his life, always threatening to erupt into disorder and confusion, into something absurd. He had begun to make lists:

Draw and paint from the great masters.
Study—Anatomy, Classics, Music, Italian.
Tuesdays and Saturdays, Classics at two o'clock.
December—Figure studies with Dorcy.
January—Paint from the model at Guérin's.

February—Study the style of the great masters, *alone*. That sort of thing.

These agendas, he had told himself, would put order into his life. But the museum and Guérin's studio had been the foundations of his strategy and now, banished from both at once, he was sure that all order and system must collapse, that his strategy must fail.

He will laugh it off, Dorcy had thought, just one more absurdity, but for Gericault it was not a laughing matter. Things happen to me, he said to Dorcy, and I don't know why. His voice broke, he was close to tears.

And all for a punch in the nose, thought Dorcy, there was no proportion. No great crime had been committed, after all; the punishment might be severe but it was surely not irreversible; there was no need to panic, there was altogether too much fuss. If only you would *think*, he said. This can be mended. Consider...

But no, Gericault would not consider. Something wells up in me, he said, and he was weeping openly now. Chaos, he sobbed. I can't master myself.

No proportion at all, thought Dorcy; and now, with growing concern, he witnessed a repertoire of strategies against chaos that seemed more likely to invite the thing than to ward it off.

Gericault rode. When all else failed, he knew that he could count on Thunder. He and Thunder always understood each other perfectly, responding to each other's thoughts before they were thought, anticipating each other's every move; it was only when he and Thunder rode together that all jumble and disorder were blotted out, that everything was reduced to one thing—horse and rider. So he went out with Thunder each morning now. He would ride to the outskirts of Paris and beyond and he would spend the day—day after day—galloping recklessly across the countryside, zigzagging back and forth between the ditches and hedgerows—no destination, no thought to what lay behind or what lay ahead, enveloped entirely in the moment of riding. He would return in the evening, mud-spattered and disheveled, when Thunder decided that they'd had enough.

On most evenings he would find Dorcy sitting with Georges-Nicolas, waiting for him. You're all right, then, Georges-Nicolas would say; there's cold supper for you on the sideboard. Then he would excuse himself, leaving the reprimand to Dorcy:

You're tracking mud on your grandmama's carpets. And your papa is distressed, Gericault. I am distressed. What the devil are you doing?

Riding, Dorcy, that is all. Just riding.

And how long do you plan to keep this up?

But I have no plan. I *had* a plan, you know, but now I have none.

And where, if I may ask, do you go on these outings?

Anywhere . . . nowhere . . .

* * *

Not so. Gericault and Thunder may have no destination in mind, but the seemingly aimless circle of their riding grows tighter and tighter until it finally draws them one evening into the courtyard at Chesnay. Having gone out in the morning without his breakfast, having given no thought to food during a long day of hard riding, Gericault is a bit light-headed and confused. Thinking vaguely that he must have forgotten an engagement with Uncle Jean and Aunt Alex, he sees to Thunder's stabling and sends the gate porter up to announce his arrival—yes, they must be expecting him.

They are at dinner when he is shown in. They look up from their soup, startled. Good Lord! says Jean. What has happened to you? says Alex. I should have washed up, he mumbles. Then the candlelight blurs, the room tilts suddenly, slides away, and he falls to the floor.

Jean calls for brandy. Alex calls for camphor. Before either can be brought, Gericault flutters his eyelashes and revives. I think I haven't eaten, he says, smiling weakly. So they have him carried upstairs and put to bed—he is limp, he neither helps nor hinders—and Alex herself comes up to feed him a bowl of broth. Like a little child, he thinks, but he doesn't protest. I will just do nothing, he thinks. He has done enough. He has made a fool of himself at Guérin's and ruined his career; he has behaved like an ass in front of Dorcy; he has disgraced himself in front of Jean and Alex; now he will just do nothing.

The local doctor comes around in the morning to examine him and assures the Caruels that there is no cause for alarm. Clear eyes, dry skin, no fever; a perfectly healthy constitution, you know, just a bit sluggish . . . phlegm, that is all; purge him . . . feed him strong broths . . . let him rest for a day or two . . .

A message is sent to Georges-Nicolas. There is no cause for alarm, they assure him, there is no need to disturb himself, but he comes down anyway, and has no more success than Jean and Alex in piercing the silence in which Gericault has wrapped himself. He will say Thank you, he will say Very kind, he will say Please don't trouble yourself . . . and not much more. He will take a little broth, and he sleeps.

Several days go by and he is still in bed. Georges-Nicolas and Jean exchange glances; they are reminded that there is a strain of instability in the family—Jean's father and his brother both sent off to be cared for by the brothers of charity at Pontorson—but they will not speak of it. They prefer the simplest, the most likely explanation—youthful excess leading to exhaustion. He has been riding every day, says Georges-Nicolas, and ignoring his meals. He hardly touches the supper we leave out for him. He's been starving himself, it's as simple as that, he says, and Alex agrees. He hasn't been finishing his broth and egg, she says. I will go back to feeding him myself, and I will insist.

Again, he does not protest. You really must finish this, Alex commands, and he obeys. When he has had the last spoonful she puts the bowl aside and puts out her hand to feel his forehead. She brushes back his curls with her fingers, she leans forward to straighten his pillows, and he is overwhelmed by her scent—Mama's cologne. He lifts his head very slightly from the pillows—or has she raised his head very slightly with her hand?—and for a moment his lips brush her bosom. It is a very brief moment—perhaps it didn't happen?—and he falls back thinking, No, I cannot master myself. He closes his eyes and there is a long uncertain silence.

I see what I must do now, he says at last. I have been thinking, you know, and I think that I must answer the Emperor's call.

Napoléon's Grande Armée is being assembled for the great Russian campaign. Gericault has drawn an unlucky number in the conscription lottery but Papa has, as a matter of course, arranged to pay for a substitute. It is a common arrangement. Papers have been drawn up promising one Claude Petit payment of a thousand francs in advance and three thousand more at the end of his obligatory two years of service. Papa has mortgaged a small farm property to do this, but he is assured that the name Gericault will not be enlisted in the Usurper's service. Gericault, of course, doesn't share his father's sentiments, but he has been happy enough to avoid an interruption in his studies. Alex is appalled now to hear that he has changed his mind.

We'll talk about this when you're feeling better, she says, deciding on the spot to invite Dorcy down to spend a few days with his invalid friend. She doubts that either Jean or Georges-Nicolas can be of any use.

* * *

I am told, says Dorcy, that there is no cause for alarm. You're not ill, then, are you?

Gericault understands that his retreat is coming to an end. He eyes his friend warily. You are going to be unkind, he says.

Dorcy is prepared for this, he has rehearsed his tone. Unkind? he asks. Just because you've come to a low fence and balked? Not I.

Gericault closes his eyes. You *are* being unkind, he says. And is that what I've done? he wonders. Balked at a jump? Suddenly he sits up in bed. Thunder, he says. Are they taking care of Thunder?

Of course they are. They are taking care of Thunder and they are taking care of *you*, and Thunder is no trouble to anyone. You, on the other hand . . .

. . . but I have told them not to trouble themselves about me . . .

. . . knowing perfectly well that they have no choice. And now you propose to repay their trouble by rising from your bed and running off to join the Emperor?

Don't be against me, Dorcy, says Gericault, pleading with his eyes, because that has always succeeded, and feeling suddenly ashamed of that little trick. Still, Don't be against me, he pleads. This is not another impulsive whim, I have given it serious thought.

He waits, and Dorcy says nothing. You yourself have told me again and again that I act without thinking, he goes on, and I know that you have been right. I know that I have acted rashly and allowed myself to be seen as a fool. I daresay they all snicker behind my back.

Again, he waits and Dorcy says nothing. You see, he goes on, you can't deny it. I am seen as absurd. I can't remain in Paris, Dorcy. I must go away. I must learn to command myself. I understand that all of you are out of sympathy with the Emperor, but if it is a way for me to find some order . . .

There are other ways, says Dorcy. Monsieur Guérin wonders why you don't seek order at the Beaux-Arts.

More school, Gericault sighs. More scenes from Homer and Plutarch.

But that is the road to Rome, says Dorcy. Monsieur Guérin wonders why you are not competing for Rome.

But that is ridiculous. Don't joke with me, Dorcy. Monsieur Guérin thinks that I, the painter of violin cases, as he so kindly put it, might succeed in the competition?

Monsieur Guérin thinks that you might succeed, says Dorcy, and so do I.

The road to Rome—the Prix de Rome—is, of course, the road to a career: a period of study at the Villa Medici, the French Academy in Rome, followed naturally by exhibition and honors at the Paris Salon, followed naturally by commissions and official patronage . . . but to compete for the prize one must enroll at the École des Beaux-Arts.

Dorcy searches Gericault's face. He suspects that he has the advantage and he presses it. You see, he says, the School is both a way to find order and a way to be taken seriously. I can tell you that all of us—your aunt and uncle, Monsieur Guérin, I myself—we will all be greatly disappointed if you don't try.

I hadn't thought of it, says Gericault, remembering Guérin's parting suggestion that he paint for the Salon, and wondering if it was perhaps a serious suggestion, not meant as sarcasm after all. I hadn't thought of it, he says.

Well then, says Dorcy, think of it.

* * *

So the contract with Claude Petit is signed, he gets his thousand francs and he goes off to serve in Gericault's place. Nine months later he is dead, and Gericault is struggling at the Beaux-Arts with 'Chryses Comes to Ransom His Daughter from the Greeks'—the subject that has been set for the Prix de Rome competition.

He has jotted the requirements—the stage directions, he calls them—on a back page of his sketchbook: 'Iliad, Book One: The scene takes place in the Greek camp. Chryses, grand priest of Apollo, comes with his entourage, bearing great treasures, to beg Agamemnon and Menelaus for the return of his daughter Chryseis. Menelaus must be seen standing at Agamemnon's side, and surrounding them we should be able to distinguish Achilles, Nestor, Ulysses, Ajax, Calchas . . . '

Gericault is fuming when he shows this to Dorcy—shoves it under his nose. You see, he says. I told you. Will you look at this nonsense?

Dorcy reads the note and nods. He sees what this is leading to, but he takes a chance. Will you let me see your sketches? he asks.

Dead, Gericault replies. Dead, and I burned them before they began to stink. I can't keep this up, Dorcy.

I suppose not, says Dorcy.

(There is an art historian's anecdote that may or may not be true: "Seeing a child scribbling on a wall one day, and being struck by the strength of the drawing, Gericault exclaimed, 'What a pity! School is sure to knock that out of him.'")

I can't keep this up, Gericault repeats, and then suddenly: Do you know that Petit is dead?

Who is that?

My substitute. Claude Petit.

Poor fellow, says Dorcy. But that was the risk, wasn't it? These things happen.

He examines Gericault's face. It has nothing to do with you, he says.

I suppose not, says Gericault, not really convinced.

* * *

In April of 1812, shortly after he had turned his back on the Beaux-Arts, Gericault's grandmother died. The men who came to make the official inventory of her personal effects listed, along with the usual jewelry, flat silver and fine linen, 2 kilos of snuff—a habit, they noted, among women of the Ancien Régime. They noted also that Madame Caruel must have been hoarding ready cash for some time—over 79,000 thousand francs in old coins and new coins and Bank of France notes, not hidden but stuffed into bureau drawers and cupboards and left lying about in boxes and bags.

Aside from that, there was a very considerable fortune, one quarter of which was left to Théodore—much more than he had inherited from Mama. In a few months he would be 21, old enough to manage his own affairs, but when he finally reached his majority he would allow the power of attorney to remain in Georges-Nicolas' hands, declaring himself to be quite hopeless about that sort of thing.

* * *

4

CHASSEUR

Afterwards, there were those who said that all Paris had been vaguely uneasy throughout the summer of 1812—something in the air, they said.

Perhaps there was a growing sense of engorgement, a sense that enough was enough. Our history-book maps of Europe in that year are largely maps of French conquest and French Empire: Territory Under Direct French Rule, or Dependent States Under French Control, or Allies of France.

The dispatches from Spain that summer spoke of nothing but French victories, but the Spanish campaign had begun four years earlier, it should have been over by now, everyone knew that something had gone wrong. The Spaniards had been ruled by a corrupt and oppressive monarchy, they might have been expected to welcome the French army as liberators—but perversely, they were refusing to be ruled by the French.

The dispatches from the Emperor himself, leading the Grande Armée into Russia, spoke of nothing but Russian retreat. But, pursuing the Russians, the Emperor and his generals moved every day farther and farther from the center of empire, deeper and deeper into an unknown northern limbo—as if the retreating Russians had something up their sleeves.

In the Emperor's absence there was grumbling and discontent (even a farcical and failed attempt at a coup) in the Paris garrison— or so it was rumored. It was a summer of rumors.

* * *

Gericault was at loose ends in Paris, and his friends conspired. Guérin, who was reluctant to speak to him directly, continued to send encouraging messages. He wonders, said Dorcy, why you don't submit something to the Salon in November.

Monsieur Guérin, asked Gericault, who wondered why I didn't try for Rome?

Dorcy ignored this. I'm thinking of preparing something for the Salon myself, he went on. 'Bajazet and the Shepherd,' I thought . . .

Racine will always give you a fine subject, said Gericault. You must try it.

And you? Dorcy asked.

Gericault shrugged.

And what do you think of these? asked Horace Vernet, laying out a random selection of oil sketches for Gericault's inspection: scenes of Polish troops, a Cossack stable, a fortified encampment, the sort of thing that he could dash off, three or four in a row, in an afternoon. What do you think? he asked. To work up for the Salon. Which one?

They're very fine, said Gericault. Why not all of them? That will keep you busy for the summer.

And you? Vernet asked.

Gericault shrugged.

He was riding again. For old times' sake he rode at Franconi's several days a week. Regretting his failure to answer the Emperor's call, he had also begun to frequent the Grenelle barracks, striking up friendships with several of the cavalry officers and joining them when they organized races in the Champ de Mars. From time to time he still rode out alone into the countryside, but more carefully now. He avoided Chesnay.

He went on like that all summer and then, quite suddenly, between mid-September and the end of October, he painted his entry for the November Salon. Another art history anecdote, a very famous one, attempts to explain the sudden burst. One tends to discount these stories, but this one has the ring of truth:

He is riding out to visit the great fair held once a year at Saint-Cloud. It is a Sunday and the Empress herself is expected at the fairgrounds to inaugurate the Dancing Waters. The road to Saint-Cloud is jammed with Parisians on holiday, wagons and carriages and single horsemen all raising clouds of fine dust that are transformed by the end-of-summer sun into clouds of light—golden light flecked with rose and . . . what? Perhaps violet, he thinks; or perhaps pale green.

He is riding alongside a large van filled with workmen and their families on a noisy Sunday outing, the men singing tipsily at the top of their voices, the children brawling and the babies bawling, the driver waving his whip about ineffectually and cursing his carthorse—a dappled gray animal, not really beautiful, Gericault thinks, but beautiful against the shimmering golden light, too beautiful to put up with this sort of thing.

The horse is evidently of the same opinion. Without any warning (though Thunder has swerved away, sensing trouble) he rises up in protest, rears up suddenly, his forelegs pawing the air, his eyes bloodshot and fiery, his nostrils flared and quivering, his white mane streaming in the sunlight. 'The artist,' says the teller of this anecdote, 'had found his picture.'

Is that how it happens? Perhaps. One goes about one's daily business, not seeking, not desiring, and suddenly something comes into view ('out of the blue,' we say), something falls into place, fills an emptiness, finishes a thought, answers a question. The instant solution to a puzzle, perhaps. Or love at first sight. Or the artist's picture.

And did he go on to Saint-Cloud? Did he see the Empress (and the King of Rome, who happened to be with her on that day)? Did he see the marvelous Dancing Waters? The story-teller doesn't say, but it seems unlikely. From the moment that he found his picture he was intoxicated. From that moment, the picture and the making of the picture filled him completely, driving out all muddle and confusion and every other thought. It was like riding Thunder in the open countryside.

* * *

The first image is a turbulent little oil sketch—the horse alone, leaping up and writhing like a flame (the mane is positively ablaze) against a dark ground. We can just make out the hastily brushed indications of a leopard skin thrown across the horse's back—the standard saddle cloth of the Chasseurs, the Emperor's cavalry; so it was a military image (and the rearing horse was meant to have a rider) from the very start.

The conception was also, from the start, ambitious. He never asked himself if he was ready for a major, large-scaled work, he simply made the leap. Up to now his most ambitious paintings had been the scaled-down copies at the Louvre. Now he bought himself a canvas that measured over nine feet by six (Dorcy's jaw dropped in astonishment) and then he rented a vacant shop on the Boulevard de Montmartre because he had only his little improvised studio at home, not enough space for the canvas itself, let alone the horse.

Yes, a horse. Not a fiery, leaping horse, to be sure, but nevertheless a horse. Thunder proved too restless for the job, nosing about the shop-cum-studio and upsetting things, so he settled for a damp and mud-spattered carriage horse whose driver was paid to bring him around every morning.

And whatever for? Dorcy protested. He can't give you the pose, can he? He just stands there and stinks up the place.

Precisely, Gericault answered. The stable smells, Dorcy, the manure, the sweat, the leather. I look at him, I sniff the air, and . . . well, it puts *horse* into my head. That is known, my dear Dorcy, as . . .

. . . working from nature? Dorcy finished for him with a smile. I daresay. And is this, he asked, to be a battle scene? They'll want battle scenes this year, I should think.

Some sort of skirmish, said Gericault vaguely.

From the earliest sketches on there is indeed some sort of distant skirmish in the background, smoke and fire and a vague confusion of battle. Gericault, of course, knew nothing about battle, but the real military action in the picture, the action in the foreground, is confined to a single rearing horse and his rider, and about that he knew a great deal. He required no models for the pose, but he did want something concrete, a physical presence, in front of his eyes when he painted, and so the carriage horse was joined by a recent acquaintance from the Grenelle barracks—Alexandre Dieudonné, lieutenant in the Emperor's Chasseurs.

The finished painting would be called, for official catalogue purposes, "Portrait Équestre de M. D . . . ", and the face was in fact Dieudonné's. Having got that far, however, Dieudonné was called to the front and baron d'Aubigny—another Grenelle acquaintance—came around to model the splendid Chasseur uniform.

It is a composite figure, then, and much has been made of the fact. Too much. It has been pointed out that D'Aubigny was a royalist while Dieudonné was a Bonapartist and a republican. It has been suggested that the composite somehow represents an inner ideological struggle, while in fact it seems to represent nothing more than Gericault's wide circle of acquaintances, the ease with which he made friends and their willingness to submit to tedious studio sessions to oblige the charming young fellow.

If there was a struggle in the Boulevard Montmartre studio it was with the paint itself. Copying from the masters at the Musée Napoléon, Gericault had learned how to deal with recalcitrant pigment, how to coax it into some sort of correspondence with the masterpiece in front of him. But coaxing it now into agreement with an image in his mind—not simply a prancing horse mounted by a posing rider, but horse and rider leaping as one, charging away from us toward the heat and clamor of battle—persuading the pigment to do that was another matter. Like getting to know a new mount, he thought: a long series of advances and retreats, compromises and concessions, victories and defeats; a series of mistakes and near misses and strokes of luck, of adjustments and discoveries and reconsiderations, while the painter and the paint negotiate an accord on what can be done and what cannot. One had to pay attention.

Dorcy, too, felt that he had to pay attention. Though he was working on his own Salon entry—his 'Bajazet'—he came around to the Boulevard Montmartre for a few hours every day, as faithful as the carriage horse; he sat quietly in a corner and he watched, and he understood what was happening in a way that Gericault himself, caught up in his struggle with the paint, perhaps did not. Dorcy saw (and he was not surprised) that from the start the painting was much more than a grumbling student's expression of discontent with the teachings of the French School; it was more than a defiant gesture, it was a clear and unequivocal declaration of independence. Independence from Monsieur Guérin. Independence from the icy surface, the cool palette, the cold, impersonal touch and rigid contour with which classical method would have frozen the horse and rider. Perhaps without realizing it, Gericault had won his struggle. His Chasseur wasn't pinned, immobilized, in an ideal moment of perfect clarity; he was carried in a furious charge toward the chaos of battle on the horizon, propelled by strokes of color and light, by splashes of scarlet, by glowing yellow and orange, by glints of gold—by the paint itself, Dorcy thought.

A violent plunge into battle, then, moving *away* from the viewer—another break with the classical conventions. But something odd and contradictory happens to this image of Imperial glory. In mid-leap, both the horse and the rider turn their heads away from their plunge, they turn to face us, and the movement is checked. The Chasseur's face—Dieudonné's face— is blank and impassive. His saber is lowered. He may be about to raise it, urging his men forward into battle (as he does in the early sketches)—but not yet. "He turns toward us," says the historian Michelet, "and he *thinks.*"

Perhaps. Perhaps the charge into battle is also a moment of introspection for this Chasseur—and for his horse as well, for they do seem to be sharing a thought; a hesitation. So perhaps there is an inner struggle after all.

In any case, once the final version was started, the painting was driven to a finish in an astonishing three weeks—in good time for the opening of the Salon on the first of November.

* * *

By that date the fierce Russian winter had set in and the Emperor had begun his disastrous retreat from Moscow. The dispatches had not reached Paris yet—it would be a month before Paris understood what was happening—but it was noticed that the crowds during the opening days of the Salon were unusually subdued. There was certainly something in the air. Nevertheless, the crowds came.

It was, as always, the event of the season. There were over a thousand paintings, more than had ever been shown before, and the interiors of the Louvre Palace had been completely done over by Messrs. Percier and Fontaine, whose names had become (under the Emperor's patronage) synonymous with Empire Style: claw-footed furniture, winged ormolu sphinxes, a great deal of Roman coffering on the ceilings and Roman grotesquerie on the walls, the Emperor's monogram wherever it could be fitted, the Emperor's bees—that sort of thing. Percier and Fontaine's renovation was the talk of Paris, and all of Paris came to see it—the beau-monde and the demi-monde, gentlemen and common clerks, prosperous merchants and neighborhood shopkeepers. The Salon was the place to be seen and, if one was still on the rise, to *make* oneself seen; it was the place to show off one's refinement and taste, to display the latest fashions (turbans and ostrich feathers were prominent that year), and to display one's marriageable daughters; it was the place for discreet assignations and indiscreet flirtations; it was even the place for a family outing on a rainy day. Not just 'le tout Paris' but all of Paris came to the Salon.

Despite the Chasseur's break with convention, the hanging committee—that is to say, Vivant Denon—had not been insensible to the talent displayed by the young debutant whom Denon himself had expelled from these galleries earlier in the year. Had he not been so busy complaining about the execrable lighting (one was expected to complain, of course, everyone did) Gericault might have taken more notice of the fact that his Chasseur had been hung (in the Salon Carré, which was an honor) as a pendant to another equestrian portrait—Monsieur Gros's tribute to Joachim Murat, Marshal of France, the Emperor's brother-in-law and now the King of Naples.

When he finally grasped the significance of this arrangement, Gericault fell silent, for he also grasped that Monsieur Gros—the one painter of the School whom he truly admired—had painted to order, had produced a feeble work, and was being subjected (perhaps deliberately) to a damaging comparison. Gros's Murat, puffed up and proud, sits astride his mount like a fashion plate and shows off his uniform, his ribbons and braid and decorations and an absurd plumed hat. His horse rears up tentatively with a worried expression, scuffing up an improbable cloud of dust with his hind hoofs. The foam at the horse's mouth is mere shaving soap lather. There is a blue Italian sky and Vesuvius smokes in the distance, but the colors are strident and the landscape is airless—a studio backdrop. The battle action in the background seems to have been arranged by a child playing with toy soldiers.

Gros's painting and Gericault's could not have been less compatible, but there they hung beside each other, those two equestrian portraits—and they were, between them, the last of their kind, the last odes to Imperial glory. On the opening day of the Salon, Murat was already on the run in Russia, along with what was left of his elite cavalry troop. Lieutenant Dieudonné, who was one of that troop, was dead at the front.

With hardly a glance, Monsieur David led his entourage, a considerable crowd, right past both of those paintings and then, stopping himself with a comical little skid, he went back to examine the Gericault. He made a great show of widening his eyes in alarm, he raised his eyebrows and looked questions at the students surrounding him, and then he moved closer to examine the horse's dappled behind. Where does this come from? he asked at last. I don't recognize the touch.

Indeed, in contrast to the portrait of Murat and much else that hung on those walls, there was—recognizable or not—a distinct and liberating touch; there was paint that presented itself openly as paint; there were brushstrokes that took pleasure in being brushstrokes; there was the artist's own hand.

For that very reason, Georges-Nicolas preferred looking at the painting from a distance. What a pity he didn't have time to finish it, he said, squinting a little to see how it would look with a smoother finish. The dear boy has always been hasty, he said. But I suppose that it does show promise?

Oh, more than that, said Aunt Alex. Much more. It is another style, you see.

Yes, another style, said Uncle Jean, who was in fact just as puzzled as Georges-Nicolas. Yes, of course. Another style. You have heard that Monsieur David spent some time examining it?

David's words—where does this come from?—had spread instantly from one end of the Salon Carré to the other. The words were ambiguous, to be sure, but they had alerted the journalists who, without guidance, would hardly have known where to turn among the thousand paintings and more. They had no trouble following the crowd to the great popular success (Lethière's 'Brutus Condemning His Sons to Death,' of course, an enormous classical pantomime) but beyond that they needed a cue. David's words led them to Gericault—but nothing could make them sense the slight tremor that David had sensed; nothing could make them see the hair-line fracture that precedes the opening of a rift.

'One more fine painter of equestrian portraits,' they wrote. 'M. Gericault's name will count for something after this exhibition.'

'In the midst of errors inseparable from a first effort,' they wrote, 'one finds strong composition, a vigorous style and a feeling for color.'

'Not without harmony,' they wrote. 'Fluent and lively. There are qualities here that will need maturing and ripening. It is said that he has wielded the brush for two years at the most.'

'The movement of the horse and the rider are rather exaggerated,' they wrote, 'perhaps a little forced, but at least there is a great vivacity of execution. The brushwork leaves nothing to be desired, except perhaps for a little more firmness here and there.'

'Warm color,' they wrote, 'but unfinished. The horse is not very well drawn.'

Faint praise, then. Yes and no. Missing the point. And nothing missed the point more thoroughly than a diatribe entitled "Letter from an Art Lover to his Cousin in the Country." 'The violent movement of No. 415,' wrote the anonymous art lover, 'led me to believe that M. Gericault would like to leap over the walls of Jericho with his charger. The tour de force that his horse executes is truly extraordinary, far surpassing what we're used to seeing at Franconi's. I challenge that riding master, for all his talent, to put a horse out of joint as well as M. Gericault does, and I challenge his best horseman to sit astride in such a forced position. If M. Gericault were to open a riding school, I don't doubt that, with his talents, he'd replace M. Franconia promptly.'

Gericault read this and, for once, he held his temper until he was alone with Dorcy. By then his temper had cooled and he was simply morose. It is a failure, he said.

You must stop reading the notices, said Dorcy. It is very beautiful. If you ask me, it is a great success.

Gericault thought about this. It is odd, he said. On some days it is a success. I come into the gallery and look at it and I think that, yes, it is right. But on most days I can only see that it is not what I had hoped for . . . not what I had seen in my mind . . . that the paint has somehow conspired to distort my thought . . .

Yet the fellows all seem to have grasped your thought very well, said Dorcy. At least, most of them. I won't say that they will all want to follow your path, but they can certainly follow your thought. Even Monsieur David . . .

Monsieur 'Where-does-this-come-from?' *That* Monsieur David? I doubt it.

Don't take that tone, said Dorcy. Do you think that Monsieur David has never looked at any painting but his own? Do you think that he has never seen a Rubens or a Van Duck? No, trust me, he understands your Chasseur very well. He may not recommend it to his students, but you can be sure that he understands it.

Gericault waved this away. What I think, he said, is that I must go and offer an apology to Signor Franconia.

An apology, as he might have known, was not required. Franconia was indeed sputtering with anger, but not at Gericault. It is a marvelous horse, he said. Why, it is the very *essence* . . . the very *spirit* . . . and does this pedant expect you to exhibit a correct anatomical chart, when you mean to give us a leaping horse? Listen, Monsieur Theo, you must challenge the fool who wrote this . . .

That, at last, made Gericault smile. I have a friend, he said, who would restrain me. Besides, I must pretend not to know the fool's name. That is the form.

Of course, Franconi hastened to add, most of the notices have been excellent.

Lukewarm, said Gericault. Tepid.

* * *

When the Salon closed, that tepid response of the journalists was reflected in the museum's jury awards. Gericault received a gold medal, but it was only one of many that were handed out, and the museum made no effort to buy the painting, as might have been expected. The genre was uncertain, and that stood against it. An equestrian portrait? A battle scene? It was unclassifiable. Nevertheless: 'A work of great promise,' wrote Vivant Denon in the citation, 'it is executed with great verve.'

Gericault assured Dorcy that the 'Bajazet' deserved a medal too if it were up to him, but their eyes didn't meet when he said it.

In any case, he said, medal or not, no one will want my cavalry officer now. Not now.

Because, by now, everyone had read the Emperor's 29th Bulletin from the front—an astonishing and shocking document. Perhaps, while writing it, the Emperor had believed that nothing could be done to soften the blow of what he had to say, that no purpose would be served by trying. Perhaps he had felt that the shame of defeat must be shared by all of France, that its citizens must be spared nothing. Perhaps he was simply collecting his own thoughts, rehearsing the disastrous events of that winter and giving no thought at all to the readers of his bulletin. In any case, whatever his reasons, he minced no words in describing his army's withdrawal from Moscow, the sudden descent of the awful Russian winter, the death in that bitter cold of artillery horses, cavalry horses—'not by the hundreds, by the thousands. In a few days,' he wrote, 'more than fifty thousand horses perished. Our cavalry found itself on foot. Without transport, we were forced to abandon most of our artillery, our ammunition and our supplies.' His troops, said the Emperor, had lost their morale, they were in shock and disarray, they were in need of rest, and their retreat was being harassed constantly by the enemy—Cossacks who seemed impervious to the Russian frost, as the French were not. He refrained, at least, from a description of the cracked skin, the bleeding hands and faces, the huddling with dead horses for warmth, the hunger, the delirium, the desertion. And he ended on an optimistic note. 'The Emperor's health,' he wrote, 'has never been better.'

How does one react to such stupefying news? The Emperor had taken more than half a million men into Russia and only a hundred thousand would return; the rest had been killed in battle or killed by the Russian winter, or they had been taken prisoner, or they had deserted. But it would be a while before the numbers—the sons and husbands and fathers and brothers who would not return—became a reality. Meanwhile, for some, the bluntness of Bulletin 29 had a numbing effect. The unimaginable had happened and, because it was unimaginable, it was possible, for a while, not to imagine it.

For some—Georges-Nicolas among them—the blow to French pride (and to the financial markets) was severe, but it was balanced by the prospect of the Emperor's downfall. Put the government, at last, into the hands of sound men and all would be well. The markets were bound to recover.

For loyal Bonapartists, it was enough that the Emperor himself was returning to Paris. He would take up the reins and, while all might not be as before, he would have a plan.

For Gericault it was a muddle. We must trust the Emperor, he said to Dorcy, who did no such thing. It is difficult, he said, but we must wait and see.

'Wait and see' had long been his family's formula for dealing with muddle, and he embraced it now. He had learned as a schoolboy that one could cope with disaster by simply not being there, not attending, and he turned his thoughts now to other things.

Where in the world, he wondered, am I to store this monstrous canvas?

Georges-Nicolas, who was going on as if nothing had happened, provided the answer. His son's Salon medal (valued at 500 francs, according to the citation) had finally got his attention. It had come to him at last that this painting business might be serious after all, and in that case it could not be pursued in a boulevard shop. The boy must have a proper studio, they must find a place to live with space that could be converted to that purpose. The faubourg Saint-Germain would be out of the question, of course, but it was only the two of them now, they were free to live wherever they pleased.

The neighborhood, in the end, was the painter's choice; Georges-Nicolas, on his own, would never have chosen the 'Nouvelle Athènes,' on the distant northern fringe of the city—a place that had been recommended by Horace Vernet, who was planning to move there himself after his impending marriage.

The nickname, 'New Athens,' was meant as a joke—but not quite. It was a tiny little maze of a neighborhood, just beginning to attract the sort of people who would turn it into a polite Bohemia: artists and writers, actors and musicians, young professional men with new families, retired military officers, all seeking to escape the strictures and obligations of middle-class Parisian life—but not quite. The residents of this Bohemia were thoroughly domestic, and they were all gentlemen.

On the lower slopes of Montmartre, this quarter was all but suburban in those days. 'One might think,' wrote Colonel Louis Bro, who was to be Gericault's nearest neighbor, 'that one was in the countryside . . . the gardens . . . the masses of trees . . . ' But it was still Paris. Only a wall separated the private gardens from the dance-hall gardens of the Coq Hardi and (somewhat tonier) Ruggieri's café. Nearby, a little theater featured the popular clown, Bobèche, who could sometimes be found performing a comical balancing act on one of the garden walls, putting on a free show for the neighborhood children. There were market stalls in the streets in the mornings, there were trinket sellers all day long, and on summer nights there were often fireworks displays put on by the cafés.

Not Georges-Nicolas's sort of place at all, but he knew that he had to compromise; he couldn't bear the thought of Théo going off on his own, they must not be separated, and the boy could be stubborn, he was quite adamant about his choice. It was here, then, that Gericault and his Papa set themselves up in a comfortable little house at 23, rue des Martyrs, with a ground-floor stable for Thunder and a building out in the back garden that would serve very well as a studio. Their garden adjoined the one that would be Horaces's before long, and Georges-Nicolas felt that having Vernet as a neighbor would not be entirely unsuitable. That young man was already the most sought after painter in Paris.

* * *

I have heard you boast, said Dorcy, that one of your horses can eat six of Horace's father's. Tell me, how many of *Horace's* horses can yours gobble up?

In the horse market, Gericault replied, none at all. I can't sell one of mine, you know, while his fly out the window like Pegasus.

Yes, light as a feather, said Dorcy.

That is mean and unkind, said Gericault.

Meanness, unkindness, jealousy, were not in Dorcy's nature, but 'light as a feather' was a fair description of Horace's dainty horses, and the great popularity that Horace enjoyed was bound to produce a certain amount of irritation in even the kindest heart. It wasn't just his horses that were à la mode, there were society portraits and fashion illustrations, there were military scenes, there were mildly satiric caricatures—he had inherited his father's smart, shallow facility as well as his social knack and his flair for publicity. 'His talent,' wrote a fawning admirer, 'is the man himself, fiery and witty . . . he paints with the dash and ease of a brilliant improviser, but always with mature thought and a rational mind.'

'Dash and ease' were certainly the words for Horace's modish brilliance, but 'mature thought and rational mind?' That kind of nonsense was surely enough to produce a degree of sourness, even in a man as good-natured as Dorcy, but Gericault would hear none of it. He couldn't help admiring Horace's bravura technique, and besides, he was fond of his old friend and riding companion—though he was perhaps a bit piqued when Horace was awarded a commission that he himself had hoped for: ten portraits of the Emperor's favorite horses in the Imperial Stables at Versailles.

You might have expected it, said Dorcy. His horses will always win out, they're so . . . flirtatious.

Yes, his father's old trick, said Gericault. There is certainly a family resemblance. Nothing to be done about it.

He made the best of it. You'll have to spend days on end in the stables, he said to Horace. You can't ride down to Versailles every morning, you must stay at Chesnay. Uncle Jean and Aunt Alex would be delighted.

You'd come along? asked Horace.

Yes, of course. Gericault had begun to think that there was really no reason to go on avoiding Chesnay; there was only something that he had imagined in a fever—a mistake.

Alas, he was mistaken.

* * *

5

CUIRASSIER

This is how it began.

Dorcy has agreed to look in on Papa, to dine with him from time to time, and Gericault has gone down to Chesnay with Horace.

The Caruels are delighted. You hardly know your godson, says Alex. It will be an opportunity.

So Horace goes off alone each morning to the Imperial stables. Jean, the man of affairs, is seldom at home. Gericault spends his days with Alex and little Paul.

The boy is not quite five, a bit younger than Gericault had been when Uncle Jean first sat him astride a coach horse, but Paul has his own pony and he allows himself now to be put through the sort of polite riding exercises that Gericault himself could never abide.

Thank you, says Alex, reaching for Gericault's hand and pressing it. Nobody has taken the trouble, she says. His father has so little time . . .

Vaguely alarmed by the pressure of her hand, by the scent of Mama's cologne, Gericault pulls away. It is a pleasure, he says, to see another horseman in the family.

But no Franconi tricks, please, says Alex.

Are there tricks? asks Paul. Show me!

You ride very well, says Gericault, but no tricks. Not yet.

If I let you see my goat?

No tricks, says Gericault firmly. But I could make a drawing of your goat for you, if you'd like.

Dear Théo, says Alex.

He fetches his sketchbook, and they go off to see the goat.

We have to be very quiet, Paul whispers. She's feeding her baby.

Shall I draw them both?

He sketches the goat and her kid, and then they go off to see the ducks, the chickens, the turkeys, the peacock.

The dogs don't like him, says Paul.

No, they wouldn't, says Gericault, and he sketches the peacock too, surrounded by the lesser fowl.

At the end of the afternoon they order bread and jam to be served in the conservatory that Jean has added to the house.

I have a new music box, says Paul.

Run and fetch it, says Alex, and when he is gone she says, again, Dear Théo, and takes Gericault's hand.

Tell me about the orchids, he says, and while he is making a show of examining them, Paul returns and sets his music box to tinkling.

Dance, Mama! Paul commands.

Alex begins to hum the tune—'Joconde'—and she takes a few tentative, dainty steps; then she breaks out of the pattern and, laughing, she pirouettes to Paul and stoops to kiss the top of his head; then she pirouettes to Gericault and kisses his cheek—her dark eyes glistening, the scent of Mama's cologne rising from her bosom.

You too, Godfather! Paul commands. You dance too!

Alex draws him to the center of the room, there is no escape, and while Paul claps his hands in rhythm, they begin to dance. Determined to make this nothing more than an entertainment for Paul, Gericault begins to exaggerate the dance pattern—*one* and, *two* and, *three* and, *four*, with comic emphasis on every step—and Alex falls in with the joke. Paul laughs and laughs, and Alex laughs, but Gericault insists on a mock-solemn expression, and they dance on like that until the music box winds down.

* * *

Horace leafs through Gericault's sketchbook. You've spent a great deal of time in the barnyard, I see . . . and the kennels as well . . . and, ah yes, the village blacksmith . . . and Aunt Alex . . . Aunt Alex . . . Aunt Alex . . . but where is your little duenna?

Duenna?

Little Paul.

Disorder rises suddenly and spins about in Gericault's head. He tries to stand up, but thinks better of it and sits down again. I cannot master myself, he thinks.

Tomorrow, he says, I will go with you to the stables.

* * *

He knows—he seems always to have known—that at any moment, for no reason at all, the world may suddenly tilt, things may scatter and spin out of control, one may be overwhelmed. He knows that any moment, any single moment, may contain the seeds of disorder; any moment may blossom suddenly into chaos and confusion.

He tries to tell himself that nothing has happened but, try as he may, he cannot dispel the sense that in fact something has passed between Aunt Alex and himself. He cannot deny the ring of truth in Horace's cruel words—'your little duenna.' Indeed, something has happened, and he wonders if he himself did not invite—whatever it was. Something impossible. He will not give it a name, but he knows that he must master himself or he will lose his footing and be swept into the treacherous tides and eddies that lie beneath the surface of things.

It is to keep his footing, then, it is to struggle against chaos, that he goes to the Imperial stables with Horace. It is either that or he must ride out into the countryside with Thunder—but Aunt Alex will almost certainly insist on coming along if he rides. Instead, he takes his paintbox and goes along with Horace. The smell of the stables, the smell of his paint, will calm him. He will set up a blank canvas, and he will escape into that blankness from the confusion and disorder that have overtaken him. He will choose a horse and watch him closely, and order will be restored by the watching itself, by the concentrated effort to see and to paint what he sees.

The Emperor's horses dazzle him in their multitude—row upon row of chestnut and bay, dappled gray and roan, milk white and ebony, their polished coats all glistening and gleaming in the patches of sunlight that fall into the stable, or glowing in the shadows. He cannot choose one. He divides his canvas into three horizontal bands and in each band he places a row of horses like a row of separate notes in a musical chord—nine horses across the top band, eight across the middle band, eight across the bottom—twenty five horses in all, and only one them is facing us. For the rest, we have nothing but silken rumps and hind legs, the forequarters are simply not painted, or they are brushed in very sketchily. Only rumps and hind legs—but that is enough. We have the color and the texture and the particular sheen of each horse's coat; we have the individual style of each horse's tail—long and flowing or cropped short, gathered in a tight knot or loosely braided; we have each horse's distinctive stance—legs apart, blunt and four-square, or hocks delicately crossed so that the hind legs form an elegant V, or one hoof tentatively raised as if considering a stride, or one hoof gently pawing the stable floor. The hindquarters alone give us each horse in all its singularity—twenty four closely observed portraits.

An interesting perspective, says Horace, peering over Gericault's shoulder. But you won't get the Emperor's attention that way, you know.

Perhaps not, Gericault murmurs, refusing to be distracted. I imagine the Emperor has more important matters on his mind at the moment.

Horace winces at this. Ever since the Russian disaster the Emperor's allies have been deserting him, a coalition against France has begun to form. Even the most loyal Bonapartists understand by now that the triumphant march from victory to victory may be coming to an end—but no one can imagine what might follow. One doesn't like to speak of it.

Horace changes the subject. In a day or two, he says, I'll be finished here and I'll be going back to Paris. Do you plan to stay on?

No, back to Paris, Gericault replies without the slightest hesitation.

Nothing to keep you here? Horace asks.

Their eyes meet, and Gericault turns his head away. You mustn't imagine things, he says. Back to Paris, by all means. I've had enough of this country life.

* * *

Alex protests. She has not, in fact, examined her own feelings, she simply wants him to stay, she desires his presence, and she is accustomed to having her way. In the course of this short visit she has come to depend on her nephew as a member of the household. She thinks of him as a companion. She relies on him for dinner table conversation (about painting, mostly—a welcome change; Jean, when he manages to dine at home, talks incessantly of business affairs and the management of Chesnay). And Théo has captivated little Paul. He is indispensable.

Can't we keep you for a few more days? she pleads. Just while Jean is in Paris? We're so grateful for the company . . . Paul and I . . .

Is it possible, he wonders, that she doesn't understand—or that she simply doesn't care? He improvises. My Papa, he says. You know my Papa. We're barely settled in rue des Martyrs, and he will fret . . . dining alone, you know . . . no one to talk to . . .

Having seen him ride, Alex expects Gericault to be reckless and impetuous. She is not prepared to see him balk, and she becomes reckless herself. And who shall *I* talk to, she pouts, left alone down here? Shall I begin to take early supper with Paul?

It can't be helped, he murmurs. He backs away in dismay from her extended hand, but she moves toward him swiftly, she comes closer to him than she had intended, confronting him with her imploring eyes, the warmth of her body, the scent of her cologne. He knows that in a moment he will begin to tremble.

It can't be helped, he murmurs again. You know that I cannot stay . . .

At last she sees his distress—he is, after all, so young!—and she too backs away. She composes herself. Of course, she agrees. You have duties in Paris. It can't be helped.

He turns and flees.

* * *

The ride back to Paris began in uneasy silence. Horace would glance at his friend from time to time, and Gericault would turn away. At one point Gericault shook his head and said quite distinctly, Nothing has happened, and Horace nodded. Nothing, he allowed, and they rode on in silence.

Dorcy found Gericault vague and distracted on his return to Paris. What happened down there at Chesnay? he asked. What's wrong?

Nothing, Gericault replied. He had learned as a schoolboy to close his eyes and say, This will not happen to *me*. By now he had learned to do that with his eyes opened.

He made himself busy. To begin with, there was the new studio in rue des Martyrs to supply and put in order. Order so meticulous that Dorcy, on his first visit, could only stare and say, Beyond belief, my dear fellow. Beyond belief. How often, he asked, have I told you that you carry things too far?

Pristine new lengths of canvas were neatly rolled and stacked according to their size and shape. New brushes were arranged in groups according to their width and thickness. New colors were laid out precisely according to their place in the spectrum. And how long, Dorcy asked, will this last?

I am no longer a slapdash student, said Gericault. This is how I intend to work. I cannot abide disorder.

Mistaking the pompous tone for self-mockery, Dorcy laughed. After a moment of puzzlement Gericault laughed too, though he was in fact quite serious in his determination to lead, henceforth, a calm and orderly life.

A new agenda, he told himself, was what he needed. Not some grand, heroic endeavor, not a new Chasseur, but a simple daily agenda, a systematic program devoted single-mindedly to intense observation, to sharpening his vision.

He spoke to Monsieur Guérin about coming around to the studio again on days when a model was posing, and found that he would be welcomed.

He began to copy at the museum again, Denon's recent medal having nullified Denon's past prohibition.

Because his mind had been cleared of all anxiety while he was painting alongside Horace at the Emperor's stables, he went on working in Horace's territory—but not quite: portraits of horses—but closely observed portraits of particular horses, not fashionable 'types' of the sort that Horace dashed off; mounted cavalrymen displaying themselves on parade or prancing about in dressage exercises—but painted with an animation, an assured elegance, a shimmering opulence of color that Horace could only envy and that he acknowledged with a certain sourness.

Splendid, he said. Really splendid . . . but perhaps a bit sketchy for the market, you know. They'll want more finish. And the backgrounds . . . they do seem a bit dark and murky . . . you don't really set a *scene* . . .

They are not meant for the market, said Gericault.

Horace found this puzzling. I understand, he said, that in your circumstances you don't depend on the market. But if not for the market, what . . . ?

Gericault shrugged. He couldn't really say.

I suppose, Horace suggested, that you could work them up into Salon subjects?

No, not for the Salon.

No. Nor is *this*, said Horace, turning to a large, crude object leaning against the studio wall. A stable door, Horace thought, or perhaps a shutter. You're thinking of giving up canvas? he asked.

It is a gift for a friend, Gericault replied.

As if to underscore his refusal to embark on anything ambitious, he had kept a promise made a month earlier to the village blacksmith at Chesnay; he had made a signboard for the fellow. Painted in broad, rough strokes on the rough wooden boards, a muscular blacksmith stood almost defiantly, raising one arm to grasp the bridle of a wild-eyed, unruly draft horse. Confident of his ability to subdue the rebellious animal, the blacksmith, without loosening his powerful grip, turned away from the horse and stared impassively into the distance.

Rightly or wrongly, much has been made of the subject matter:

animal passion calmly and coolly restrained by human will. Even Horace may have found some significance in that. I see, he said. Everything under control.

Anxious to change the subject, Gericault averted his eyes. As you can see, he said, I've been busy. He began to fiddle with the drawing pencils on his table. In fact, he said, I haven't looked at a journal in days. You must bring me up to date. Is there more bad news from General Bonaparte?

From the Emperor?

But we are told that he leads the troops himself. *General* Bonaparte will do.

It was not the first time that Horace had detected a note of disaffection in Gericault's tone, and he refused to encourage it. There's no news of any importance, he lied, though he supposed that Gericault knew perfectly well that there had been bad news once again.

*   *   *

Indeed, for some time there had been nothing but bad news from Bonaparte. After the Russian debacle, everything had turned against him. France's Prussian ally had deserted him, forming an alliance with Russia that turned rapidly into a larger coalition embracing England and Sweden and finally Austria. Since the summer of 1813 France had been engaged in what seemed to be a war against everybody, and by now the French people had begun to desert the Emperor in their own fashion. They had begun to chafe at his increasingly autocratic ways, and they were weary of endless war, of continual conscription, of ever increasing taxes, all for the sake of an empire that gave them . . . exactly what? In the midst of war they were becoming—and what can be worse for a military enterprise?—indifferent.

In October, at Leipzig, Bonaparte had fought the coalition in the longest and perhaps the fiercest battle he had ever fought (history books call it The Battle of the Nations), and he had lost. France had lost over 70,000 men.

The Emperor called for a new army of 300,000 men and he managed to scrape together a mere 50,000. Murat, who owed the throne of Naples to his brother-in-law, the Emperor, deserted him. A remark by Germaine de Staël began to be whispered in certain Paris salons: that her heart's desire was to see the Emperor victorious . . . and dead. Everyone sighed.

In December the allied forces crossed the Rhine into France and started toward Paris, proclaiming that their quarrel was not with the French people but with Bonaparte. Their progress was slow, but they never retreated.

By February refugees from the countryside began coming into Paris, first a trickle and then a stream—terrified families bundled into carts and wagons along with odds and ends of furniture and bedding, pots and pans, sacks of potatoes. And then, in March, came the worst; for days on end, a straggling parade of wounded from the retreating army. They came by the wagonload, rattling down the boulevards and trickling blood onto the paving stones. They came on foot, wounded cavalrymen dragging by the bridle horses too exhausted to carry them; injured soldiers using sabers and muskets as crutches. 'On both sides of the boulevard,' one Parisian eyewitness reported, 'we sat in chairs and watched . . .'

Dorcy and Gericault would not sit. They stood among the spectators, Gericault sketching furiously while Dorcy shivered with rage. I don't see how you can do it, Dorcy whispered (for no one in that crowd spoke aloud). My hands are trembling so, I couldn't hold a pencil.

Gericault, who had taken out his sketchbook precisely to prevent himself from trembling, only shook his head and went on sketching. It was something he could not explain.

By the 30th of March the coalition forces were at the gates of Paris.

On the morning of the 30th Horace appeared in Gericault's studio, flushed and disheveled and out of breath. The National Guard, he panted, is going to turn them back at the Clichy gate. There is a call out.

He waited, but there was no response. I am going to join them, he said.

Yes, Leonidas at the pass, said Gericault. Yes indeed. Bravo. But Leonidas failed, you know. You will not turn them back.

Indeed not. A fierce battle was fought at the Clichy gate, but on the 31st an armistice was signed and the first of the allied forces entered Paris—a company of Cossacks followed by Tsar Alexander himself. There was a certain amount of discreet cheering.

On April 2nd the Senate voted to depose Bonaparte, and four days later it voted to restore the Bourbon monarchy. On April 11th Bonaparte submitted his formal abdication, and on the following night he tried to poison himself. Having botched that too—his own servants refused to give him more of the stuff when he demanded it—he prepared to go into exile.

On May 3rd the new monarch entered Paris: Louis Stanislas Xavier comte de Provence, now Louis XVIII—an obtuse, lackluster, gout-ridden man who had promised (half-heartedly) to accept a constitution (of sorts). He rode into Paris in Bonaparte's own carriage (painted over with the royal coat of arms) and he was escorted by a troop of Bonaparte's generals (for treason, as Talleyrand remarked at the time, is only a matter of dates).

Again, there was discreet cheering.

By the end of that summer British troops were encamped in the Bois de Boulogne. Cossacks on their ponies were mingling with Parisian horsemen on the Champs-Elysées. At a dinner party Horace's father (who had stood with his son at the Clichy gate) referred to these foreigners as 'our friends, the enemy,' and before long all Paris was saying 'nos amis' with a wink.

*   *   *

Our friends the enemy. Precisely. Where is one to stand? Which way is one to turn? We are a city of girouettes, says Horace. Weathervanes.

Horace's loyalty to the Emperor remains unshaken, of course, but before long he finds that his military subjects have great appeal to the officers of the occupying armies. One must study their uniforms, he tells Gericault. They are a market, after all. And he has to admit that their behavior in Paris has been impeccable.

Dorcy, on the other hand, is overjoyed to see the Emperor gone, but as a patriot he cannot reconcile himself to the foreign troops in the streets. I almost wish, he says, that Bonaparte had turned them back. Almost.

Uncle Jean, who had prospered under the Emperor, has no real quarrel with the man. But there is no reason to suppose that he will not continue to prosper under the king—and now he sees the possibility of a title in the future.

Aunt Alex, born into aristocracy, smiles at her husband's aspirations. She assumes that the Bourbon restoration must be a good thing, but it isn't something that she has longed for passionately. She pays little attention to such things. She smiles and shrugs.

Only Georges-Nicolas is unambiguously fervent and delighted, and he is puzzled to find that his son seems only . . . puzzled; that he will not discuss the great affairs of the moment, and spends his days riding Thunder through the streets of Paris.

* * *

In the past, riding Thunder has always served as an antidote to disorder, but now the strategy fails. Gericault rides along the boulevards and through the Bois de Boulogne, and everywhere he sees Cossacks and Prussians, Austrians and Englishmen. Chaos and confusion, he thinks, and nothing can be done. Thunder himself seems confused and tentative in his movements. They cannot find their usual harmony.

We have been like schoolboys on a patriotic holiday, he thinks— the high emotion, the passion that the Emperor inspired, the dreams of heroism—and now we are like schoolboys facing the mess on the day after and wondering what we have done.

As for himself, he thinks bitterly, he has done nothing. When he was called, he sent another man to die in his place. He would not follow the Emperor into Russia. He would not go to the Clichy gate. He has done nothing, and now there is nothing to be done.

Hearing his name called, he looks up to find that Baron d'Aubigny—the young officer who had modeled the uniform for his Chasseur—has come up alongside him. He nods.

A sorry sight, says d'Aubigny. All these foreign outfits.

A sorry sight, he agrees.

They ride along for a bit in silence, and then d'Aubigny says, You want cheering up. If you'll come along with me to the barracks, I'll show you something . . .

Gericault doubts that the Grenelle barracks can be a very cheering place at the moment, but d'Aubigny insists. Come along, he urges. Come along. You'll see.

What d'Aubigny wants to show him is only a military uniform displayed on a tailor's dummy, but it is a uniform that Gericault (who thought that he had seen them all) doesn't recognize.

Very fine, he says—and indeed it is: the scarlet coat and the jet black tunic are heavily encrusted with gold embroidery; the silvery helmet is embellished with golden oak and laurel leaves, and topped with an egret's feather and a flowing mane of horsehair; the cream colored leather breeches cling smoothly to the dummy's thighs, soft and supple as a lady's glove. Very fine, Gericault says, feeling a sudden hunger for scarlet and gold. But what . . . ?

Maison Rouge, d'Aubigny explains. His Majesty's household cavalry, you know . . .

One of His Majesty's first official acts had been the revival of this elite personal guard which conferred the rank of lieutenant on all of its members (regardless of the position they might hold in the regular army) and ranked the King himself as their captain. To insure loyalty, this guard was chosen largely from members of the old nobility—elderly returning émigrés and titled adolescents. "Old men and children," wrote Alfred de Vigny (who was one of the adolescents), "as if the Emperor had taken all the rest and killed them off." To fill out these ragged, if prestigious, ranks, exceptions were made for young men from well established bourgeois families if the young men were tall enough—at least five-foot-six—and if their families could pay the price. They must be guaranteed an annual allowance of 1500 francs, with an extra 600 francs to be paid annually into the company fund; they must provide their own mounts and pay for their own uniforms and trappings—a small fortune; and they must, of course, be properly sponsored.

Our company is The Grays, says d'Aubigny. Gray Musketeers. The color of our mounts, you know, and we're all having the devil of a time finding suitable animals of just the right shade. Whereas you, with Thunder, would have no trouble at all. If you would allow me to put you up . . . ?

Scarlet and gold, Gericault thinks. Scarlet and gold on the finest gray mount in the Maison Rouge, riding down the Champs-Élysées with his fellow Musketeers . . . riding in formation on the Champ de Mars with Thunder in the lead . . .

The best men in the company would sponsor you, says d'Aubigny, and he ticks off a list of noble titles. The best men. There would not be the slightest question . . .

Gericault remains silent and d'Aubigny takes another tack. We're not in barracks, you know, one sleeps at home. And one doesn't lack time for one's own pursuits . . .

He waits, but Gericault seems lost in thought. An old friend of yours has joined us, he goes on. Auguste Brunet. I believe you were together at the Lycée Impérial . . .

Still no response, and d'Aubigny changes course. In showing that we support His Majesty, he says, we can end this foreign occupation. At long last, we shall have some order and stability . . .

Perhaps, says Gericault. At long last. All at once he sees scarlet and gold as the colors of order and stability.

Perhaps it is that—not patriotism, not royalist sentiment but a longing for order. The Emperor had ended by creating chaos and confusion; perhaps this new regime . . .

Or does he hope that, escaping into this world of horses and military trappings, he will dispel the disorder and confusion in his own life?

Or perhaps it is the scarlet and gold pure and simple, the glitter of the uniform, for we know him to be something of a dandy—and what a figure he would cut in front of Aunt Alex and the rest of the family, how he would dazzle them!

Or perhaps it is the thought of the Gericault name on the roster of the fashionable Grays; Gericault in the company of 'the best men,' the grandest titles—for he is a man of fashion, after all, and not immune to snobbery. And wouldn't Papa be pleased!

Or perhaps it is only a flea in his ear, a whim, another ill-considered impulse.

In any case: You would be kind enough, he asks, to put my name down for the Grays?

* * *

Again, the art historians can't resist quoting Molière: "Que diable allait-il faire . . . ?" they ask. What the devil did he think he was doing? Enlisting in the Musketeers, they say, seems out of character. As if 'character' were a fixed and stable thing, a constant, not changeable, not mutating, not a process in a state of flux. As if we could say "this was not like him, in light of what we know," rather than "this is one more thing that we know. He was this, too."

Still, what the devil did he think he was doing?

For Papa, at least, the question did not exist. Eager to see a Gericault on equal footing with the Rohan-Chabots and the Talleyrand-Périgords of the Maison Rouge, he offered to bear the expenses himself (though he would have to mortgage a small farm in Normandy to do it) and his son (who could have born his own expenses without much trouble) accepted the offer without giving it a thought.

Horace, as might have been expected, raised the question at once. What the devil are you doing in that uniform?

I thought that you might understand, said Gericault. After all that has happened . . .

Horace eyed the splendid uniform, the scarlet and gold. Oh, I think I understand, he said. But now? he asked. Now, when so many loyal fellows who served the Emperor are being dismissed at half pay?

Do you suppose that I give no thought to those men? Gericault asked. I saw them, you know. I saw them or their brothers returning to Paris from the front, broken and bleeding. It was the Emperor who brought that upon them . . .

And you think that serving the King now will heal their wounds and set things right?

Gericault avoided his eyes. One must do something, he mumbled.

And is this the thing? Horace asked. It is a very fine uniform, but those half pay fellows will jeer at it in the streets. They will stand on the sidelines and mock you while you play at being soldiers on the Champ de Mars . . .

I know, he confessed. They have done so already.

And can you blame them?

He had to admit that it was understandable.

Then he went to show his splendid uniform to Dorcy. And what, Dorcy asked, do you think you're doing?

But that, Gericault protested, was Horace's question. I thought that you, at least, would understand.

Dorcy dismissed Horace with a wave of the hand. To Gericault's surprise, he dismissed the Musketeers as well. The Grays are a fine company, he said, I applaud your intentions, but you know perfectly well that there is a Salon announced for November. You should be preparing for that, not playing soldier.

I have nothing for the Salon, said Gericault.

You have several months.

* * *

So joining the Musketeers had not dispelled doubt and confusion after all. He had hummed a military tune while he put on his new uniform, taking note of how well it suited his figure; he had gone about to show himself off, and before the day was over he found himself questioning what he had done.

He had thought that, serving in the Grays, he might redeem the unquestioning enthusiasm he had always shown for the Emperor. Now he wondered if it was only an ineffectual gesture. And those half-pay pensioners: vaguely, he had thought that serving the cause of order and stability would somehow redeem the agony they had suffered for the Emperor's sake. Now he wondered if he wasn't mocking them instead.

For the first time since he had rolled it up and stored it in a corner, he took the canvas of his Chasseur and unrolled it on the studio floor. Perhaps that too had been a mockery, that fiery leap into battle. The reality had been those broken men he and Dorcy had watched straggling into the city. Perhaps he would have done better to paint a wounded officer.

He circled the canvas slowly, refusing to let his eyes linger on those passages in which he took some pride (the leopard skin, the officer's jacket, the horse's head), seeing only the leap into battle. He turned and began to circle slowly in the opposite direction, and slowly he came to a decision. Because the November Salon had been hastily called, permission had been granted to exhibit pictures that had been shown before. He would exhibit the Chasseur again, then, and he would paint a wounded officer to exhibit at its side. He would redress the balance.

* * *

Did he think that the patrons of that Salon or its public or its critics wanted to be reminded of Imperial glory and Imperial defeat? No, the walls that year were hung with scenes from French history, but dynastic history, not the recent past. Beyond that there were landscapes, there were official portraits of the new courtiers, there was a scattering of nymphs and dryads and glimpses of antiquity. And then there was his Charging Chasseur with its new companion, 'A Wounded Cuirassier Leaving the Field.' It was a most unwelcome sight.

The Cuirassier is not, to tell the truth, an easy picture to admire. The composition is in fact a mirror image of the signboard that Gericault had painted for the blacksmith at Chesnay, but something more than the figures has been reversed. The blacksmith had stood with his feet on the ground, firm and defiant, controlling his horse. The Cuirassier, a dismounted cavalry officer, struggles to lead his balking horse down a slope, away from the distant battlefield; he seems to falter, he is slipping, sliding, grasping at the horse's reins with his right hand and supporting himself with the scabbard in his left. He turns his pallid face to look back at the battlefield with what some have seen as a tortured, tragic gaze and others as an empty, vapid stare. The Chesnay blacksmith had looked off into the distance calmly and impassively.

The Cuirassier is painted on the same grand scale as the Chasseur, but Gericault had rejected the sweeping movement, the luminosity, the loose touch and flashing brilliance of the earlier picture. The colors here, despite the red lining of the officer's cloak, are somber. The figure of the officer is solid and heavily modeled—boldly sculptural to some eyes, bulky and ponderous to others. The gleaming helmet and breastplate, the muddy boots, the soft leather breeches and the gloved hand are painted with a marvelous physicality, but the horse is a fiasco. It seems that he couldn't be made to fit, even after a strip of canvas had been added to widen the picture. Gericault had not been hasty, he had corrected and corrected, squeezing and foreshortening, but the solution was finally beyond him, it is clumsily done. The horse's hindquarters are scrunched up abruptly against his forequarters and the intervening figure of the Cuirassier does not disguise the fact that there is no middle at all. Our modern eye, to be sure, does not demand verisimilitude, but this painting is not meant to be looked at in that way and the horse seems absurd.

Monstrous, said the critics. The drawing was full of errors. The painting as a whole was only a careless sketch, and one hoped to see improvement in the final execution. Perhaps one could admire the painter's vigor, his virile and bold touch, but one had to admit that in this case the boldness had gone too far. The brush strokes were hardly disguised, one had best stand fifty steps away to look at this work. This young man's first painting had given rise to great hopes, but those hopes had yet to be realized. He had been advised to moderate his touch, but the advice seemed to have been lost on him.

Gericault stood fifty steps away and watched two of his fellow officers examining his painting. One of them shrugged, the other guffawed, and they walked on.

We've all been in the same fix, said Horace, everyone scrambling to produce something on short notice. Never mind.

But finish it, said Dorcy. You can correct the errors.

Gericault stood in front of the painting with Papa and the Caruels, and wished that he were anywhere else . . . at home . . . safe in his bed . . .

Oh dear, said Papa, and Uncle Jean said, I say! You've tried to do something different, said Aunt Alex. It must have been very difficult.

Damned calf's head with a great stupid eye, said Gericault under his breath.

There was no medal.

6

ONE HUNDRED DAYS

The Bourbon restoration may have been greeted at first with a muted sigh of relief, but that was followed quickly by a sigh of resignation. What more, after all, could one have expected? "To go from Bonaparte and the Empire to what followed them," wrote Chateaubriand, "is to fall from reality into the void, from a mountain peak into an abyss." The new King, in short, was not an inspiring man. His most ardent supporters could only describe him as the best that one could hope for under the circumstances.

It can be argued that Louis XVIII was not a fool. There are those who would argue otherwise, but no one would deny that, fool or not, he had been dealt a bad hand. The other players at the table all held high cards.

To his right sat his own brother, the ultra-royalist comte d'Artois, who had rallied around himself the clergy, the nobility returning from exile and expecting their privileges and properties to be restored, anyone who scoffed at the notion of constitutional rights and believed that all could once again be as before—before the aberrations of the revolution and 'The Usurper,' Bonaparte.

To his left sat a vast and nebulous population—men of every class who had learned in the revolution to call themselves Citizens; men who adamantly refused to relinquish the rights that they had gained in the revolution and who believed that Bonaparte, for all his errors, had confirmed and consolidated those rights; men who questioned the authority of the King, and rallied around his free-thinking cousin, the duc d'Orléans, whose father (known as Philippe-Égalité) had voted for the death of Louis XVI.

And what cards had the King to play from his own hand in the middle? Men who called themselves moderates, men who believed in the possibility of a liberal monarchy and saw it as the best way, under the circumstances, to preserve their constitutional rights. They were not comfortable allies for a man whose early decrees were dated not as of the first year of his reign but as of the *nineteenth*, as if he had been on the throne since 1795 and there had been no break in the monarchy, no revolution, no empire.

Beyond the moderates, the King had Bonaparte's generals—or so he hoped. They had, to be sure, sworn allegiance to him—but could they be trusted?

In the event, many of them could not. On the first of March in 1815 Bonaparte, encouraged by dissension among the allied forces, defied his exile, landed at Golfe-Juan on France's southern coast, and began a march toward Paris so triumphant that he himself was astonished. People who had wept at his exile, but been relieved to see him go, now wept with joy at his return. They lined the roadside to embrace him and to cheer the ever growing army that marched north with him. Soldiers, sent to arrest The Usurper, kept their muskets on their shoulders and joined the march. General Murat and General Ney, sent by the King to stop him, fell into his arms.

And what can the King have expected? asked Horace when he heard the news. The generals have grown accustomed to treason. Vive l'Empereur!

And would Paris hold? The King swore that he would defend the city with his life, and he called on his loyal troops to stand with him. Loyal! said Horace. Weathervanes all. They will welcome the Emperor with open arms and we will be well rid of fat Louis.

And if he goes, Gericault asked himself, do we follow him? He was disturbed by the thought that in other times no man in the King's household guard would have seen it as optional.

On the 19th of March Benjamin Constant, that most furiously spinning of all weathervanes, published a stirring polemic in the *Débats* calling Bonaparte the enemy of France and all humanity, a man whose reappearance threatened the country with misery and misfortune. He himself was a liberal, said Constant, he believed in liberty, and he believed that only the King could preserve it.

The next morning Constant notes in his diary: 'Bad timing. Complete disaster. Confusion and cowardice everywhere.' The King has fled in the middle of the night, calling on his household guard to follow him.

And do we follow? Gericault asks. He has not discussed the matter with Dorcy, who would surely have said, Yes of course, one has no choice, though the question does not arise for him. He has not asked Horace, who would surely have said, You must be mad! Certainly not! He puts the question instead, at the last minute, to his old school friend and new comrade-in-arms, Auguste Brunet. Brunet has begun to make a name for himself as an economist and a student of politics. He will have studied the matter, he will understand the dilemma that is clouding Gericault's thoughts and weakening his resolve.

The household guard has been called to assemble in the courtyard of the Tuileries on the night of Palm Sunday, the night of the King's flight. There is a driving rain, but everyone understands that the rain itself does not account for the absence of many of their fellows. They have not been told, but everyone has guessed at what is about to happen.

And do we follow him? Gericault asks. Indeed, the confusion of that scene at the Tuileries, the shouting, the scurrying back and forth, the commands and counter-commands, might lead one to think that, with the best will in the world, these hastily trained officers cannot follow anyone.

It was easy enough, Brunet replies, to guard the King when there was nothing to guard against. Following him now would seem to be our purpose.

Into defeat? asks Gericault. Shall we follow him into defeat?

And do you think that our friends . . . do you think that the allied forces will allow the King to be defeated? It is our business, Gericault, to take him to firmer ground, and then we shall see.

Gericault ponders this in silence, and Brunet approaches the matter from another direction. The King or Bonaparte? he asks. Which one is the tyrant? Answer that, and you will see who to follow. By the time Bonaparte was finished he was ruling by decree, by his own whim. The King, at least, has granted us a charter, and he would do more, you know, were it not for the ministers . . . were it not for d'Artois. But they can't prevail if we give him our support. The King is not one of your ultras.

All at once the clamor in the courtyard subsides. Brunet and Gericault turn to see what has happened, and there, tottering down the stone steps, barely able to stand but supported by two of his ministers, is the King himself, bloated and grotesque in the swaying lantern light and drenched by the rain as he is led, shivering and stumbling, to his coach.

He will not make a stand, says Gericault. *He* is running away from *us*.

He is running away from men he can't trust, says Brunet. And would you trust his generals to make a stand? If he can trust no one else, Gericault, let him at least trust us.

The royal coach rolls away with an enormous clatter, and that sound is followed at once by the clatter of muskets falling to the ground. There are men in that courtyard who are quite prepared to simply throw down their arms and walk away.

Years later Gericault explained his own actions on that night. When I saw the cowardice of those soldiers denying their oath, he said, I resolved to follow the King.

* * *

The rain never stopped. It was raining when they rode out of Paris early on the morning after Palm Sunday and it went on raining for the rest of that Holy Week.

It was hardly an organized cavalcade. They followed the King in confusion and disorder, and in a perpetual drizzle interrupted regularly by drenching rain. And where *was* the King? Headed north, that was certain—but to Calais? Dunkerque? The Belgian border? His route was as uncertain as his destination—partly because the King himself was uncertain, partly because he trusted no one. Before long his escort, lagging behind and unsure of its orders, began to disintegrate. Small groups of stragglers and single men became detached from the main body, wandering about in that everlasting rain. "I could hear nothing but rain," wrote Alfred de Vigny, "and the sound of my horse's hoofs stumbling in the rutted, muddy road. My boots were coated with a thick layer of yellow mud, and inside they were filled with rainwater. I looked at my brand new golden epaulets, my pride and joy, and it grieved me to see that they were shaggy and sopping wet . . . " That lovely operetta uniform!—as unfit for such an expedition as the men who wore it.

Gericault and Thunder traveled that same rutted, muddy road under the same leaden sky. There were moments when the gray sky would turn suddenly white and for a time pale sunlight would filter through the rain, creating a sparkle and dazzle that Thunder and Gericault would stop to admire. Then the sky would turn leaden again and they would ride on, getting wetter and wetter. Once he had realized that no amount of effort, no farmhouse fire, would ever make him dry, that he would live in his squelching boots forever, he had become quite content to be wet. This is not happening, he thought, to that miserable fellow, that failed painter who became a musketeer; this is happening to some rain-soaked body in a sodden uniform, that is all. Every hour that he rode on took him farther and farther from Gericault.

My poor Thunder, he said, understand that this is not happening to the noble Thunder; it is happening to a dapple-gray, mud-spattered coat, that is all.

And for less and less reason they went on riding north. On the day that Bonaparte had entered Paris the King's party had been at Abbeville. They had hesitated there, they had considered waiting for the household guard to appear, but the moment had passed and impatience had prevailed. They had hurried on ahead, leaving the guard to straggle on behind them, floundering toward the north in the yellow mud and never catching up.

By the end of the week the King was at Lille, not far from the Belgian border, and somehow the drenched and exhausted stragglers, or most of them, had come together just behind him at Béthune. The Grand'Place there seethed with men who had no orders, no notion of whether they were to assemble or where, whether they were to stay or move on, and at first there were as many rumors as there were men. Before long, though, there was only one rumor, and then there was a proclamation to confirm it:

His Majesty bid them all farewell. He thanked them for their loyalty, and he now relieved them of their oaths. They were free to return to their families and wait for better times . . . or if they wished, they might follow his Majesty into Belgium, with the understanding that one could not bear arms into foreign territory . . . and of course there was no longer an exchequer to provide stipends . . .

Standing dazed in that crowd, Gericault became, in one blow, himself again. For no reason at all, he said. We have come all this way for no reason at all. The King will not make a stand.

To be sure, there were cries of Vive le Roi! . . . but these men had been relieved of their oaths, there were also cries of Vive l'Empereur! All at once the French impulse toward oratory took hold, and the crowd resolved itself into a dozen clusters to debate what historians still call 'La Grande Question:' the King or the Emperor?

Standing on a cannon at one end of the square, the most eloquent speaker of all was young Alphonse de Lamartine, who had yet to publish his first poems. He was a monarchist, said Lamartine, but above all he was a Frenchman. In the worst days of the revolution his noble family had never emigrated, never made common cause with the enemies of France. He was prepared to fight for the King, but he would not leave French soil to do it. Republicans and royalists were united, he said, they *must* be united, in the cause of liberty. If they were to rally the French people against tyranny, against Bonaparte, they could not do it from foreign soil, under a foreign flag; the people would not trust them. So far, he said, they had taken the path of loyalty and honor, but one step farther, one step onto foreign soil, and they would denationalize themselves. 'If we emigrate,' he concluded, 'we accept defeat on the very ground where we must stand and fight. I will not cross the border.'

Muddle, said Gericault. He and Brunet had found each other in the crowd, and they stood together listening to the eloquent young poet. That fellow makes a very fine speech, said Gericault, but his thought is muddled.

Perhaps, said Brunet, who had been moved and disturbed by Lamartine's words. Is our own thought any less muddled? he asked. Do you propose to follow the King?

The King will not make a stand, said Gericault.

Then you intend to go back?

In this uniform?

No, said Brunet. I am told that there's a little shop near here that sells second-hand clothes . . .

That is what it had come to: incognito.

The necessity was obvious. Even before he had reached Paris Bonaparte had issued a decree that put Paris and its environs, and the neighborhood of any imperial residence, off limits to soldiers of the King's household. But that was before the King had conceded everything to the Emperor; now it seemed likely that no part of the country would be safe, at least for a while. One did not want to be recognized.

For the time being, said Brunet, we had better lie low. Do you have some place to go?

I thought Mortain, said Gericault. My Uncle Bonnesoeur. You would, of course, be welcome . . .

Bonnesoeur the regicide? Brunet asked with a smile. You *are* well connected. I'm afraid that I'm traveling in another direction, but I daresay we'll meet again in Paris before long. In a few months, you know, no one will ask any questions. It will all be forgotten.

So Gericault put on a wagon driver's felt hat and shabby clothes and Thunder became an unconvincing cart horse. It is only a game, Gericault assured him. Bear with me, my dear, and get us to Mortain, and then we can ride as we please.

He looked up at the sky. At least, he said, the rain seems to have stopped.

* * *

Uncle Siméon understood at once, he cut Gericault's explanations short with a wave of the hand. But that's a very poor masquerade, he said. I would have spotted the two of you a mile off as suspicious characters.

We had very little choice, said Gericault, getting down from his seat on the wagon. The stock of old clothes was thoroughly picked over by the time I got to it. You can't imagine the number of fellows . . .

I can imagine, said Siméon, and the two of them embraced.

At least these old rags got us here, said Gericault.

And a good thing, too, said Siméon. We were afraid that you might have gone . . . the other way . . . to Belgium, you know. You were wise to come here. I take it you understand that you must stay away from Paris?

I understand, said Gericault as he began to unhitch Thunder. And my Papa . . . ? he asked.

He'll be frantic with worry, of course. You must write to him at once.

They're not intercepting letters?

We are told, said Siméon, that there is to be no more of that.

Yes, said Gericault. We are told many things.

Remembering the boy filled with fervor and enthusiasm, Siméon looked at Gericault in surprise. Sarcasm, he said, does not become you. Has fat Louis turned you sour?

Gericault ignored this. Before he wrote any letters, he said, he must take care of Thunder and then they must have a ride. They hadn't had a proper ride in a week.

I suppose, said Siméon, that we can expect the two of you to be out from dawn to dusk every day?

It clears my head, said Gericault.

Indeed it did. They rode every day, fiercely and deliberately, from dawn to dusk as Siméon had expected, and while they rode his head was emptied of every painful thought—as if he were seventeen again and the two of them had never left Mortain.

In the evenings he and Siméon played piquet and talked of horses and the weather and everything under the sun but the subject that lay between them. From the start it had been clear to Gericault that Siméon still held his allegiance to the Emperor—still saw in him the embodiment of the revolution and the republic. From the start it had been clear to Siméon that Gericault could not find where his allegiance lay. They were too fond of each other to want a confrontation, but as the days passed they grew increasingly uncomfortable. They couldn't go on talking of horses and the weather forever.

It was Siméon who finally broached the subject. This musketeer business, he said, à propos of nothing. It was your Papa's doing, wasn't it? Or your Uncle Jean's?

Do you find it so hard to believe, asked Gericault, that the choice was my own? Because it was, you know. Is that so hard to understand?

Siméon thought about this while he rearranged the cards in his hand. I think I understand, he said at last. You believed in the King's charter, didn't you? You gave your trust to a man who was too weak to hold it. And now, of course, you've been hurt.

I gave my trust to the Emperor, Gericault replied, and then I gave my trust to the King. Neither of them could hold it, and now it seems to me that it's France that has been hurt.

Perhaps, Siméon allowed. Perhaps she has. But surely the Emperor and the King can't be equally to blame?

I blame the Emperor, said Gericault. Then he said, I blame the King, and he tried to collect his thoughts. I don't know, he said. I blame everything that has happened.

Everything, Siméon echoed, and once again he fiddled with his cards. You understand, he said after a while, that the Emperor will manage things very differently now?

And still be Emperor?

There is talk of a new constitution, said Siméon. I grant you that mistakes were made, but after all that has happened he can't be the same man. This time, I think, he can be what we will make him.

We? asked Gericault.

The patriots who will rally to him now, said Siméon.

Ah yes, said Gericault. The patriots. When I rallied to the King I thought that I was a patriot. Are you sure that you can tell me where patriotism lies now?

Siméon nodded. On the one hand, he said, you have a man who could not rest easy until he set foot on French soil again. On the other hand . . . *your* man, who couldn't rest until he was on *foreign* soil, surrounded by our enemies. That is where he is comfortable. *Your* man is a born émigré.

Gericault put down his cards and stood up. Doubt and confusion flooded him, he was adrift. Uncle, he said, forgive me but I cannot choose. I have taken off one uniform, I won't put on another.

You will stand aside then?

I will paint, said Gericault, who until that moment had thought that he would not paint again. Still, I will paint, he said, though he doubted it.

The Emperor, said Siméon, has always favored painters. Monsieur David . . .

No, I leave the Emperor to my friend Horace, said Gericault. He can paint one uniform on Monday and another on Tuesday, he can paint whatever comes marching down the street. I leave that to him. I will paint for myself, he said, not really knowing what he meant by that and, in any case, not really thinking that he would do it. It was a way to end the conversation. I will paint for myself, he said. And now, if you'll excuse me . . .

* * *

The fellow is in distress, Siméon said to himself, let it rest. But he couldn't let it rest, every day brought news that kept the subject alive for him. The allied coalition had begun to assemble a joint force in Belgium, determined to rid Europe once and forever of the man they called The Ogre. Determined to act before the coalition forces were at full strength (as usual, there was a great deal of squabbling and delay), Bonaparte was preparing his own forces for a pre-emptive strike. Siméon went about murmuring, Momentous times, momentous times, and Gericault began coming in later and later from his rides, hoping to avoid being drawn into a discussion of the day's news. He did not want to argue with his uncle. He did not want to argue with himself. He did not want to form an opinion.

They went on like that, uneasily, for almost a month. Then, in the middle of May, Siméon's daughter Rose was married, and the scene in the small parish church affected Gericault in an unexpected way.

He had been sitting in the family pew, waiting for the ceremony to begin and looking about: at the young people laughing together, flirting, sharing jokes and secrets back and forth across the aisle; at their elders, shushing the young ones and looking about as Gericault was doing, nodding vague recognition at distant relations and whispering explanations to their neighbors; and all at once it came to him that in this whole web of crisscrossed ties and connections he had no place. In that small church the scent of the wedding flowers was mixed with, was almost overpowered by, the familiar scent of cologne, and suddenly he was filled with a longing for his own familiar world, for Dorcy, for Horace, for

Papa, for Aunt Alex, for everyone. He was, quite simply, homesick.

He spoke to Siméon that evening. Uncle, he said, we have imposed on your hospitality long enough. It's time, I think, for Aunt Alex and Uncle Jean to share the burden.

Alexandrine? Siméon was horrified. Jean-Baptiste? But Chesnay's much too close to Malmaison . . . to St. Cloud . . . You know that you're not to go near an Imperial residence.

Uncle, Uncle, Gericault said chidingly, we can be discreet. And so much time has passed . . . this will all blow over before long.

I daresay, said Siméon. Meanwhile, you know perfectly well that you're not a burden here, and you know that Chesnay is a mistake. What's got into your head? But Gericault only said, Uncle, Uncle, I will write to them in the morning, and Siméon understood that he had lost. A mistake, he repeated, but clearly there was no reasoning with the fellow.

* * *

A mistake. Having dismissed Siméon's objection, he has convinced himself that there is no other reason to avoid Chesnay. If there ever was a reason, it is now a thing of the past. And perhaps there never was a reason, only a foolish idea that Horace had put into his head. A misunderstanding.

He leaves Mortain, then, with a light heart, looking forward to his reunion with Aunt Alex and little Paul. The situation at Chesnay, he thinks, is perfectly simple. Uncle Jean is forced to spend too much time in Paris. Aunt Alex is forced to spend too much time alone. The change in government will, if anything, have prolonged Uncle Jean's absences; now Aunt Alex will want company more than ever and they will both be delighted to see him. Pleasant company for Aunt Alex, that is all. There is, he feels certain, no more to it than that.

Until Alex greets him on the steps at Chesnay, until she stoops to retrieve the shawl that has slipped from her shoulders and brushes his hand with her bosom as she rises again. Then, as if flowing from her body into his, a sudden agitation fills him, a churning, a trembling—chaos—and in an instant, there on the steps, he is forced to understand the calamity that he has refused to understand.

He begins to stammer. It . . . it . . . it's been a long ride. If I can rest for a while . . . and we'll talk later?

An hour's rest in the familiar little room that has always been his at Chesnay; an hour's rest, he tells himself, and he will be able to bring order to his disordered thoughts—but the room itself conspires against it. Can it always have been so small? Were the pink and yellow stripes of the wallpaper always so oppressive? And there is something new, something that seems terribly out of place, on the familiar writing table; a little terracotta by Clodion, a piece that had turned up in an odd lot of bibelots that Jean had bought at auction—a lucky find. Charming, Jean had said. Very fine, he had admitted—but really, it was the taste of another time. Nowadays, he had insisted, the subject was only suitable for a bachelor's rooms.

Indeed. The sort of thing that Clodion was famous for: a nymph and a satyr carousing, ardent and abandoned in an explicit way that suggests, to be sure, the libertine taste of an earlier time—'ancien régime.' The nymph's flesh is modeled with such sensuous physicality that one can imagine the sculptor's fingers trembling as he worked. And she is not the least bit demure, she is as eager as her partner, rushing into his embrace and nearly toppling him over, thrusting herself between his goats' legs and bringing an ecstatic smile to his lips.

Gericault lies on his narrow little bed and stares at this debauchery and, now that he has allowed impermissible thoughts to enter his head, he allows himself to imagine Alex as that ardent nymph.

Later, he sends down word that he is quite exhausted, he offers his apologies and asks if a little supper might be brought up to his room. He will be better company in the morning.

* * *

Simply staying in bed is, of course, a possibility, but then Alex would be drawn to his bedside, and the thought—Alex leaning over him with a bowl of broth, Alex with her hand on his wrist, with her hand on his forehead, caressing his cheek—the thought is too disturbing. He dresses and goes down for breakfast.

Jean has already left for Paris—he will be gone for several days—and they are alone at the breakfast table. Alex begins to chatter: the family is so proud of their brave musketeer . . . how awful it must have been, she can't bear to think of it . . . and how awful now to be unable to move about freely . . . Jean will of course tell Georges-Nicolas that he must come down to visit him at Chesnay . . . and who else? Monsieur Vernet? Monsieur Dedreux-Dorcy? . . . but first she must have him to herself for a few days . . . she insists . . .

And all the while she smiles what he takes to be a knowing smile; her eyes are fixed on his as if they are reading—oh Lord! he is certain of it—the improper thoughts that have broken loose in his mind. For he has lost control of his own thoughts, he is defenseless.

I insist, says Alex. For a few days, anyway, all to myself, before Jean comes home and they all come down from Paris to see you.

Oh Lord!

* * *

She has indeed read his thoughts, and she makes no effort to conceal her own. Neither of them now has the slightest doubt, but everything remains unspoken. For three days they are alone together (Paul is now six years old and occupied with his tutor) and for three days they never touch.

They wander the estate together, they inspect the barnyard, the kennels, the little parish church that Jean is having restored, and each of them puts up a screen of sorts: Alex chatters constantly; Gericault has helped himself to one of Jean's blank account books and uses it as a sketchbook wherever they go.

Together they visit the village blacksmith to see the signboard that Gericault had sent down as promised.

Some fellow offered me quite a sum for it, says the blacksmith proudly, but I wouldn't part with it.

You should have let it go, says Gericault. That would be the first sou that anyone has paid for my work.

Monsieur Gericault could have made you another, says Alex.

They ride together—no farther than the boundaries of the estate, for he accepts that limitation on his freedom—and he discovers that, red-faced and hair flying, she will take the same jumps and ride just as recklessly as he. Amazon! he exclaims, and she says, Just let me ride Thunder and I'll show you!

In the evening, at Alex's insistence, they read "Paul et Virginie" to each other. 'Virginie!' Gericault intones, 'sans elle je n'ai rien . . . ô ma chère Virginie! . . . elle n'est plus! Elle n'est plus!' His voice trembles.

For three days they go on like this. They exchange glances, they look deep into each other's eyes, they tremble, they tremble constantly, and they never touch.

Then Jean comes home, bringing Georges-Nicolas with him, and together they step back from the brink on which they have tottered. With a sense of relief, they retreat into decorum. They are innocent. They have done nothing to bring this about. They have done nothing.

Decorum and innocence on the surface—but a tide of unruly desire suddenly floods the back pages—what Gericault now thinks of as the secret pages—of his sketchbook. Taking Clodion's nymph and satyr as his theme, he begins to imagine convulsive and violent embraces for the carousing couple: the satyr takes his nymph roughly from behind, spreading her legs with one hand and grasping at her bosom with the other; or, facing him, she straddles his goat's legs and thrusts with her hips, throwing her head back in desperate ecstasy; that sort of thing.

Gericault has discovered what pornographers have always known: no experience is necessary; once one permits oneself, one is able to imagine these things with no trouble at all.

* * *

Dorcy and Horace come down. They take a look about, they sniff the air, and they become alarmed. You are in great danger here, says Horace. You should really go back to Mortain.

As if suddenly welcoming chaos and confusion, Gericault says, lightly, But you're mistaken, my dear, I'm perfectly safe here.

In fact, says Dorcy, you're in danger and you're rather enjoying it, aren't you . . . the danger?

That is nonsense, says Gericault.

Of course, it is not. Beneath the surface decorum there is the faint buzz of recklessness and danger and, like riding Thunder, it is a pleasure. Given time, disaster is inevitable, but in mid-June they are saved from that by the news from Waterloo.

The news is greeted at Chesnay with a mixture of regret and relief. Another defeat, another humiliation—but still, things can't go on and on as before, one can't be at war with the whole world forever. Perhaps it is just as well.

In any case, with Bonaparte defeated there is no longer any need to avoid Paris, there is no longer an excuse to stay on at Chesnay.

* * *

Back at the rue des Martyrs he discovers that Papa has kept his Musketeer's parade helmet polished and on display on the dining room sideboard. Dear Papa, he says. But I'm afraid that's over now.

He takes the helmet and packs it in a box and puts it away.

* * *

7

RUE DES MARTYRS

On the 22nd of June Bonaparte abdicated once again, once and for all, and with a sour sense of anticlimax the French prepared to welcome back the man who everyone now called Louis the Unavoidable.

Just you wait, said Horace. D'Artois and his gang of ultras will have the upper hand now.

And so they did. The second Bourbon Restoration began on a note of revenge—what came to be known as White Terror. Men who had sworn allegiance to Bonaparte on his return from Elba were suddenly fair game—hunted down and in many cases simply massacred, or tried and executed, or hounded into exile like Monsieur David; like Uncle Siméon. Even Dorcy, a Bourbon supporter, had begun to waver in his allegiance to the King. For Gericault, there was no longer any possibility of allegiance. Having resigned his commission, he resigned himself now to doubt and uncertainty, to unease and anxiety—the ailments of his generation. 'Mal de siècle,' Alfred de Musset called it.

For a generation born in revolution, every dream had failed—first the ideals of the Republic, then the glory of Empire. It had all ended in defeat and dishonor and the moral squalor of the Bourbon restoration. Patriots like Siméon were sent into exile. Loyal young officers were dismissed at half pay while ageing

181

émigrés who had fled the revolution crept back from their hiding places and were awarded positions for which they had no qualifications. Every day one heard of some new outrage—of men like the Comte de Chaumareys, who had never followed a naval career but, because he had attended the naval academy twenty five years before, now demanded a position as a ship's captain and, incomprehensibly, was put in command of the frigate Medusa.

There was a sense of disgust, then. A sense of despair. A sense of stymie. 'Mal de siècle.'

Beyond malaise, however, there was an active, if clandestine, opposition led by the King's cousin, Louis-Philippe, duc d'Orléans. Louis-Philippe would indeed be brought to the throne one day and he would be called (for a while) the Citizen King, but for the moment he was nicknamed Monsieur Valmy (having taken part in that famous battle) and his followers—young artists and writers, politicians with liberal and Bonapartist leanings, pensioned off Napoleonic veterans—tended to gather at Horace's studio, just across the garden from Gericault's.

"As I approached," wrote a visitor to that studio, "I heard an indistinct noise that grew louder and louder with every step that I took and finally became a bizarre uproar. I opened the door just a crack—and what a sight! I was frozen with astonishment . . ." Horace himself painted the scene. The room is crowded with half-pay officers standing about and chatting or reading what are presumably political broadsides. In the midst of this crowd Horace is smoking a pipe and fencing with one of his students, both of them holding a palette and brushes in their unarmed hands. Two other students, stripped to the waist, are resting between rounds of a boxing match, and still another is painting at an easel. Someone is playing the piano, someone is blowing on a trumpet and someone else is beating time on a drum. The studio dog is barking at what appears to be a young fawn, and in the corner, next to a bust of Horace's father, a fine horse is tethered to the wall. There is, however, no sign of the monkey or the bear that witnesses assure us put in an appearance from time to time.

I stay away from that hullabaloo, Gericault told Dorcy, but that wasn't quite true. He knew that Dorcy, though he had begun to call himself a liberal, didn't approve of the Bonapartist crowd that gathered at Horace's studio. He himself had begun to take a rather haughty attitude toward Horace's great commercial success (when someone came looking for Horace but knocked on Gericault's door by mistake he would say, No, Vernet's the shop across the way). Still, he was not out of sympathy with the politics of Horace's crowd, and it was something of a point of honor to defy—to be *seen* to defy—the secret police who, it was assumed, kept Horace's studio under surveillance.

Besides, there was the attraction of a certain Baroness Lallemande.

What had happened? At Chesnay he had allowed disorder, a sudden tide of reckless desire, to flow into the back pages of his sketchbook, and now, back in Paris, he found that he could not prevent that same wild desire from swamping his thoughts and saturating his work. It is something that happens to every young man—a time when, quite beyond his control, every moment, every single thought, is charged with erotic implication, abuzz with confused longing. He would begin to draw a scene of lovers entwined, lovers embracing tenderly, and as he went along it would become, despite himself, a scene of combat, of violent struggle—though never rape; the women are always eager partners. He tried to contain the violence with a rigid classical line, but the style is strained and coarse, even brutal. One can't really say that these couples are entwined and embracing, making love; one can only say that they are screwing, tearing off a piece.

Horace, who had no objection at all to the subject matter, found the violence (and the aggressiveness of the women) somewhat disturbing. But I begin to draw a woman, Gericault complained, and she becomes a lioness. I can't help it. Then Horace was astonished to hear him say, Anyway, the two of us, we both like big rumps, don't we? (But no, the phrase he actually used was 'grosses fesses' and, given the coarseness of the remark, one can only translate that as 'fat asses'). Disorder, then. And Caroline Lallemande.

According to Colonel Bro, Gericault's nearest neighbor and a regular at Horace's studio, she was, if anything, rather too slim—but very pretty, really. A Creole, of course . . . elegant . . . carefree . . . coquettish. Everyone thought her charming and everyone sympathized with her situation.

Charles-Francois Lallemande had found her while serving the Emperor in San Domingo, putting down a colonial rebellion. A fervent Bonapartist, Lallemande had risen rapidly to the rank of General and to the title of Baron, and he had never forgotten his obligations, never trimmed his loyalty to the Emperor. During the exile in Elba and after the defeat at Waterloo he had managed to entangle himself in various more or less crack-brained conspiracies to restore the Emperor to power, and at the end he had put himself forward to accompany Bonaparte to St. Helena. He might have considered himself lucky when the British refused the offer and exiled him to Malta instead, but he did not. He might have done better to accept Malta and lie low for a while, but he did not. He was a restless man, determined to have a mission. Before long he would turn up in Turkey, then in Persia, then in Egypt, and eventually in the United States, where he planned to found a colony in the Texas territory for pensioned-off Napoleonic veterans. It was to be called 'le Champ d'Azyle,' but in the long run nothing would come of it and he would found a girl's school near New Orleans instead. One can't say that the man didn't try to create his own destiny.

Through it all, Caroline Lallemande remained in Paris, promoting her husband's destiny and creating her own. She was entirely dependent on the kindness and generosity of the political opposition, the sort of men that one met at Horace's studio, and she became a regular visitor there, encouraging support and soliciting funds for her own upkeep and for her husband's schemes.

She continued to honor Lallemande, then, and everyone understood that, to remain faithful, she could not take fidelity too literally. One has to get along from day to day, one does what one must. 'According to the scandal-mongers,' wrote Colonel Bro (who had set her up in a little house in the rue des Martyrs, rent free), 'she had special favors for Vernet, for Gericault, for others . . . '

Gericault had seen her first at Horace's. Surrounded by a circle of admirers (including the duc d'Orléans—'Monsieur Valmy'), she was reading aloud from one of Charles-Francois' letters— declaiming, actually, for Charles-Francois described his trials and his ambitions in a declamatory style. When she was finished it was hard to tell whether the applause was for her husband's valor and enterprise or for her performance.

A brave man, says Valmy. The fates may appear to be against him, but with the help of this brave lady . . . and of course, we must all do what we can . . .

With this signal Caroline's allowance is assured—nothing so vulgar as passing a hat, but before the afternoon is over everyone in that circle has pressed something into her hand, a contribution to her upkeep and to Charles-Francois' dream of founding a colony for pensioned off veterans.

Alas, says Gericault, I go about with empty pockets. If you'll just come around to my studio later on . . .

He might easily go to the studio himself to fetch his purse, it is only a few steps away, but no: If you'll just come around, he says, and the alternative never occurs to him.

* * *

With the same seemingly deliberate thoughtlessness he has left his drawings lying about the studio; Caroline can hardly be blamed for noticing and leaping to conclusions. As he offers her the contents of his purse she asks—straightforward; matter-of-course—Shall I pose for you, Monsieur?

He has heard all the gossip and the un-gentlemanly innuendos at Horace's studio, he hasn't the slightest doubt about what is being offered. The warm scent of cologne rises from her barely covered bosom and suddenly he finds himself whirled about in a confusion of desire and doubt. Alex . . . he thinks . . . Alex's cologne . . . Mama's cologne . . . He runs his hand over his face, he begins to stammer, and he is surprised to hear himself say, Indeed, Madame, that would be charming.

Whatever you command, she whispers.

She is, after all, a General's wife.

* * *

Coming from the islands, says Horace, she is so much freer . . . so much less restrained. That Allemande woman, he says, is an education. And so she is. She comes to Gericault in the afternoons and together they explore the path that leads from lustful, violent abandon to measured, calculated abandon to, finally, tenderness and constraint. Because, for him, Alex is always a presence in their bed—in his mind they are, somehow, not two but three—and, after the initial burst of passion, her unseen presence imposes a certain constraint.

The drawings, too, become less violent. The nymphs and satyrs are coyer, more coquettish, less ravenous; the embracing couples seem to be caught in that tender moment just before passion is fully aroused, or in the moment after it has been satisfied.

In one small painting the third presence actually appears. Naked to the hips, she is lounging serenely at the foot of the bed and observing the entwined couple, cool and impassive.

* * *

One might expect that his afternoons with Caroline would dampen his desire to see Alex—it is what he himself expects—but no, he finds that he is still burning and abuzz with longings that he cannot dismiss. He becomes as incautious, then, as he had once been cautious, riding Thunder down to Chesnay at any hour of the night or day, on the spur of the moment.

Both Horace and Dorcy absolutely refuse to ride down with him. Horace begs off politely (so much work to finish, you know . . . and my new bride . . .) but Dorcy won't disguise his disapproval. We're not talking of an amusing escapade, he says. I get no pleasure, watching you flirt with disaster.

Disaster? asks Gericault. What *are* we talking about?

Recklessness, Dorcy replies. Just plunging ahead with no thought . . .

If you're complaining about my riding again . . . says Gericault, and Dorcy is finally obliged to understand the futility of his argument. His friend is indeed riding blindfolded at the edge of a precipice and he is smiling and enjoying the risk—as usual. There is nothing to be done about it now. The regrets, the despair, will come later.

Dorcy shrugs helplessly. It's not your riding, he murmurs. Never mind.

* * *

Chesnay itself provides all the pretexts that he needs. He has promised a set of decorative wall panels for the Caruel drawing room, he must see how the light falls in that room, he must examine the boiserie that will frame the paintings . . . and of course he must see little Paul, he has been neglecting his godson.

Uncle Jean is hardly ever at home. Now that the monarchy has been safely restored he spends a great deal of time in Paris, sniffing about in court circles, lobbying for a title . . . perhaps de Saint-Martin, his wife's family name; that would do very nicely. Alex refuses to join him in this, she finds his snobbery faintly comical; she will not join him in Paris, she stays resolutely at Chesnay and Gericault's visits are, for her, a godsend. The servants have already learned to treat him as a member of the household, and his visits become longer and more frequent.

They resume their dangerous game, then, gazing into each other's eyes and trembling whenever they are alone together, but never speaking of it, never touching.

If Jean happens to come down from Paris, Gericault turns his attention to excursions with Paul—cautious rides in the countryside (the six-year-old has not outgrown his pony); visits to the riding school at the royal stables; visits to the picture gallery at the Trianon (it is not too soon to start forming the boy's taste)—and what could be more fitting? A Godfather doing his duty. But the visits to the Trianon go beyond Paul's education, they manage to turn him, once again, into a little duenna.

To begin with, wanting to see Poussin's *Arcadia*, Gericault had gone to the Trianon alone. Jean, for once, was down from Paris.

Gericault had decided to take Paul along with him to the Trianon, and then at the last moment it occurred to him that the painting of shepherds reading their own mortality in a tombstone inscription—*Et in Arcadia Ego*—was not, perhaps, the best way to arouse a child's enthusiasm. He went alone.

When he arrived, the gallery was already occupied by two young ladies—Mlle de Montgolfier and her friend, Mme Belloc—painting copies, as it happened, of the Poussin. Many years later Mlle de Montgolfier, speaking to the historian Jules Michelet, recalled the encounter: "It was a fine autumn afternoon," she remembered. "He knocked so politely that one simply had to let him in . . . and such a lovely smile . . . "

In short, the two ladies were charmed.

As for Gericault, his afternoons with Caroline Allemande had done nothing to dispel the lascivious thoughts that might flood his mind at any moment, the sudden, tingling desire to embrace whoever stood before him . . . anyone, it seemed . . . in ways that he barely understood

He began to babble. He praised the ladies' copies; he told them that he himself copied at the Louvre whenever he could, it was the only way to learn.

In that case, said Mlle de Montgolfier, he must have been greatly distressed, after Waterloo, to see the allied coalition reclaim so many of the Louvre's treasures.

He could not argue the justice or the injustice of that event—the paintings and the statues were, after all, loot—but yes, he had indeed been distressed, and he saw now that a display of that distress would go down very nicely with the young ladies.

"With great animation," Mlle de Montgolfier remembered, "he

told us how indignant he had been, after the allies entered Paris, to see them packing up our masterpieces at the Louvre to send back to . . . wherever they came from. His voice was choked with emotion," she said. "He had stood in the courtyard through the whole thing, to see the paintings leave and to mourn them one by one."

Truly, he had wept at the time. Now, at the Trianon, he let a tear fall, he wiped his eye, and he wondered if he had perhaps carried it too far. But no . . .

"We wept too," Mlle de Montgolfier remembered, "and it was impossible to remain strangers after that. We should have been worried about what people would say, young and alone as we were, but instead we gave him permission to visit us again while we were painting at the Trianon . . . "

At first he thought that he would not. Riding back to Chesnay he found it impossible to dismiss the sort of improper thoughts about those two proper young ladies that would make it impossible to meet them again without blushing. With a smile, he thought of Cherubino at the opera: '*Ogni donna cangiar di colore, Ogni donna mi fa palpitar.*' It might seem rude, he thought, but he'd better not go back to the Trianon.

Then, at dinner that night, he mentioned the two copyists that he had met at the Trianon and Uncle Jean began to tease. Yes, yes, he said. Two young Arcadians, to be sure. And no doubt they appreciated your—professional advice? And no doubt you promised that you would return to observe their progress?

Seeing him blush, Alex too began to tease. But of course you must, she insisted. The young ladies will be quite lost without you.

Well, perhaps I will, he mumbled, stung by Alex's sarcasm.

"And when he returned," Mlle de Montgolfier remembered, "he was thoughtful enough to bring along his little godson . . . to spare us the embarrassment of what people might say, you know . . ."

On their way across the park he had filled a pocket with fallen horse-chestnuts, and while he chatted with the ladies he used his pen-knife to incise the outline of one of Poussin's figures on the surface of one of the chestnuts. It was meant to keep little Paul amused, of course; but equally, it was a way of showing off for the ladies, and little Paul sensed that. He did not have his godfather's full attention—or rather the attention that he got seemed somehow to pass right through him and go to the ladies.

He frowned. He put his hands in his pockets and he began to shift from foot to foot. Someone, said Mlle de Montgolfier, is a little chilly.

Paul nodded his head and came right out with it: It's cold, he said. It's time to go, godfather.

I suppose we must, said Gericault. Just give me a moment, he said. He put the final touches then to his chestnut carving and, with a little flourish, he offered it to Mlle. Montgolfier. Will mademoiselle accept this little token . . . ?

Gladly, she replied, and then she saw Paul eyeing the chestnut. But perhaps the little one . . . ? she asked.

Paul held out his hand.

Altogether, it had been a disagreeable outing for him, but he did keep the chestnut as a souvenir and showed it to Mama as soon as they got back to Chesnay.

Cousin Théo made this for you? Asked Mama.

Paul shook his head. He made it for the lady, he said, and she gave it to me.

The lady . . . ?

And at that moment Alex decided to take matters into her own hands. She had never in all her life doubted her ability to have what she wanted, and in all her life she had never been denied a thing—except a passionate lover. She turned to face Gericault and he understood at once the decision that she had made.

Uncle Jean? He asked.

Gone back to Paris, she replied.

So there was no escape. He thought for a moment that he might faint again, he was so weak with desire.

*   *   *

One mustn't imagine a dramatic scene of high passion—in the stable, say, with Thunder rearing up on his hind legs and whinnying while they tumble in the straw. No, she simply comes to Gericault's room and it is in fact rather hurried and clumsy, impeded by clothing that they are too impatient to remove and punctuated by coarse breathing and rasping moans.

Afterwards, he lies with his face in her bosom, inhaling the scent of Mama's cologne and thinking that everything in his life has been an accident, a mistake. For no reason, he thinks, for no reason at all, they are lovers now, and once that line has been crossed they can never be anything else to each other. From now on they can only be lovers. It is like a terrible net that has dropped from the sky and trapped them both.

* * *

He flees. He goes back to Paris, but not to Caroline Allemande. A vague notion of fidelity to Alex prevents that. Instead, to give himself an agenda that won't allow him a moment to think about his predicament, and as a kind of self-punishment, he decides to try again for the Prix de Rome.

And why not? asks Dorcy, though his expectations are not high. If you think you can bear it?

For all his contempt, Gericault is quite aware of the prize's prestige. We shall see, he replies.

The subject set for the first round of the Prix de Rome competition is 'Venus Preventing Aeneas from killing Helen, who Seeks Refuge at a Statue of Vesta.' The usual nonsense, Gericault says, but he manages to get through that round successfully (though he announces to Dorcy that he despises the drawing and he will not show it to him).

The subject set for the final round is 'Oenone Rejecting the Dying Paris.' Oh Lord, says Gericault wearily, but he applies himself, he sketches the composition in a dozen ways—Oenone to the left, Oenone to the right, Paris supine and pathetic, Paris pleading with outstretched arms—and then he just stops. It's no use, he says to Dorcy. Paris and Oenone mean nothing to me. I can't do this, and damn the Academy anyway.

He goes back, then, to riding Thunder into the countryside— riding wildly and aimlessly, but bound, sooner or later, to end up at Chesnay.

I cannot stay, he announces, but he allows the servants to show him to his usual room and bring him warm water, and no sooner has he washed and stretched out on his bed for a rest after a hard morning's ride than Alex comes to him.

This time she leads him slowly, deliberately, teasingly, until they are both naked and trembling in each other's arms, and when he begins to moan she covers his mouth with her hand.

He is frightened. He flees back to the rue des Martyrs and, for a time, he tries to distract himself at the salons and soirées of fashionable Paris. This charming, smartly dressed, well connected young man has only to show his face to be flooded with invitations.

You've become quite impossible, Dorcy finally complains. You expect me to drop everything at a moment's notice to go along with you to some theater, or to drink tea at someone's 'afternoon,' or to dine out here and there . . .

. . . And you think that I should abandon this frivolous society, Gericault says. And you will be happy to learn that I agree with you. I have decided that I must leave all that behind me.

He has decided that Paris is too close to Chesnay, that the proximity can only lead to chaos and disorder. He may have withdrawn from the Rome competition, he tells Dorcy, but he can certainly afford to travel to Italy without that assistance. Any painter, after all, must travel to Italy sooner or later.

Dorcy is taken by surprise. What brought this on? he asks.

I have put myself in a most awkward position, Gericault says. Then, after a pause, I am a monster, Dorcy. A monster . . .

Guessing at the nature of Gericault's problem, and realizing that the poor man has begun to weep, Dorcy moves closer to him, he puts a hand on his shoulder. Gericault throws an arm around Dorcy's waist and clings to him. He buries his head in the ruffled bosom of Dorcy's shirt and sobs. And Dorcy, overwhelmed with pity for his friend, begins to stroke Gericault's hair gently, murmuring, Don't, don't, it will be all right, as one might to a weeping child . . .

. . . and then, as if on a signal, they both draw back. Gericault turns his head away and tries to compose himself. Dorcy straightens his waistcoat.

There is always an element of desire, even if only a trace, submerged in any friendship. There is always the possibility that the trace will rise suddenly, unbidden, to the surface—the possibility of a hand held a shade too tenderly, an embrace or a searching look held a moment too long, a meeting of the eyes . . . perhaps no more than that. It happens all the time between friends and, whatever men may say, it is always understood.

Both Gericault and Dorcy understand what has happened—the sudden, unexpected rush of desire—and they both make an effort to leap back and start all over again.

Italy, Gericault says. Then, to suggest that the moment between them may not actually have happened and so cannot stand as an impediment, he asks Dorcy if he will consider coming with him to Italy. It is the natural question to ask, after all. It would seem odd *not* to ask.

Yes, of course, says Dorcy, a bit too hastily. If I can, he says. There are family matters that I must see to . . .

* * *

Gericault too had family matters to deal with. Papa was both hurt and puzzled by the proposed journey. Why? he asked. To go among those foreigners? And besides, you know that I don't like to dine alone . . .

Friends will come in to dine with you, Gericault assured him. I will see to that.

But why? Papa wanted to know. What is the point?

It was hopeless. He would never understand.

Alex, on the other hand, understood perfectly. When she heard the news she came up to Paris immediately and sent him a note asking him to call on her at l'hôtel de Cambacérès, the Caruel townhouse.

She received him in her little upstairs sitting room—curtains drawn, the lamps unlit, the only light coming from a low fire in the grate. At first he didn't see her in the shadows at the far side of the room, but then she spoke. What are we to do? she asked very softly—almost a whisper. What are we to do?

He had already determined that there was no great range of possibilities to choose from. We must stop, he said. I must go away.

She dismissed that with a wave of her hand. Come and stand by me, she said, and tell me that that is what you really want.

And what *did* he want? He wanted to go away and never see her again. He wanted her not to exist—and at the same time he wanted to rest his head in her lap and stay there forever while she comforted him as Mama used to do—and at the same time he wanted to put his lips to her bare shoulders, to smell her scent and to take her on the spot, standing there in front of the sitting room fire.

What I want? He asked. You know very well what I want. My mind is filled with you, I think of nothing else. But it isn't a question of what I want, it is what I must do . . .

Nevertheless, he found that he had obeyed her command, he had crossed the room to stand at her side. He bent down to kiss her shoulder, and she put her arms about his waist and drew him to her. Jean is not coming home, she said—though she had no way of knowing that. The truth was that, at that moment, she didn't care. We are alone, she said.

That stopped him. He pulled back and said, That must not happen again, choking a little on the words.

And if I tell you that I will die?

You mustn't talk like that. This is not 'Paul et Virginie.'

But it will be something like death, she said. If you abandon me, I will have no one. I will be alone.

Yes, he said as he retreated toward the door, we will both be alone.

At that point she recognized the futility of pleading; they both understood that there was nothing more to be said.

* * *

His life, he thought, was a chaotic jumble of mistakes and accidents, but there was one area where he could impose some order, exercise some control. He began the preparations for his journey by labeling and numbering the entire contents of his studio—not just the finished work but everything, every study, every sketch, every single scrap of paper with a scribble on it.

The thought of doing that would put me off traveling entirely, said Dorcy. I shall leave my things just as they are.

In any case, it wasn't long before Dorcy reneged. Family affairs, he explained. He was obliged to play the young scion in Paris for a time . . . and then, perhaps, he could follow Gericault . . . join him later in Rome . . .

Was his own impetuosity to blame? Gericault wondered. His want of self-control? By now he had almost convinced himself that there had been no embarrassing moment, that nothing in fact had passed between him and Dorcy—but perhaps he was mistaken?

He must not, in any case, allow Dorcy to see his disappointment. Nuisance, he said. I suppose I must find someone else, then. With no more Italian than what one gets at the opera, it will be more agreeable to travel with a companion.

I *will* try to join you later, said Dorcy. But meanwhile, we must look about for someone. I'll ask around.

A few days later he said, Tell me, do you know Théodore Lebrun? Does a bit of painting himself, I'm told.

Yes, of course, said Gericault. We were at the Lycée together. I was much younger, but he and Brunet used to allow me to tag along with them. Schoolboy condescension, you know. And now he's taken up painting?

Evidently, said Dorcy. I've been making inquiries, and his name has been mentioned several times—contemplating a trip to Italy. Shall I get word to him to call on you?

By all means.

* * *

Much later, Théodore Lebrun would become headmaster of a school at Versailles—he came from a family of academics—but at the moment he still hoped to become a painter, and he was pleased and flattered to be sought out by Gericault. His obvious pleasure, in fact, was the first sign that Gericault had that his two Salon paintings had made a reputation for him in certain circles.

It began well, then, but it ended in a muddle. Shortly before they were scheduled to leave, Lebrun, like Dorcy before him, found that family matters obliged him to remain in Paris, and Gericault once again blamed himself.

I may have given the wrong impression, he told Dorcy. It seemed that Lebrun had called on him one evening to discuss their final plans, and he had found Gericault dressing to go out, sitting in front of a mirror and combing out his curls as he removed the 'papillotes'—the paper curlers—from his hair. Clearly, Gericault said to Dorcy, Lebrun doesn't want to travel with a dandy, a fellow in curlers . . .

I doubt that, said Dorcy, but Gericault persisted. It never occurred to me at the time, he said, but yes, I must have given . . . the wrong impression.

When Lebrun learned of the interpretation that Gericault was putting on his defection, he hurried around to assure the fellow that nothing could be further from the truth. He explained the family business that kept him in Paris, he hoped that Gericault would understand . . . and yes, of course he understood, Lebrun mustn't give it another thought. But Gericault remained unconvinced. It was those damned papillotes, he said to Dorcy, and there's a lesson for you: it is a mistake to seem too soigné.

So he was once again without a traveling companion and he doubted that he could find one now. He resigned himself to traveling alone, and there was no reason for any further delay. He had finished the inventory of his studio. He had asked M. Guérin for letters of introduction to be used in Italy, and Guérin had surprised him by writing that he had the highest hopes and expectations for M. Gericault. He had taken Thunder down to be stabled at Mortain, and he had resisted the temptation to stop at Chesnay on the way. He had even wrung a grumbling acquiescence from Papa. There was nothing to keep him in Paris any longer.

* * *

On the tenth of September, 1816, a brief notice appeared in the Paris *Moniteur Universel* announcing that, at three o'clock on the afternoon of July second, in fair weather, the frigate *Medusa* had been lost off the coast of west Africa. The ship's six launches and lifeboats had been able to save most of the crew and passengers, but of 150 men who had tried to save themselves on a raft, 135 had perished.

That was all, so brief that it might have escaped anyone's notice, and Gericault was, in any case, already on his way to Italy.

* * *

8

LA COURSE DE CHEVAUX LIBRES

In signing the foreign visitor's register he did not put himself down, as might have been expected, as *artiste-peintre*. All the Prix de Rome fellows at the Academy called themselves *artiste*. He, on the other hand, had come to Italy without official sponsorship, and he was rather proud of that. He was, after all, not a student at the Academy and he was not a professional, he was only a gentleman-amateur who had never sold a painting, and he might as well be proud of that too. He put himself down in the register as *propriétaire*—landowner.

* * *

He wrote to Dorcy, he wrote to Horace, he wrote to Papa, but in all the time that he was in Italy he never wrote to Alex. Much as he longed for her (the longing would flood his bosom suddenly at unexpected moments, making him gasp, filling his eyes with tears) he never inquired about her, never even mentioned her name.

He wrote to Dorcy from Florence: "In the coach on the way to Italy an old lady assured me, with the aid of cards, that my voyage would bring me honor and prestige. She also promised me letters from my friends, but alas! she was mistaken. I haven't seen a single one, and I'm distressed, as you can imagine . . . not a word from my father. If you see him, do me a favor and tell him seriously that it isn't right to neglect me so . . ."

And: "Come, come, my dear friend, hurry and join me. I am alone in the most beautiful of Italian cities, surrounded by admirable things and lacking only a companion to be able to enjoy them. I am bored . . . I don't know what to do with myself . . ."

On the other hand: "Yesterday night in the French ambassador's box at the opera, though my boots were soiled and my clothes were a mess, I had the place of honor next to Mme la duchesse de Narbonne, who had to leave the next day for Naples and made me promise to come and visit her there. She went on and on about my modesty, and assured me that it was the true gauge of talent. You can judge for yourself if I found that flattering . . ."

And: "I shall wait for you here, I want to set myself up in Florence for a while. I shall regret it for the rest of my life if I don't bring back sketches of all the beautiful monuments here . . ."

And there you have it: he was at loose ends and lonely in a foreign city, he was homesick—but at the same time he had set about charming the beau monde of that city, and was doing a good job of it. And the masterpieces of Florence were having their effect.

The great revelation was Michelangelo, whose work he had known only in inadequate engravings that emphasized and exaggerated the twisted poses and the over-developed musculature. Mistaking brute force for strength, he had admired those engravings and he had allowed their distortions and coarseness to invade his own drawing, as if to confirm the belief at the Academy that Michelangelo was a pernicious influence.

The moment he saw Michelangelo's sculptures in the Medici chapel, however, he understood that the engravings were in fact travesties—feeble attempts to duplicate Michelangelo's furious energy. Bit by bit, in sketching those figures, his line lost the tense, jagged harshness it had assumed, becoming firm and fluid and supple again.

He was doing what he had come to Florence to do, then—learning from the masters and, in particular, the master whose influence was so feared at the Academy. It should have been exhilarating. For the first time in his life he was truly on his own and independent, he was welcomed in the very best Florentine circles—and suddenly, without warning, he fled to Rome.

"It's true," he wrote to Dorcy, "that I said I intended to stay longer in Florence, but one doesn't really think straight when one is so far from everything one loves. I was alone, you see, and I came to Rome to find a familiar face . . . someone who could speak and understand my language . . . "

His homesickness, a longing for anything French, had overwhelmed him, and all the Frenchmen were in Rome.

* * *

He did indeed find a few familiar faces: Dorcy's half-brother, Pierre-Anne Dedreux, an architect at the Academy; Jean-Victor Schnetz, whom he had met at Horace's studio in Paris and whose painting—particularly his way with pure white highlights—he admired. On the whole, however, Rome was not an improvement. Stendhal, who was in Rome at the same time, wrote of it: "I don't understand a thing that I read about the pleasures of Roman society. There is not a trace of society. This evening I was reduced to playing whist with some Englishmen . . . "

As for the Roman art world, it was moribund. "Correct, decorous and cold," according to Stendhal. "The Italians are beneath us now," wrote Gericault.

Not that he had a high opinion of the Frenchmen at the Academy. "It's wonderful to know Italy," he wrote, "but one needn't spend as much time here as is said. One year well employed seems to me to be sufficient. The five years given to the Academy pensioners do them more harm than good. Their studies are prolonged at a time when they had better be doing serious work, and thus they become accustomed to living at the government's expense, spending the best years of their lives in peaceful security. They come out of that having lost their energy, unable to exert any effort. The best encouragement for these talented young men would be government commissions, frescoes, monuments to decorate, prizes, financial rewards, not five years of a *cuisine bourgeoise* that fattens their bodies and destroys their spirits."

Cuisine bourgeoise. This does indeed describe the Academy's table, but it also describes the obligatory student exercises that are crammed down the pensioner's throats. He congratulates himself on being free of all that.

He is free to spend his days with the detested frescos in the Sistine Chapel, where Michelangelo's *Last Judgment,* that hallucination, that fever dream of chaos and despair, makes him tremble as he hasn't trembled since he was a child, but cannot make him turn away. A painting can be that too, he thinks: not heroes, not grandiose figures from mythology, but men, ordinary men, horrified and without hope as their twisted bodies fall through chaos. Even the saints safe in Michelangelo's heaven are only ordinary men with ordinary bodies. And what did it cost the painter to tell that kind of truth? He has heard that, to study the human body, Michelangelo kept cadavers in his studio until the stench drove his visitors into the streets. Must one abandon all polite society, then, and all decorum?

He begins to wander the streets of Rome with his sketchbook, determined to find a subject in ordinary Romans and the daily life of the city. Herdsmen and butchers at the cattle market, churchgoers on their knees at a shrine, carpenters at work, street dancers and street musicians, street beggars and a public execution—all are recorded simply as matters of fact, no heroic attitudes, no mythological disguises, no pathos, no sentiment, no symbolic meaning at all. Each stage of the beheading—the prisoner prepared for his execution by three monks, the prisoner led through the streets to the scaffold, the prisoner mounting the scaffold, the severed head displayed by an impassive headsman—each stage is shown with neither sympathy nor revulsion, approval nor disapproval. It is simply a fact.

But these are only sketches. "I have it in mind to paint a picture or two, to save me from boredom here," he writes to Dorcy, but the same letter makes it clear that he still hasn't organized his life in Rome in a way that would make painting a picture possible. He has, for the time being, taken rooms with a family in the Via S. Isidoro on the Pincian hill. "But I still don't know where I'm going to set myself up," he writes. "I've found several places that might serve as a studio, but each one has its advantages and its disadvantages. I weigh them against each other and I can't decide . . ." He will find a place, he tells himself, when he has found his subject and knows what he will need.

No subject, then, no painting, no studio—and add to that a hitherto unsuspected tendency to spoil, with erratic behavior, the useful introductions that people make for him.

* * *

At Gericault's request, Victor Schnetz has taken him to see Monsieur Ingres, whose painting is somewhat out of favor at the moment and who is supporting himself with pencil portraits of prominent visitors to Rome. No one of any consequence leaves Rome without a portrait drawn by Monsieur Ingres.

Madame Ingres shows Gericault and Schnetz into an ante-room

whose walls are covered with portrait drawings, and she goes to fetch her husband from his studio. When Ingres comes out to greet his guests he finds Gericault studying the drawings on the wall, so absorbed that he barely acknowledges his host's Bonjour, messieurs. Schnetz jumps in to thank Ingres for permitting this visit, and finally Gericault murmurs, Extraordinary . . . extraordinary . . .

To Ingres, those drawings (which some, today, would call his finest work) are only bread-and-butter drudgery. There are paintings next door in the studio, he says, struggling to remain polite. If you'll come with me . . .

Schnetz has positively to take Gericault by the arm and lead him into the studio, though he keeps looking back at the drawings as he goes. And in the studio they are greeted by a display of Ingres' mannered classical scenes (the paintings that he thinks of as his *real* work) that Gericault hardly looks at. There are also preliminary sketches for a *Venus Born from the Sea*, and Gericault heads straight for these.

Your drawing . . . your line . . . extraordinary! He keeps saying, oblivious to the fact that Ingres is seething.

Finally Ingres cannot contain himself. One does not, he says, visit a painter's studio to admire his drawings.

Afterward, in the street, Gericault turns to Schnetz and says, Prickly, that friend of yours.

He and Ingres—perhaps the two greatest draftsmen of their time—will not meet again.

* * *

I shall never be able to draw like Monsieur Ingres, he complains, but in fact his own drawings have begun to attract some attention.

When it comes to that, says Schnetz, you have your own way. You needn't envy anyone, he says, and he brings the sculptor Jean-Jacques Pradier around to Gericault's rooms to have a look and to confirm his opinion.

Pradier is indeed impressed. Examining a pen-and-ink drawing of Hercules taming the Cretan bull he murmurs, But you are an artist, Monsieur . . . a master . . .

Gericault bows his head modestly and blushes—but as soon as Pradier has gone he begins to examine the Hercules drawing, and he suddenly finds it full of faults: the right hand . . . the left leg . . . the bull's belly . . . surely Pradier had been mocking him, surely he was being sarcastic?

He is convinced that he has been insulted, and he insists that Schnetz call on Pradier on his behalf to demand either an apology or satisfaction.

This is nonsense, says Schnetz. You mean to challenge the man over a *compliment*? But Gericault insists and Schnetz finally decides that it would be best to go around and explain the misunderstanding to Pradier.

The two of them have an uneasy laugh over the matter—is the fellow really mad?—and Pradier good-naturedly agrees to visit Gericault and straighten things out.

He assures me of his sincerity, Schnetz reports back to Gericault. He plans to call on you, if that will convince you . . . ?

Not that it takes much convincing. After Pradier has spoken his piece, Schnetz is astonished to see Gericault suddenly embrace him, saying, Is it really true, then . . . you think I have talent?

One can only call it erratic behavior. His loneliness in Rome has made him 'difficult.'

* * *

Can one make too much of the fact that, when he finally finds it, his subject has to do with horses? Perhaps. Nevertheless . . .

The days before Ash Wednesday—the days of carnival—came that year in mid-February, and Gericault (who like most Parisians considered himself to be worldly) had never seen or imagined anything like the Roman carnival.

Tohu-bohu, Schnetz had warned him. Total chaos. The entire population is in the streets, you know, one simply can't move, and one can't see an inch of pavement for the confetti. And the disguises! You might expect Harlequins and Columbines, but rich young men prancing about in beggars rags? Or disguised as women? Or women disguised as men? And nothing is forbidden, you understand. Absolutely *nothing*. One is licensed to do *anything at all*, and next week it will be forgotten. It never happened. You can't imagine . . .

Oh, I can imagine, said Gericault.

He knows how easily—in an instant—one can tumble into chaos. The ease with which he can imagine '*anything at all*' rather frightens him. Nevertheless, he allows himself to go out into the carnival streets—in the spirit of observation, to be sure. He is still seeking a subject, after all, and he is in any case curious to see the scene that Schnetz, with rolling eyes, had described.

No sooner has he set foot in the street than he is accosted by a pair of *saltarello* dancers—the boy, in tight britches chosen to display plump thighs, carrying a mandolin that he hasn't the elbow room to strum; the girl, in a deeply ruffled skirt covered by a filmy apron, carrying a tambourine that she rattles in Gericault's ear. They may really be country folk, he thinks. The girl's handsome face is sun-browned and she has allowed her thick brows to grow shaggy. Not a city face. The boy, on the other hand . . .

But it is impossible to think. The air is thick with confetti and crude, jangling music and the din of the crowd. The *saltarello* dancers are squeezed up against him on either side, they are carrying him along in the crowd, smiling and whispering incomprehensible Roman street slang in his ears, and he realizes that their free hands are all over him.

They are not clever pickpockets, and he has deliberately dressed to foil pickpockets, but their fluttering fingers—are they really pickpockets, he wonders, or are they up to something else?— their fingers arouse him and he allows himself to be carried along, thinking, How can it matter? He finds it exhilarating.

After a while his hands too, hidden by the jostling crowd, have done some exploring. He has come to the conclusion that the boy and girl are in fact a girl and boy, and yes, he understands exactly what this sort of thing can lead to. He understands what carnival means—the refusal, for once, to control, to rein in, to tame—and, just for once, how can it matter?

He thinks of riding Thunder at a gallop, loose-reined and free— but of course, riding like that, he would know that the reins were in his hands and he could use them whenever he wanted. Now, with his *saltarello* dancers, he is not so certain.

Still, he allows himself to be carried along. Despite the crush of the crowd, he finds that one of his arms is free to encircle the girl's (that is to say, the boy's) waist, and then he finds that the boy has embraced his own waist in return—a slithering, clearly lascivious caress that produces a sudden tickle of desire and, at the same time, a sharp physical memory of Alex. All at once he shudders and a wave of self-disgust washes through him. He knows that if he loses control now he is lost. He drops his arm to his side and no longer allows himself to be carried along, though the press of the crowd carries him along anyway, willy-nilly. Still, the boy and the girl sense that he is no longer playing, and they lose interest at once. It will be so easy to find another—and, improbably, they vanish into the crowd.

At that moment he catches his first glimpse of the carnival racehorses (wild African ponies imported from the Barbary Coast and called *barberi*) rearing and plunging behind their starting rope while their grooms struggle to restrain them. The dancers have led him into the Piazza del Popolo—the starting point for a race of the riderless *barberi* that is run late in the afternoon on every day of carnival.

The excited ponies wear stylish little plumes between their ears, and their rumps are covered with cord netting that carries little spiked balls that will bounce about and serve as spurs, and strips of tinsel whose rattling will do the same. Once the starting rope in the Piazza del Popolo is dropped, the riderless *barberi* are released to stampede down the length of the narrow, crowd-lined Corso, ending up in the Piazza Venezia where, with some difficulty, they are recaptured and the winner is awarded a golden banner—the *palio*.

* * *

He never considered the race itself as a subject, though the horses' manes streamed out behind them and their hoofs struck sparks from the paving in a thoroughly picturesque way. He did consider the recapturing of the ponies at the end, but quickly decided that it was too much of a groom's melee, there were too many comical pratfalls, the horses themselves were too bewildered. No, from the moment he saw it, it was the struggle of the grooms with the wild *barberi*, kicking and rearing and biting behind the starting rope—animal passion controlled (but just barely) by human will; chaos contained.

There was nothing particularly original about the *barberi* race as a subject. It had long been a favorite genre scene for tourist-market engravings—picturesque views of Roman street life that were sold in souvenir albums called, perhaps, "A Year in Rome" or "Italian Scenes." In that spirit, Horace's father had painted the scene many years earlier, and many years later Horace himself would paint it in the same way, his usual delicate and nervous horses prancing rather flirtatiously behind the starting rope. Indeed, Gericault's own preliminary studies have no great force, they are not much more than notations on an observed scene, grandstand and excited crowd and starting rope and grooms and horses all accurately set down with very little energy or passion. But, bit by bit, as the studies progress from one version to the next, Gericault begins to eliminate the things that identify the scene as a particular event tied to a particular time and place, he eliminates the things that makes it a common genre scene, a scene of the moment—the race course, the spectators, even the clothes that the grooms wear—and what is left is the struggle between men and beasts, between the grooms and their violent horses.

A chaotic scene, but Gericault's developing composition is never allowed to become chaotic. In his search for the essential grandeur in this commonplace event, in his attempt to find the timeless at the heart of the everyday, he begins to treat the scene as a classical frieze—disciplined, ordered and controlled despite the ferocious intensity of the grooms and their horses. He begins to make a painting in the 'Grand Manner.'

Grand indeed. He bought a canvas nearly thirty feet wide, he rented a studio that would accommodate it, and he began to transfer his composition to the canvas at larger-than-life scale—a scale that was thought at the time to be appropriate only for scenes from the classics, battle scenes and pictures of great historical events. To depict something like the start of the *barberi* race—a genre scene—on that scale was unheard of. To reduce the scene to an abstract struggle—no mythical story, no historical context—would puzzle the critics and enrage them. The painting would be seen not as new and original but as radical and transgressive, it would be seen as subversive of everything that was taught and held to be true at the Academy—but, in fact, the painting would never be seen. Indeed, it would never be finished.

Perhaps he was too young and inexperienced, perhaps he was not as independent as he liked to think; he was only twenty five, after all. Perhaps it was simply a failure of nerve. As he worked on the painting he became doubtful and uncertain, he began to wonder if he had really resolved the contradictions that he had poured into it—Roman street scene . . . classical tableau . . . timeless struggle. He lost his concentration, then, and he began to fiddle away his time. Faced with uncertainty he was capable of 'exquisite laziness,' as Madame de Pracomtal had noted, remembering her lazy childhood playmate. Uncertainty had always produced in him a strong desire to just do nothing, and for days in a row now he would neither paint nor leave his studio.

On some days he would fuss about the place, arranging and rearranging his brushes and pigments, moving the large canvas into a more favorable light, raising it, lowering it, any kind of studio housekeeping to avoid working on the *barberi* painting.

On other days he would lie on his bed all day long, dressed carelessly or not at all, thinking, I will get up now and wash my face and get to work, but continuing to lie there, flooded with longing . . . longing for Alex . . . longing for Dorcy . . . longing for any kind of loving embrace . . .

. . . and one day, on the spur of the moment, in a burst of busyness, he got up and packed a bag and boarded the coach to Naples, where his letters of introduction, and the recommendations of la duchesse de Narbonne, would give him instant access to a world that he had always known how to charm.

Indeed, every one of his Neapolitan hostesses would write to someone that 'we all found him charming,' though one of them would complain that his artistic excursions took up far too much of his time. For he did make a point of seeing all the sights. He took his sketchbook to the ruins at Paestum, he took it to the new excavations at Pompeii and Herculaneum, he spent long hours drawing the antiquities at the *Museo Borbonico*, and he spent even longer hours negotiating permission to have a plaster cast made of a Roman horse's head in the *Borbonico* collection.

Handsome as Thunder, he thought, when Thunder could be coaxed into presenting himself and showing off. A handsome model for my *barberi*, he thought. And, abruptly, he left Naples and traveled back to Rome, carrying the cast of the horse's head with him, thinking that it would help him return to the huge canvas with a fresh eye.

Instead, he found that the painting had died.

It can happen. The emotional force seeps away, the impetus, once broken, cannot be restored. On returning to the canvas, it is immediately clear to him that he has not resolved the painting's contradictions. What had seemed to work in the smaller studies somehow has resisted enlargement. The violence, the turbulence of the action, are not contained by the classical composition, they are frozen. To be sure, he could make adjustments, he could suppress a groom-and-horse group here or bring it forward there, he could add a fallen groom or one more leaping horse, but he sees that he is making a static picture of action, he is not painting movement itself, and he has no desire to go on.

* * *

Toying with the language of despair, he begins to draft a letter to Dorcy, just to try it out, just to see how it would sound ("I am wandering, I have gone astray . . . nothing is solid, everything escapes my grasp, everything deceives me . . .") but he pockets the draft when a letter arrives from Dorcy.

At last! Dorcy announces, he has finished his business in Paris, there is nothing to keep him from joining Gericault now, he is looking forward to painting in Rome and to studying the great masters together with his dear friend, and he is already arranging his passage.

Reading the news, Gericault experiences a little shudder of pleasure, and he is rather frightened by the physical intensity of his anticipation, by the intensity of his need to see Dorcy again, to embrace him. He realizes vaguely that he is afraid to be alone with Dorcy in Rome.

But it is really Alex, he tells himself. He can no longer stay away from Alex. If he were to stay on in Rome he would have Dorcy but not Alex. If he returned to Paris, on the other hand, he would have Alex but not Dorcy. Neither prospect pleases him, but his fear of being alone with Dorcy in Rome is growing.

"My Dear Dorcy," he writes, "I am deeply grieved to be leaving here without having the pleasure of welcoming you . . . it's another one of those disgraceful things that happen only to me. After a year of sadness and vexation, just when you are about to arrive and I might be happy again, I am obliged to leave. I am leaving behind some things that you may find useful . . . an easel, a paint box, some prepared canvases. Once you've settled yourself, start to work at once. It's the only way to avoid anxiety . . ."

Then he crates up the Neapolitan horse's head, arranges for it to be sent to the rue des Martyrs, and he flees.

* * *

The god of coincidence sees to it that their paths cross in Siena, both of them stopping at the same inn, Dorcy just arriving in Italy and Gericault just leaving. They greet each other as might be expected of dear old friends—warmly, but nothing excessive. They embrace in the usual way but, rightly or wrongly, Gericault senses a certain coolness, a certain standoffishness on Dorcy's part.

You came anyway, says Gericault.

Yes, of course, Dorcy replies. He wants a year in Rome and he knows that he will never win it in the Prix de Rome competition. He, like Gericault, will have to manage it on his own.

Well then, says Gericault, you must ignore the advice of those fellows at the Academy, you must keep your eyes open, you must look at everything. And you must work. Without that, you may be very lonely here.

They have only a day before they must both move on, and they spend most of it looking at the *barberi* studies that Gericault, at Dorcy's urging, has unpacked.

You can see, says Gericault. A wasted year.

Dorcy has his usual response to his friends' paintings, he's not at all sure that he understands what Gericault is trying to do, but he can honestly say that he finds the pictures very beautiful.

Are they beautiful? Gericault asks. I don't know if that's what I wanted. I wanted something grander.

Something grander. But in a few days, on his way back to Paris, he is confronted by the grandeur of the Swiss Alps and it doesn't occur to him to take out his sketchbook. To be sure, he is preoccupied, thinking of Alex, thinking of Dorcy, anticipating his meeting with the one (a meeting that should not take place, though he is sure that it will) and beginning to regret his behavior toward the other. And he has just found in his pocket the draft of the letter that he never sent to Dorcy: "I am wandering, I have gone astray . . ."

Preoccupied, then. Distracted. Still, to barely notice the Swiss Alps . . .

* * *

9

FAITS DIVERS

November of 1817, just as Gericault was returning to Paris, the printer de Hocquet announced the appearance of an account of the shipwreck of the frigate *Medusa* written by two of its survivors, Alexandre Corréard and J.-B. Henri Savigny. Despite the government's efforts to suppress the story, it had been whispered about for some time that the shipwreck was not so much an unfortunate accident as a disgraceful scandal, and the book was an instant success.

* * *

"One morning," wrote Antoine Montfort many years later, "a young man entered the studio of my master, Monsieur Horace Vernet. The two of them flew into each other's arms and I gathered from what they said that the young man was a painter who had just returned from Italy . . .

"He was a tall, elegant fellow," wrote Montfort. "His face was animated and energetic, his eyes and his voice were kind and gentle, and he blushed easily. He and Monsieur Horace went on about Italy and about artists, about painters like Schnetz, whose names I had never heard . . .

"Another student whispered to me that this must be Monsieur Gericault, the painter of a mounted chasseur and a cuirassier that had been shown at the Salon a few years before, but I had only the vaguest recollection of those paintings . . .

"When I finally saw them in Monsieur Gericault's studio I was very enthusiastic about them, but this other student insisted that Monsieur Horace was the better painter and, later, he said so to Monsieur Horace in so many words. 'But the horse's head,' said Monsieur Horace, 'the tiger skin saddle cloth . . . there are very fine passages in those paintings.'"

* * *

So Horace had taken to patronizing Gericault's paintings, and his student, Montfort, had only the vaguest recollection of them. That is what comes of being out of it for a year.

Still, Horace was eager to see what a year in Rome had produced. He knew that his friend would not have returned from Italy with nothing but 'Italian Scenes.' He expected something a little odd—the sort of thing that he would have to admire without necessarily understanding or approving—and he was not disappointed.

All the *barberi* studies—mostly oil paint on treated paper—were neatly arranged in chronological order, first to last, in a large portfolio. In his haste to leave Rome, however, Gericault had packed them up before the oil paint was quite dry, and by now the sheets had begun to stick together. He and Horace had to peel them apart carefully, one by one, and Horace was able to concentrate on the delicacy of the task without commenting on the paintings themselves.

Finally, Gericault felt that he must offer some explanation. It was to be very large, he said. I wanted something grand and noble . . .

But what is the subject? Horace asked. He could have understood a colorful rendering of the street scene in the Piazza del Popolo at the start of the race. Failing that, he looked for an anecdote, a central incident, a story, but he found only a composition of men and wild horses struggling in a vaguely classical setting. What is happening here? he asked.

Gericault fumbled for words. The ponies . . . he said. The grooms . . . well, it doesn't seem to work, does it?

And so you gave it up and hurried back to us, said Horace. Lallemande will be delighted to see you again.

No, said Gericault. That is not what I had in mind.

* * *

Before he was thoroughly unpacked, Gericault took the coach down to Mortain to collect Thunder.

He was happy enough to see his Bonnesoeur cousins again but he had longed to see Uncle Siméon, and Siméon was still banned from French soil, living abroad. The government's vengefulness, what Horace's friends called the White Terror, had not been relaxed.

As for Thunder, he was extremely haughty at first but Gericault knew that he was bound to give in sooner or later. Indeed, Thunder couldn't hold a grudge for long and, after a certain amount of coy sparring, the two of them took off into the Mortain countryside, riding as if a year hadn't passed since their last ride together.

When it came time to leave Mortain, Gericault announced that they would not ride back to Paris directly, they would ride to

Chesnay first. Uncle Siméon might have stopped them, but Siméon was in Belgium at the time.

And at Chesnay, as you might suppose, it would start all over again.

* * *

Alex knew, of course, that he had returned from Italy—that he had returned, in fact, a year early—and she thought she knew why. She did not, however, come rushing up to Paris, she made no effort to contact him, no welcome-home note, no invitation to Chesnay, nothing at all. She simply waited and, sure enough, as if nothing had changed, as if all was as before, he and Thunder came trotting into the courtyard at Chesnay one fine afternoon.

Uncle Jean was at home for a change and so their meeting, while cordial, was proper and polite. Jean seemed not to notice the tension that hung palpably in the air between his wife and his nephew.

You have been missed, Jean said. Your Aunt Alex has missed your visits, and your Papa has missed you most awfully. Will you stay put now for a while?

Yes, stay put, Gericault mumbled, and with that thought the pleasant tingle of anticipation gave way suddenly to panic and regret. He ought to have stayed away. He might have traveled directly from Mortain to Paris. He might have stayed on in Italy, to begin with. He might have . . . what? . . . traveled to the Orient. But now it is inevitable, nothing on earth can stop what is going to happen . . .

Tell us all about Rome, says Alex, and he begins to babble: . . . the provincial social life that one led in Rome . . . his loneliness there . . . his homesickness . . . his longing to speak French, even if it meant putting up with those Prix de Rome fools at the Academy, men who turned their backs on Michelangelo and learned only to paint like each other . . .

Indeed, says Jean. Perhaps you'll want to rest for a bit before supper?

Yes. Grateful for the respite, he goes upstairs and falls asleep at once and sleeps soundly until he is called. Then, at supper, he continues to babble—his views on Florence, his views on Naples—until Jean excuses himself. He has to rise early in the morning, he is off to Paris for several days, there are important affairs that he must see to (he is still lobbying for his title), and so he leaves Alex and Gericault facing each other across the table—facing the inevitable.

Once they have happened, of course, things can indeed seem to have been inevitable,. It is when they seem inevitable in advance that one should be wary.

Alex, however, is all anticipation, she is not the least bit wary. It is like 'Paul et Virginie,' she thinks. It is fate. It is destiny. We must not fight it.

Gericault is wary but to no avail. He feels helpless. It is like a terrible accident rushing toward us, he thinks. We can no longer prevent this disaster. It will happen . . . but where? he asks himself.

That is always the question with adultery, isn't it?

Where? He asks himself, and then he realizes that he has said it out loud.

Well, one finds a place.

He never comes to my room, says Alex. I will go up now, and you will follow me in half an hour . . .

By the time half an hour has passed they have both abandoned any lingering sense of decorum, of reticence, of caution, that they might have had. They resist nothing.

Afterwards, he rests his head between her full breasts and breathes deeply. Mama's cologne.

* * *

When Uncle Jean finally returned from Paris, Gericault went back to the rue des Martyrs and sat down immediately to write the letter of regret and apology that should have been written to Dorcy long ago.

Searching for a convincing tone, he re-read the unsent Roman draft that he still carried in his pocket ('I have gone astray . . . everything deceives me . . . ') and he found that its plea for sympathy was just right. "My dear Dorcy," he wrote, then. "I am a monster, as you well know, but if I say it myself, if I accuse myself, you may be moved to forgive me. I so regret the way I've behaved toward you . . . you could hardly hate me more than I hate myself. Still, you will pity me when I can finally sit you down and tell you about the terrible situation into which I have recklessly thrown myself . . . I haven't many friends who will listen to that kind of outpouring . . . but you have always understood me and I have loved you . . . why does a contrary fate keep us apart? Left to myself, I'm capable of nothing . . . nothing is solid, everything escapes my grasp, everything deceives me. Our hopes and desires are only vain fantasies . . . if anything is real it is our suffering, our pleasures are only imaginary . . . "

Dorcy was used to this kind of thing, he thought that he understood his friend. Receiving this letter in Rome, he didn't see it as a kind of love letter, nor did he take it seriously as a *cri de coeur*. He thought, Oh dear, he does overdo things, and he thought, Oh Lord, they're seeing each other again . . .

* * *

Having written that letter, Gericault felt suddenly unburdened, as though the letter itself had been a kind of penance. Now he could give himself to the inevitable without a struggle, he could continue to visit Chesnay, to go back and forth as often as he chose—though he made an effort, to be sure, to time his visits to Uncle Jean's absences.

Georges-Nicolas could hardly complain—Chesnay was *family*, after all—but these frequent absences were most distressing. The Roman year had been a misery for him. Now that Théo had come back he might at least give some time to his Papa instead of rushing down to Chesnay at every opportunity.

Still, Georges-Nicolas understood that at Chesnay they talked about pictures in a way that he could not—yes, that must be it—and he decided that he would no longer doze off when Théo and Horace were talking shop. He would keep his ears open and try to make sense of their talk.

What he heard, among other things, was Théo praising the work of Victor Schnetz and the wonderful, luminous effects that he achieved with the clever use of white paint.

I keep trying for it, said Théo, but I just can't get Schnetz's whites. It's very frustrating.

Well, Georges-Nicolas was prepared to do whatever was necessary to prevent his dear boy's frustration. He ran to all the art supply dealers that he knew of and pleaded for Schnetz's whites, and finally he appealed to Horace.

You're his friend, he said. Will you do us a great favor? Find out where they sell Schnetz's whites and, whatever the cost, I'll get them for him. The poor boy is so unhappy . . .

Horace suppressed his laughter and tried not to make the solicitous old man feel like a fool. No one has been able to get Schnetz's whites, he said, but if I hear of any, I'll let you know at once . . .

And Théo went on riding down to Chesnay quite regularly.

* * *

At the same time he began work, in Paris, on what he came to think of as his Italian Painting—*The Cattle Market,* sometimes called *The Butchers of Rome.*

It is an odd, even an alarming painting. In a dark band of shadow that is cast across the bottom of the canvas there is a violent, writhing tangle of half-naked men, vicious dogs and frenzied cattle. Improbably, the men, with nothing but clubs and a pike and their bare hands, seem to be subduing the cattle, who outnumber them; the men are as ferocious as the cattle and it is a fierce struggle.

The violence crowded into the foreground at the bottom of the picture is extreme, but it is taking place in an entirely peaceful, bucolic landscape. In the background, the upper two thirds of the picture, we see a rustic wall flooded with sunlight, a serene blue mountain reposing in the distance, a beautifully pearly sky.

Perhaps one can make too much of the struggle between man and beast, perhaps one is going too far to see it as the artist's struggle to impose order on chaos, but it is certainly a recurrent theme: the Roman butchers, the *Barberi* studies, *Hercules Subduing the Cretan Bull* . . . animal violence subdued by human will . . .

And what is one to make of the idyllic landscape in the background?

Is it an effort to dislocate the scene, to detach it from any particular time and place? Is Gericault, unable to free himself entirely from the prejudices of his time, trying to generalize the scene, to elevate it, even to classicize it? Just as the *Barberi* grooms were stripped of their everyday work clothes, so are the butchers of Rome, for a realistic depiction of the everyday, of the actual cattle market in Rome, detailed and specific, would have seemed both puzzling and shocking to most people. Why would anyone want to paint *that*? Not a fit subject. No, not at all—but then, is the painting that he actually painted any less puzzling, any less shocking?

* * *

Not a fit subject. Does subject, then, count for more than we might like to think? In our own time we have seen painters turn their backs on cubist guitars and colorist arabesques, declaring that the only fit subject for a painting was the act of painting itself. We have seen painters revolt against that revolution, turning their attention from their own action to the miscellanea and minutia of the quotidian. It seems (though we may not like it) that here is seldom a drastic change in style without a corresponding change in subject matter. The painter who refuses to paint in the same old way may also refuse to paint the same old thing. Often, in fact, it is the new subject that demands and creates the new style.

There are painters who can smell change in the air, who can sense it as if with antennae, who will follow the new trend so swiftly that they will be thought to have set it. Then there are painters who deliberately set out to create change, quite willing to walk blindly into unexplored territory. And Gericault?

He did not consider himself to be a rebel. He did admire Monsieur David, he was quite prepared to learn from the past— but he was not prepared to be bound by it. He felt that in his Italian painting he had failed to achieve the fusion of grand style and natural subject that he was seeking. He felt that he was at an impasse, a dead end, and he could only find his way out through finding a new subject: a modern subject that was not dictated by convention; a subject that evoked the human condition as ordinary men experience it, joy or despair, bravery or folly—something that he could respond to with authentic emotion. But still, something that could be painted on a grand scale and in a grand style.

Contradictory aims? No wonder he has been called a Realist, even a Classicist, in the same breath that also calls him the first of the Romantics.

He would not have called himself any of those things, of course. He could not, in fact, put into words what he was looking for, but he did set out quite deliberately to find a new subject.

The Salon wants Plutarch, he told Alex. They want the lives of the saints and medieval kings—something exemplary. I can't do that.

She reminded him, then, of his *chasseur* and his *cuirassier*, and he sighed. It is ironic, he said. The Emperor gave us a subject . . .

* * *

Indeed, in a way that would not have pleased him, the Emperor continued to provide a subject.

There was a general sense of betrayal in the air. The Emperor's promise of glorious victory had produced only adversity and defeat. After that, the promise of a liberal monarchy had been sacrificed to the conservative *ultras* who surrounded a weak king. Whenever Gericault visited Horace's studio the air was filled with the grumblings and grievances of the *demi-soldes,* the Napoleonic veterans pensioned off against their will at half pay, who gathered there regularly. Little wonder, then, that betrayal and defeat became for a time his subject.

On his return from Italy Horace had introduced him to the new technique of lithography. In the course of its short life (the process had been demonstrated for the first time only twenty five years earlier) lithography had come to be looked down on as best suited for popular prints and political commentary in the press—the sort of thing that Horace dashed off at a moment's notice to keep the pot boiling. In addition, the simplicity of the process gave it a special appeal to amateurs. Many of the regulars at Horace's studio dabbled—even the future Citizen King, the duc d'Orléans, 'Monsieur Valmy.'

Gericault took lithography more seriously. Attracted by the rich tonal range that it made possible, and by the fact that one could draw one's image directly on the stone with one's own hand, no need for an engraver, he set to work on a series of images from the Napoleonic wars—not scenes of great glory, not the sort of sentimental Bonapartist propaganda that Horace turned out, but ordinary scenes of battlefield life and images of defeat, images of suffering and endurance. No great shining heroes here, but common ragged soldiers making a last stand against the enemy, or maimed and vanquished and in retreat: a cartload of wounded men; a blinded soldier on horseback being led by a companion who has lost an arm.

Monsieur Valmy bought every one of these prints. He made a point of patronizing the liberal opposition that met at Horace's, currying favor and seeking support wherever he could against the day when, as Louis-Philippe, he would wangle his way to the throne.

* * *

For the grumbling veterans at Horace's, the Napoleonic wars were, of course, the great subject, but as Gericault worked on his lithographs he began to realize that the veteran's nostalgic stories were turning those wars into ancient history. They were stories of another time, of a distant past when one could still speak of honor. Times had changed and the wars were no longer a modern subject. He began to scour the newspapers, then, for another kind of story and he finally hit upon what they were calling The Crime of the Century—not the first crime to be called that, and certainly not the last: *l'affaire Fualdès*. Rightly or wrongly (and most likely wrongly) this sensational affair was believed, in liberal circles, to demonstrate the depraved vengefulness of the White Terror.

On the 20th of March in 1817, in the town of Rodez, a certain Antoine-Bernardin Fualdès—a former Imperial Magistrate, generally supposed to be a Bonapartist—had somehow (it was a puzzle) been drawn to a house of ill repute owned by a Monsieur Bancal, where he had been set upon by a gang and robbed and then butchered in a peculiarly atrocious fashion. His blood had been drained from his body into a large tub and it had been fed to a pig brought in specially for that purpose. So much blood, it was reported, that the pig had been unable to finish.

All this was garnished with exactly the sort of colorful tidbits that the public appetite demanded. There was the criminal as sentimental monster: the assassin who had cold-bloodedly decided to murder his little daughter (a dangerous eyewitness to the crime) and then repented at the last minute, falling to his knees and embracing the child. And there was the Woman of Mystery: another possible eyewitness, Madame Manzon, who may or may not have been hiding in the kitchen during the butchery, and who may have been dressed at the time (for unknown reasons, though there was certainly speculation) as a man.

If the Fualdès trials had a celebrity star witness, it was Madame Manzon. The daughter of a respectable judge and the wife of an officer from whom she was now separated, la Manzon lived what the French call *une vie galante*, a loose life, bouncing from officer to officer in the local garrison. She dressed like the expensive trollop that she was (a lithograph in the press shows her going to court in ermine-trimmed clothes and too many ostrich plumes), she made dramatic courtroom scenes and she seemed determined to implicate herself as a witness to the crime. As she changed and embroidered her story constantly, it was impossible to untangle her contradictions or to believe anything she said, but the readers of the popular press couldn't get enough of her. What would she say next?

In addition, and perhaps most important, there was a conspiracy theory. It was rumored that this was a crime of political revenge carried out by a gang of royalist ultras against a former adherent to the Emperor—a crime that had been planned at such high levels that the King himself wanted the truth suppressed. There was never the slightest bit of evidence to support this unreasonable speculation, but it was widely believed, and Gericault enjoyed a sense of liberal righteousness when he chose the Fualdès affair as a subject. He was determined, however, to avoid the sensational reportage and the political comment of the lithographs that had begun to appear in the press. He was determined to treat this common subject in an elevated style, as tragedy. He had decided to produce a painting for the next Salon.

In a series of wash drawings he examined the possibilities of several moments in the gory tale—the assassins plotting the crime, Fualdès dragged into Bancal's house, the murder itself, the assassins throwing Fualdès body into the river, the assassins escaping—and in every case the figures are naked or very scantily draped. They have been stripped of their everyday clothing, stripped of any facial expression, stripped of their particularity, generalized and classicized into blandness and unreality. The drawings are bloodless, they convey very little, and certainly no emotion; they are nothing but arrangements of figures.

It is the poverty of the subject, the discrepancy between the public's assumptions and the actual facts of the case, that defeated him. In the end, the Fualdès affair is only an exceptionally brutal homicide committed by ordinary thieves. It is not a timeless subject, not a tragedy. It is nothing but a vulgar *fait divers*, a sordid news item that cannot bear the weight of a grand style. It will not give him a painting for the Salon.

* * *

In January of 1818 Uncle Jean is finally granted the right to add his wife's family name, *de Saint Martin*, to his own name, and he is determined to mark the event with a season of receptions and entertainments at *l'hôtel de Cambacérès*, his house in Paris. Under the circumstances, it is not possible, as it has been in the past, for Alex to refuse to come up from Chesnay. She is obliged to come to Paris, then, at exactly the moment when she most needs to see Gericault but least desires it—because she has begun to live in fear of what Jean may understand, or what he will certainly come to understand in a very short time.

There is a great deal of coming and going at the Paris house— newly hired servants popping up in every corner, well-wishers dropping by at any hour to leave their cards, luncheon parties, dinner parties, evening parties, musicales—it is impossible for Alex and Gericault to meet there except in a roomful of people, and at first Alex is glad of that. Every day, however, the need to meet privately with her lover becomes more and more urgent, and one afternoon, after announcing to Jean that she intends to pay some calls, she instructs her coachman to take her to the rue des Martyrs.

She is greeted at the studio door by Mustapha in his turban and Turkish robes and she has a moment of panic, imagining that she has come to the wrong place. But Gericault's face appears over Mustapha's shoulder and he motions for her to come in at the same time that he dismisses his servant with a whispered, That will be all.

You were startled, he says to her when they are alone. If I had expected a visit I would have warned you.

And is this the latest fashion? she asks. Living *turquerie*?

Isn't it a wonderful face? he replies. There was a whole gang of them, you know, selling sweets in the Palais Royale arcade. The crew of a Turkish ship, so they said—the only survivors when the ship went down outside the harbor at Marseille. I thought that all of them would make excellent models for the *Mameluke Massacre* that Horace is painting for the Salon, but one of them took me aside and said that the others were all thieves and he wanted to get away from them . . . and so we have Mustapha. Most attentive, you know. Curls up and sleeps on the floor outside my bedroom door, that sort of thing, though he frightens the wits out of Papa. Shall I bring him down to Chesnay next time I come?

I'm afraid, she says, that you may have to stop coming down to Chesnay.

Thinking that she is joking, he asks, Will you continue to come to me here, then? Is this visit to be the start of a new regime?

Listen to me, she insists, I'm quite serious.

Uneasy silence then while he takes that in, and it dawns on him for the first time that they may be (where in fact they have always been) on the brink of disaster. Uncle Jean? he asks at last in a hushed voice. He's taken notice?

If not yet, then very soon, she replies. I am going to have a child.

And they are over the brink, tumbling into chaos and disorder, beyond any hope of rescue, beyond any might-have-been. And for no reason at all, he thinks. But can they not have known that this might happen? Haven't they been tempting it, daring it to happen?

You understand, she adds, that it cannot possibly be his. He will not say a word—not now, not ever—but he will draw the obvious conclusions and, knowing Jean, he will refuse to acknowledge the child.

Gericault's gaze is not so much horrified as bewildered. She lowers her eyes to avoid meeting that gaze, and he keeps his distance, he makes no move to take her into his arms. He shakes his head and murmurs, What will happen?

Alex knows exactly how such matters are handled. Very shortly she must go back to Chesnay and she must remain in seclusion— there will be no visitors; Jean will remain in Paris—until she comes to term. Then, if it is physically possible, a clandestine trip to Paris where there are private birthing establishments that guarantee anonymity. That arrangement must be made by Gericault—Jean will not lift a finger. After that it will be up to Gericault to find a country family to raise the child, and he will, of course, provide them with suitable funds. And I, she says, will remain shut up alone at Chesnay. Jean will never speak of it and I doubt that he will ever speak to me of anything at all—not that he has very much to say at the best of times. So for me, you see, it is the end . . .

Little Paul, he murmurs, but she shakes her head. He will be sent away to school, she says, I will have no one, I will be quite alone.

Quite alone, he echoes with a shudder, and then, with a sudden burst of indignant bravado, I will not allow that!

Do you imagine, she asks, that there is anything you can do to prevent it?

Only then does he open his arms to her and, trembling, she buries her face in the warmth of his bosom. After a while, though, she collects herself and pulls away and speaks very calmly. We won't see each other again, she says, and again she turns her eyes away to avoid his bewildered stare. If I could have something of yours for remembrance, she says, one or two very small things ... drawings ... water colors ...

And that is all. Knowing themselves to be helpless, each of them is suddenly reluctant to let the other see his helplessness. They refuse to weep, they refuse to rage against fate in each other's presence. Their hearts may be broken, they may be choking with pain, but Alex's realistic view prevails: it is over and nothing can be done. One must be calm. There is no drawn out, passionate farewell. There are no tearful regrets, no bitter recriminations, no defiant confrontations. Instead, they allow themselves to play the game of silence that their world has invented, impetuously submitting to the rules just as they had once impetuously trampled on them. There is another way, of course, but in the end they are not made for *la vie de bohème.*

* * *

Claiming a vague illness, Alex alarmed her husband by insisting on returning to Chesnay, where she went at once to her own little apartment—a bedroom and a sitting room—leaving instructions for her meals to be sent up. Certain that Jean would never visit her there, she took Gericault's drawings and water colors and propped them up on the mantels, on the bureau, on table tops here and there, and then she lay down to rest, content to be alone now after her days in Paris and actually feeling relieved. Despite her realism, she could not possibly have imagined that 'I will be quite alone' would mean, literally, the rest of her life in these rooms—fifty-seven years.

As for Gericault, he alarmed his Papa by resuming his day-long rides into the countryside—reckless riding, deliberately inviting the wind to sting his face and bring tears to his eyes (as though he needed the wind). But Thunder, allowed to run free, kept pulling them toward Chesnay, and he was afraid that sooner or later he would find it irresistible, he would let Thunder have his way. He gave up riding, then, and alarmed his Papa further by claiming exhaustion and a fever and taking to his bed; but he found that lying there all day with nothing to distract him from his grief was quite maddening, as was Papa, who insisted on nursing him with broths and gruels and ointments and flannel vests. After two days of that he got up and put on his clothes and went about his business—and how can one contain a chaos of grief and still go about one's business in a seemingly normal way, holding in the grief, walling it off, and functioning as if nothing has happened? It is amazing, but it is done all the time.

Gericault might have confided in Dorcy—he would not hesitate to weep or to rage against fate in front of Dorcy—but Dorcy was still in Rome. You would think, then, that in his friend's absence he would have turned to Horace for support and advice on making the necessary arrangements, but no. Horace could not be fobbed off with the usual 'friend of mine,' he would understand at once that the lady in question was Gericault's Aunt Caruel. Gericault didn't really mind for himself, and no doubt the time would come when Horace must be told—but not yet. For as long as possible, Alex must be protected with anonymity, and so he spoke of the plight of 'a friend' to his old school friend and fellow musketeer, the economist Auguste Brunet.

Well, said Brunet, these things will happen. Poor fellow . . . your friend. And the lady . . . ?

The lady, said Gericault, relies on our discretion.

Sooner or later, of course, Brunet would guess at the lady's identity, but for the moment he simply gave useful advice and he took it upon himself to make the necessary arrangements. 'A friend of a friend' would add one more layer of anonymity.

Brunet sought out and engaged doctor Danyau, an *accoucheur* who was both prominent and discreet, and he traveled to Normandy where he found a childless couple, a farm family—monsieur and madame du Bois—to raise the child. And what, asked Gericault, can I possibly do to repay you?

Well, as a matter of fact, Brunet wondered if Gericault had read the account of the *Medusa* shipwreck written by monsieur Corréard and monsieur Savigny?

Indeed, anyone who visited Horace's studio with any regularity had heard of this book that was always in the hands of the anti-royalists one met there. Gericault had not, in fact, read it but he had heard monsieur Valmy praise it highly (a perfect example, he had said, of the government's irresponsibility)—and did Brunet have some interest in the book?

Well, yes. Or at least, in one of its authors—monsieur Corréard—who, under the patronage of the banker, Jacques Lafitte, had just set up shop in the Palais-Royale arcade as a printer and publisher, calling his press *Au Naufragé de la Méduse*. (And what was a prominent banker doing, sponsoring this trouble maker who was supposed by many to be a member of the Carbonari—that secret society of anti-royalist agitators that had spread from Italy to every country in Europe? Was this an early example of radical chic? Or was it that the rising *haute bourgeoisie* had every reason—and better reasons than most—to challenge the power and authority of the monarchy?) In any case, Corréard was setting out to publish liberal, even radical, political pamphlets (Saint-Simon was one of his authors), and he would shortly publish Brunet's *Aristocracy and Democracy*. In addition, he was contemplating a new and expanded edition of the very successful account of the Medusa shipwreck and he hoped to have it illustrated with lithographs, if he could find a sympathetic artist . . .

Yes, of course, said Gericault. That is, I shall certainly read the book and we shall see.

* * *

Before he had finished the book he had made his decision. Here was a subject that could engage him and numb his grief and keep him occupied for many months, creating order out of a tale of chaos and disorder. Here was a modern subject that could not be dismissed as an ordinary *fait divers*; there was nobility here, there were innocent men who had been made to suffer, there was a story that could be elevated into tragedy by simply painting the awful physical reality of what had happened and painting it on an heroic scale. One had only to choose one's scene.

Somewhere in this story, he said to Brunet, there is a moment to be painted. But first I must speak to the authors. Can you bring them around? Tell monsieur Corréard that he can have his lithographs for the price of an interview.

And before he ever met with Corréard and Savigny he was planning to buy a wall-sized canvas and he was looking about for a studio large enough to accommodate it. He had his subject.

* * *

10

CORRÉARD AND SAVIGNY: A VOYAGE TO SENEGAL

He found it impossible not to tell his father—at the very least, Papa would have to be informed of the necessary financial arrangements—and at first Papa misunderstood. That is to say, he was delighted. Alexandrine! he exclaimed. Why, good for Jean-Baptiste!

No, not Uncle Jean, said Gericault.

It always took a moment for Papa to grasp anything at all, and anything unpleasant took a bit longer. It wasn't until Gericault had repeated, Not Uncle Jean, that he begin to sputter, But . . . but . . . but . . .

Gericault held up a hand to silence him. I have agreed, he said, to take responsibility.

But that's impossible, said Papa. The family . . . ! Why would you want to do that?

For the best of reasons, Papa. You must trust me.

In the moment of silence that followed Papa furrowed his brow and shook his head and then, quite suddenly, he guessed at the situation. But the family . . . ! he exclaimed again. Alexandrine is your aunt!

By *marriage*, Gericault insisted, not by blood—as though that made a difference. He knew perfectly well that their world would call it incest.

This is really too wicked of you, said Papa. Now, how can I ever speak to Jean-Baptiste?

Again, Gericault held up his hand. I suppose, he said, that everyone in the family will know sooner or later, but it is my belief that no one will want to give it a name; no one will want to acknowledge the facts and so no one will speak of them. (And did he think that this would make an untenable situation tenable? Well of course, if everyone agreed to play the game . . .) In any case, he went on, *arrangements* have been made . . . very *discreet* arrangements . . .

Shortly after that Papa learned that Gericault planned to move to a larger studio (as soon as he found one) for an indefinite period of time. Blow upon blow.

But I'll be back, Papa, said Gericault. It's not permanent. And at least you'll be rid of Mustapha for a while . . .

And in fact, thought Papa, it might make it easier for him to deal with the rest of the family. Quite a bit easier.

* * *

Before Gericault has found his studio in the faubourg du Roule, Corréard and Savigny come repeatedly to be interviewed at the rue des Martyrs, though they are not without certain reservations. They are bitter men, after all, they have been treated unjustly, they have been abused, they have been forced by circumstances to eat human flesh . . . and what can this dandified young painter know about that? But Corréard's anger has turned him into something of a professional survivor, he lives to publicize the injustice that has been done him, and the promise of a painting at the next Salon—a painting that will show the world how they have suffered, a painting that will give them their place in history—cannot be resisted. Corréard argued, then, for suppressing their doubts, and in the end they come to the rue des Martyrs despite their reservations.

It is Gericault's idea to question them and to sketch as they talk, trying out possible moments in the story, possible compositions.

But it's all in the book, Corréard protests.

Yes, and I've read the book, Gericault replies, but still . . . your own report in your own voices . . . it will make it easier for me to *see*, you know . . . if you'll just start at the very beginning . . .

That, of course—the beginning—was long before Corréard and Savigny came into it:

France had occupied the West African territory of Senegal since the seventeenth century, and then she had lost the territory to England during the Napoleonic wars. After Napoleon's defeat, however, the Treaty of Paris had allowed her to recover her lost land—a triumph for the negotiating skills of Talleyrand, whose doctrine of 'legitimacy' seemed to mean, in this case: 'If I was there once it must be mine forever.' The Senegalese were not consulted.

The French took their time about repossessing their territory. 'The Minister of the Marine,' wrote Corréard and Savigny, 'after having long meditated, and taken two years to prepare an expedition of four vessels, at last gave orders that it should sail for Senegal.' Does one detect a note of irony there? 'Long meditated?' 'Two years?' One might well. Neither Corréard nor Savigny was inclined to say anything favorable about the Minister of the Marine.

They were even less inclined to speak favorably of the convoy's captain, Hugues Duroy du Chaumareys. Chaumareys, to be sure, seemed to have no qualifications at all for his position, but that was not unusual. He was a *reentrant*—one of those noblemen who had gone into exile during the years of revolution and empire and who had returned now, sniffing about for position and advancement; men who were being given preference quite indiscriminately, regardless of their qualifications, to reward their loyalty to the crown. Chaumareys, for example, had spent a few months at the naval academy in his youth, and that had been his only experience with ships. It did not prevent him now, twenty five years later, from seeking a naval commission, and being rewarded with his own ship, the Medusa, not to mention the command of the entire convoy to Senegal. Aside from the frigate Medusa, he had overall command of the Argus, the Loire, and the Echo, a brig, a flute and a corvette.

On meeting the officers of these ships for the first time Chaumareys had smiled nervously and said, I hope that you fellows will show some indulgence . . . that you will make allowances . . . hoping to defuse their resentment and failing entirely. The officers and crew under his command, all of whom had served under the Republic and the Empire, resented any *reentrant* automatically—any man who had come back from years in exile to block someone's career and discount his years of continuous service—and they had a very keen sense of Chaumareys' inability. They grumbled, but they understood that Chaumareys was under orders to punish severely any talk against the Crown, and so they grumbled in private.

The distrust and contempt that the crew felt toward their Captain was equaled only by the distrust and contempt that he himself felt toward the troops that he was to transport to Senegal—three battalions, two hundred and fifty three men in all, most of whom were believed (with some justice) to be hot-heads and criminals recruited from who knew what God-forsaken jails. Chaumareys confided his concerns to his most prominent passenger, the governor-designate of Senegal, Julian-Dasyure Schmaltz, who shared his views of the riff-raff that they were to travel with. These men, they agreed, might become restless and dangerous in the confines of a ship at anchor, making tedious preparations to sail. It would be best to put off boarding them until the very last minute.

Before that, the entire establishment that was to run things in Senegal (and the lower orders that were to serve the establishment) had come on board. Besides Schmaltz, with his wife and daughter, there were clerks and curates and schoolmasters, hospital directors and surgeons and apothecaries, bakers and engineers and agricultural experts and even a gardener; and among them were Monsieur Savigny, who was assistant to the chief surgeon, and Monsieur Corréard, official geographer of the expedition.

Two thirds of this party embarked on the Medusa itself, which became an instant microcosm, a little floating France with all the tensions and cross-currents, all the animosities and allegiances, of the mother country—a perfect metaphor, a perfect symbol, sailing toward a perfectly symbolic event: unimaginable extremity.

(But Gericault is not setting out to paint a symbolic event or a metaphor, any more than he is setting out to deliver a moral lesson. He is determined only to paint what actually happened—the extremity itself and the nobility of the suffering—and to get it right. He has not yet noticed that his informants, and Corréard in particular, have other expectations. Go on, he urges them . . .)

There was trouble from the very start aboard the Medusa. It began as they were approaching Madeira, when they suddenly found themselves surrounded by a school of porpoises, leaping and dancing in a ring about the ship, and nearly everyone rushed up on deck to enjoy the circus. One of the cabin boys, a lad of fifteen, clambered up to a fore porthole for his own ringside view, but the poor boy leaned out too far and lost his footing and fell headlong into the sea. There was a cry of Man Overboard! and one of the sailors immediately threw out a life buoy, but after that everything went wrong. An attempt was made to fire a gun to signal the other ships in the convoy to be on the lookout, but none of the guns was loaded and ready. The sails were lowered and the ship hove too, but the captain had waited too long to give that order and when he finally did the maneuver was clumsily executed and took much too much time. Finally, a rescue boat was lowered, but there were only three men at the oars in a boat that called for six. In the end, the cabin boy was lost, and one could only pray that he had not in fact been able to swim to the life buoy, which would only have prolonged his agony.

After that, Chaumareys dropped all pretense of trusting his officers. He quarreled repeatedly over trifles with his second in command, Lieutenant Reynaud, threatening to replace him with Second Lieutenant Espiaux—but while both Espiaux and Reynaud were perfectly competent officers, neither of them was well born and they were both undoubtedly Bonapartists. Chaumareys refused, in the end, to trust either of them. He chose instead to take advice in matters of navigation from a fellow named Antoine Richefort.

(A puzzle, says Gericault, interrupting. Your narrative doesn't quite explain this Richefort, you know. Who the devil was he?

We were told, says Corréard, that he had been a marine officer in the past and that he knew these waters well. We were told that he had been ten years in England . . . as a prisoner . . . or perhaps as an exile . . . we were told many things.

An exile, says Gericault, would have appealed to Chaumareys, wouldn't he? And if he had an understanding of navigation . . .

Claimed to have an understanding of navigation, Corréard corrects him. That was not the impression of the ship's crew. They called him the God of Misrule, you know, after the fellow who dresses up as Neptune for that farce the sailors put on when they cross the Tropic.

And your course was set by this God of Misrule? Gericault asks. But what the devil was he doing on that ship, sailing to Senegal?

Corréard and Savigny stare at each other blankly.

Was he a member of the official party? Or did you carry commercial passengers?

No and no, Corréard replies.

Then where on earth did he come from and what was he doing there? He can't have been there for no reason at all . . . ?

In fact, no one could ever pin Richefort down. No one ever knew for sure where he had come from, but as for what he was doing there—well, the expedition's mining engineer, Monsieur Bredif, wrote in his journal that before they even reached Madeira, their provisioning way-station, 'the vessel was worked almost entirely according to the advice of this passenger.')

Madeira shocked even the rowdiest of soldiers and randiest of sailors from the Medusa. The women of St. Croix—housewives, shopkeepers, *all* the women—thought nothing of standing brazenly in their doorways, inviting the passing Frenchmen to enter. *'The depravity of morals is extreme,'* Corréard and Savigny wrote in their book, noting that the jealous husbands of the town were forced to accept their wives' behavior by the monks of the Holy Inquisition, who pacified the men with sermons preached on *'conjugal mania—the persecution of Satan'* and the duty to combat this mania with religious sentiments. As for Corréard and Savigny, they attributed the moral depravity to passions inflamed by the burning tropical heat, *'and not to abuses facilitated by a religion so sublime as ours.'* One supposes that this was meant as sarcasm but it is hard to tell.

After Madeira the officers and crew of the Medusa knew that they were in trouble. Sailing in water that was known to conceal dangerous reefs, Richefort insisted on steering too close to shore— within half a cannon shot, according to Corréard and Savigny; one could see the surf breaking on the shore, one could see enormous outcroppings of dangerous rock. When members of the crew expressed their concern, Richefort would reply, We know our business, now you go and tend to yours. When they protested the ship's course to Chaumareys he drew himself up and said that it was the King's order. He commanded by order of the King, he said, and while they were at sea he *was* the King. The man was hopeless.

So too, it turned out, were the charts that were supposed to aid their navigation, but in any case the charts were ignored. Egged on by Richefort and Governor Schmaltz, Chaumareys decided that it would be great sport to pull ahead and reach Senegal before the rest of the convoy that he was responsible for, and before long he had lost all contact with the Argus, the Loire and the Echo. He was sailing blind, or close to it, through notoriously treacherous waters. He never even noticed when the color of the water began to change, becoming clearer and greener.

The officers and the crew of the Medusa understood what that meant. They understood what it meant to see great masses of seaweed and swarms of fish at the ship's side—and sand, according to some, swirling in the current. In a perfectly calm sea, in perfectly clear weather, in shallow water, they were sailing toward disaster. The sounding lead showed eighteen fathoms . . . then nine . . . then six—and suddenly they were all overcome with a kind of torpor, a kind of stupor, a silent terror. A terrible thing was happening, a terrible calamity seemed to be falling out of the sky, a terrible, meaningless calamity. Nobody doubted that they were going to their doom and nobody imagined that anything could be done about it. Nobody lifted a finger. Nobody said a word.

Well yes, at the last minute someone did exclaim: That man is no more a sailor than my sister! He's going to lose us all!—and with that the ship gave a little leap and a shudder and it ran aground on a sandbar within sight of the African shore.

(So you see, says Corréard, the villainy that was practiced on board that ship.

What is worse, thinks Gericault, it was not really villainy, it was only folly. Chaumareys and Richefort were nothing more than fools who believed that they were in the right, and their righteous folly carried all those souls into catastrophe, into chaos and disorder . . . for no reason at all . . .)

Corréard and Savigny were struck by *'the extraordinary changes impressed on every countenance'* as they ran aground. *'Some persons,'* they wrote, *'were not to be recognized. Here you might see features become shrunk and hideous; there a countenance that had assumed a yellow and even a greenish hue; some men seemed thunderstruck and chained down to their places, without strength to move. When they had recovered from the stupefaction with which they were first seized, numbers gave themselves up to despair, while others uttered imprecations against those whose ignorance had been so fatal to us . . . Two women alone seemed insensible to this disaster; they were the wife and daughter of the governor. What a shocking contrast! These men, who for twenty or twenty-five years had been exposed to a thousand dangers, were profoundly affected, while Madame and Mademoiselle Schmaltz appeared insensible, as if unconcerned in these events.'*

Bit by bit the thunderstruck men came to their senses and set about trying to save their ship. They began by attempting to drag it off the reef using capstan and anchor, but the bottom was too sandy to hold the anchor, and the anchor was in any case too small for the job. It was then proposed that they lighten the ship and float it off the reef by dumping gunpowder, cannons and barrels of flour, but Governor Schmaltz wouldn't hear of it. How was he to keep order in Senegal without gunpowder and cannons? How was he to establish civilization in that primitive land without good French flour? Schmaltz, who was now effectively in command (Chaumareys having fallen into a state of stunned silence), proposed an alternative. A raft was to be built, a very large raft made of planks and beams and spare masts and spars lashed together, to be placed in the water, fastened by cable to the stranded ship (but at some distance) and loaded with as much of the heavy cargo as it would bear. If this lightening of the load failed to move the ship off the reef, if it became clear that the ship would have to be abandoned, the raft would serve another purpose. The Medusa, you see, carried only six boats (in dubious condition) for over four hundred passengers. If they had to abandon ship, the raft would accommodate the overflow, and it could be towed to shore by the six-boat flotilla.

Corréard and Savigny had to admit that this was a well laid plan, that it might even have been crowned with success, but *'unhappily these decisions were traced upon loose sand,'* they wrote, *'which was dispersed by the breath of egotism.'*

The raft was built, but by the time it was finished the ship was showing signs of breaking up, it seemed wisest to abandon her before she could be lightened, and the disembarking was pandemonium. The plans for an orderly evacuation never had a chance in a general atmosphere of *'sauve qui peut'*—words that were in fact never spoken by Schmaltz or by Captain Chaumareys, who continued his policy of silent dithering.

Below decks there were murmurs of mutiny among the soldiers, who had got it into their heads that they were about to be abandoned. Once their officers had convinced them that this was not so, they turned their attention to the casks of wine in the hold and to looting the belongings that their fellow passengers were forced to leave behind.

On deck it was every man for himself, with very little attention paid to the boat assignments that Schmaltz had worked out. There were those who crawled down the side of the ship on flimsy ladders, there were those who swung away from the ship on ropes, there were those who simply threw themselves into the sea—all in a mad, panicked scramble for a place in one of the boats.

In the rush to disembark, and in the absence of a firm commander, everything that could be bungled was bungled, everything that could go wrong went wrong. Most of the provisions that had been intended for the boats and the raft—casks of water and wine and barrels of biscuit—were left lying on the Medusa's decks. At one point the raft slipped its mooring and began to float away; they had to row after it and tug it back to the side of the ship. The only thing that went smoothly was the evacuation of the Schmaltz family. They sat calmly in velvet armchairs and were hoisted by block and tackle over the side of the ship, followed by case after case of the ladies' dresses and the Governor's uniforms.

Once those distinguished passengers had been seen to, Captain Chaumareys saw no reason not to go to his own boat. Quite simply, he abandoned his ship while others had yet to disembark. Later he would claim that when he left the ship no one remained on board except the seventeen soldiers who, either too drunk or too doubtful of the seaworthiness of the boats, absolutely refused to leave the Medusa, but that was not how the other survivors remembered it. They thought that Chaumareys was lucky not to have been fired on by those still waiting at the ship's railing to disembark.

(And where, asks Gericault, was Richefort during all this?

Again, Corréard and Savigny stare at each other blankly. They have to admit that for the first time on that voyage they had no idea of Richefort's whereabouts and never stopped to wonder. In our haste, says Corréard. In all that confusion . . .)

When they were finally ready to pull away, the boats, leaking at every seam and in danger of being swamped, were deliberately underloaded, while the raft they towed—sixty five feet long and twenty eight feet wide—carried one hundred and fifty passengers; one hundred and fifty *standing,* you understand, some of them waist deep in water, for with that heavy load the raft did not float, it wallowed. The officer who was to command the raft had taken one look at it and then disappeared into one of the boats. The soldiers who boarded the raft had no such choice and they were in an ugly mood. While they had been forbidden to carry their muskets, they did carry their sabers, and the tow-boat people were happy to keep their distance from the raft.

They were hardly under way when the passengers standing at the front of the raft noticed that the distance to the tow-boats was growing wider. As the unthinkable does not become thinkable in an instant, they were at first only puzzled, and then their attention was distracted by the raising of a flag in the lead boat and by the cries of *Vive le Roi!* that arose from all the other boats. One couldn't tell if they were cries of hope or cries of despair, or if the men in the boats were only cheering to cheer themselves up, but in any case, *Vive le Roi!*

(And we joined them, says Corréard. *Vive le Roi!* We were slow to understand that the solidarity had been breached, that the compact had been broken. But sooner or later we had to notice that the distance to the tow-boats was growing wider and wider by the minute. With *Vive le Roi!* still echoing in our ears, we began to understand what was happening to us.

And what exactly *was* happening? asks Gericault. It seems so uncertain . . .

What is certain, says Corréard, is that the towlines were dropped.

In all fairness, says Savigny, we must grant that one line may simply have snapped under too great a strain. We were a heavy load, after all. And one line may have been severed when a boat ran across it . . .

But the lines were dropped by all six boats, says Corréard. All six.

Of course, Savigny points out, we were sailing against the current. The tide was against us, and our raft was a considerable drag on the whole flotilla . . .

The tide would have turned, says Corréard, but they would not wait for it. They were determined to reach land before nightfall, they did not want to spend a night at sea in open boats. One by one the lines were dropped . . . they dropped the lines . . . and they sailed away . . .

It is true, Savigny has to agree. The compact was broken . . .)

Intentionally or not, the boats certainly did sail away, abandoning the raft and its hundred and fifty passengers (a hundred and twenty soldiers and thirty others, one of them a woman) with only two small casks of water, six barrels of wine, a barrel of water-logged biscuits and an improvised mast and sail. No charts, no compass, no anchor, no rudder, no oars.

Nevertheless, the first reaction was anger, not despair. To a man, they all swore that from now on they would live only to inflict vengeance on those who had deserted them. They had yet to ask themselves if any of them would live at all. They were certain, with the spirit of vengeance sustaining them, that they would somehow be rescued and somehow reach the shore, that they would survive.

That certainty, alas, like many of their comrades, did not survive the first night. *'The wind freshened, the sea rose considerably,'* wrote Corréard and Savigny. *'In the middle of the night the weather was very bad; very heavy waves rolled upon us, and often threw us down with great violence; the cries of the people were mingled with the roaring of the billows . . . lamenting our misfortune, certain to perish, yet still struggling for a fragment of existence . . .'*

They fastened ropes to the planks of the raft and they bloodied their hands clinging to them. They tore the flesh of their fingers clinging to the planks themselves. They clung to each other in violent embrace, stranger to stranger, friend to friend, as if it were the last embrace they would ever know. In the morning, when the sea had calmed, they found that twenty had been lost overnight—some swept into the sea, some trapped between the boards of the raft and trampled to death—and they began what was to become a familiar duty: throwing the dead into the sea.

Despite this unpleasant duty, the new day's tranquil sea brought new hope to everyone on the raft—everyone but two young boys and the ship's baker who, maddened and disoriented by the violent sea of the first night, were convinced that the violence would return and that nothing could save them. They went about saying their goodbyes politely and then, quite calmly, they stepped off the raft and into the calm sea. The rest of the raft's passengers spent the day preparing to board the rescue boats that were sure to appear at any moment. There were some, in fact, who repeatedly saw rescue ships on the horizon, but their sightings owed more to wishful thinking and short rations and the beating sun than to reality.

'*The evening came,*' wrote Corréard and Savigny, '*and the boats did not appear. Despondency began to seize all our people, and a mutinous spirit manifested itself by cries of fury. The wind, which during the day had been rather high, now became furious, and agitated the sea. If the preceding night had been terrible, this was still more horrible. Mountains of water covered us every moment, and broke, with violence, in the midst of us. Before and behind the waves dashed with fury, and carried off men in spite of all their resistance. At the center, the crowd was such that some poor men were stifled by the weight of their comrades, who fell upon them every moment . . .*'

In the midst of this tempest, delirium descended on many of the raft's passengers and on many others a drunken thirst for violence.

The delirium first: '*Some became furious; others threw themselves into the sea, taking leave of their comrades with great coolness; some said "Fear nothing, I am going to fetch you assistance; in a short time you will see me again." In the midst of this general madness, some unfortunate wretches were seen to rush upon their comrades with sabers drawn, demanding the wing of a chicken, or bread to appease the hunger which devoured them. Many fancied themselves still on board the Medusa. Some saw ships, and called them to their assistance. M. Corréard fancied he was travelling through the fine plains of Italy; one of the officers said to him, gravely, "I remember that we have been deserted by the boats; but fear nothing; I have just written to the governor, and in a few hours we shall be saved . . ."*'

Then the violence: '*The soldiers, terrified by the presence of an almost inevitable danger, gave themselves up for lost. Firmly believing that they were going to be swallowed up, they resolved to soothe their last moments by drinking till they lost the use of their reason. They fell upon a cask which was in the middle of the raft, made a large hole at one end, and with little tin cups they each took a pretty large quantity. The fumes of the wine soon disordered their brains...* 'Mad and unreasoning, their thoughts turned at first to mutiny. They were determined to rid themselves of the officers whom they blamed for their predicament, but as their drunkenness grew on them, and as the sea grew more violent, they decided instead to end their ordeal, and to end everyone else's ordeal as well, by destroying the raft itself. With their knives and sabers they began to hack at the ropes that lashed the planks together—someone even produced a small hatchet—and the sight of this madness seemed to dispel the delirium that some of the passengers suffered. Men who, a moment before, had been lost in hallucination, suddenly awakened to the common danger and joined together to face the mutineers with knives and bayonets and sabers. *'The fury of the soldiers suddenly abated, and gave place to extreme cowardice: many of them fell at our feet and asked pardon, which was instantly granted them.'*

The subdued soldiers retired, grumbling, to a corner of the raft and for an hour it seemed that order had been restored. Not so. *'After an hour's apparent tranquility, the soldiers rose again: their senses were entirely deranged; they rushed upon us like madmen, with their knives or sabers in their hands. They were entirely deaf to the cries of reason... and soon the raft was covered with dead bodies. Those among our adversaries who had no arms, attempted to tear us with their teeth; several of us were cruelly bitten; M. Savigny was himself bitten in the leg and shoulder...*

'It is here the place,' wrote Corréard and Savigny, *'to observe and to proclaim aloud for the honor of the French army, that most of these wretches were not worthy to wear its uniform. They were the scum of all countries, the refuse of the prisons, where they had been collected to make up the force charged with the defense and the protection of the colony. When, for the sake of health, they were made to bathe in the sea, the whole crew had ocular demonstration that it was not upon the breast that these heroes wore the insignia of the exploits which had led them to serve the state. Reason at*

least seems to demonstrate that it is dangerous to entrust arms for the protection of society to the hands of those whom society has itself rejected.'

(Can that be shown? Asks Corréard. Can that point be made?

Show the marks of the branding iron on the soldiers' buttocks? Only, says Gericault, suppressing a smile, if I paint them without their breeches and cast moonlight on their behinds . . .

To be sure, he has been considering the Battle on the Raft as a subject, and many of the figures in his preliminary sketches are indeed quite naked. They owe something to the tumbling nude figures in the *Last Judgments* of Michelangelo and Rubens—the terrifying fall into Hell—but they also owe something to Gericault's belief in the Davidian dictum that one must study the nude figure before one can paint it clothed. He is not the least bit interested in painting naked, branded buttocks to make a point, and he is in fact beginning to lose interest in the battle itself. His sketches are tangles of incident, they are ludicrously busy, too much is happening all at once—struggling figures, despairing figures, praying figures, dying figures, mourning figures, swooning figures falling into the sea, maddened figures throwing themselves into the sea—with no central action to focus on.

Too crowded, he explains to Corréard and Savigny. Too complicated. I must find a scene with the numbers reduced.

Soon enough, says Corréard. Soon enough . . .)

'At length daylight came, and disclosed the horrors of the scene: we found that between sixty and sixty-five men had perished during the night; we calculated that, at least, a fourth part had drowned themselves in despair. We had lost only two on our side, neither of whom was an officer.'

(We did what we could, says Corréard, to make a decent marine burial for the dead.

For most of them, murmurs Savigny, and in some cases, to be honest, for the dying as well. And for the badly wounded, as well, he thinks. That had begun already.

To be honest, says Corréard, with no rations to speak of and no rescue ship on the horizon, how many of us do you think would have survived if all of us had survived?

I know, says Savigny, I know—but he knows, also, that a necessary triage can easily be seen as a heartless massacre. He has never been able shake the thought that, even when it is justified by absolute necessity, it is always wrong. And there was worse to come . . .)

'We soon discovered a new misfortune; the rebels, during the tumult, had thrown into the sea two barrels of wine, and the only two casks of water that we had on the raft. Two casks of wine had been consumed the previous day; we had only one left and we were above sixty in number. We resolved to employ all possible means to procure fish. We collected all the tags from the soldiers, and made little hooks of them; we bent a bayonet to catch sharks; all this availed us nothing; the current carried our hooks under the raft, where they got entangled. A shark bit at the bayonet and straightened it. We gave up our project. An extreme resource was necessary to preserve our wretched existence . . .'

(There are certain things, says Corréard, that need not be shown . . .)

'We tremble with horror,' they wrote, *'at being obliged to mention that which we made use of! We feel our pen drop from our hand; a deathlike chill pervades all our limbs; our hair stands erect on our*

heads!—*Reader, we beseech you, do not feel indignation towards men who are already too unfortunate, but have compassion on them . . .*

'*Those whom death had spared in the disastrous night, fell upon the dead bodies with which the raft was covered and cut off pieces, which some instantly devoured. Many did not touch them; almost all the officers were of this number.*

'*Seeing that this horrid nourishment had given strength to those who had made use of it, it was proposed to dry it in order to render it a little less disgusting. Those who had firmness enough to abstain from it took a larger quantity of wine. We tried to eat sword belts and cartouche-boxes.*

We succeeded in swallowing some little morsels. Some ate linen. Others pieces of leather from the hats, on which there was a little grease, or rather dirt. A sailor attempted to eat excrement, but he could not succeed . . . '

(Say what you like, you can't deny that cannibalism, while it may horrify us, is usually presented in ways that make us giggle. Tasteless jokes about the Donner party. Cartoon drawings of missionaries stewing in large soup kettles. The famous shipwreck in Lord Byron's 'Don Juan' (which seems to have been based on a reading of Corréard and Savigny). As Byron tells it, lots are drawn to see who will be devoured, and the lot falls on Juan's tutor, Pedrillo. To make light of that horror, Byron refers to the scene in Dante's 'Inferno' in which Count Ugolino chews on the skull of his enemy, Archbishop Ruggieri:

> '*And if Pedrillo's fate should shocking be,*
> *Remember Ugolino condescends*
> *To eat the head of his archenemy,*
> *The moment after he politely ends*
> *His tale. If foes be food in hell, at sea*

> *'Tis surely fair to dine upon our friends*
> *When shipwreck's short allowance grows too scanty*
> *Without being much more horrible than Dante.'*

This is a way of not looking at the facts—the chunks of raw flesh covered with blemishes and sores and wounds; the drinking of blood and urine. But at the same time, it is a way of acknowledging that, of all taboos, this is the least absolute; it is all too easily trumped by necessity.

Despite Corréard's admonition, Gericault makes one stab at the subject—a sketch that is usually called 'Despair and Cannibalism on the Raft:' a pyramid of despairing figures, and one fellow who is too busy chewing on another fellow's elbow to share in the general despair. Sure enough, it is faintly comical, and it demonstrates clearly that cannibalism cannot be treated as one incident among many. If you are going to show it, you must make it central; if it cannot be central, best forget it. Only one sketch, then, and Gericault never returns to the subject).

The sea was calm on the third night, but the load had yet to be sufficiently lightened, they still wallowed in water up to their knees and had to sleep standing, *'pressed against each other to form a solid mass.'*

The fourth morning's sunrise revealed a dozen new corpses trapped between the planks of the raft. They were promptly extricated and consigned to the sea, *'reserving only one, destined to feed those who, the day before, had clasped his trembling hands, vowing him an eternal friendship.'* Now, to make it more palatable, his flesh was cut into strips and hung on the ropes to dry.

Later that day the raft plowed into a school of flying fish and many of the tiny things were caught between the planks—several hundred, in fact, but so small that each man's ration had to be supplemented by a portion of the reserved human flesh, and from that time on no one balked at the forbidden diet.

The soldiers took note of that and, concluding with some justice that when worst came to worst they would be the first to be eaten, they rose up in a new mutiny. *'A terrible combat again ensued, and both sides fought with desperate fury.'* One must imagine it: vicious hand-to-hand combat on a raft wallowing in the sea. *'Soon the fatal raft was covered with dead bodies and flowing with blood. At length, after unheard of efforts, the mutineers were again repulsed, and tranquility restored. The sea water had almost entirely excoriated our lower extremities; we were covered with contusions or wounds, which, irritated by the salt-water, made us utter every moment piercing cries; so that there were not above twenty of us who were able to stand upright or walk. Almost our whole stock was exhausted; we had no more wine than was sufficient for four days, and we had not above a dozen fish left. In four days, said we, we shall be in want of everything, and death will be unavoidable . . .'*

(It was really as if we were dead already and removed from time, says Savigny. One remembers that things happened . . . events, one after the other . . . but somehow one cannot be certain of the time in between . . . it might have been minutes or hours or days . . .)

Only one barrel of wine was left. Two soldiers, hidden behind it, bored a hole in the barrel and began to sip the wine through a reed (one wonders how they came to be carrying a reed). When they were discovered they were, by general agreement, thrown into the sea. The rules of behavior had been laid down.

On the same day a young sailor boy named Léon, barely twelve years old, *'died away like a lamp which ceases to burn for want of aliment. His angelic countenance, his melodious voice . . . his youth . . . filled us with the tenderest interest for this young victim.'* When madness had driven the poor child to running about the raft crying for his mother and trampling on sore and wounded feet, no one had complained. He had, in fact, been fed extra rations ungrudgingly. Nevertheless, he died in the loving arms of a fellow named Coudin, who had taken an interest in the young sailor and had tried to protect him.

(But Lord Byron gives the scene as father and son:

> 'And o'er him bent his sire and never raised
>   His eyes from off his face, and wiped the foam
> From his pale lips, and ever on him gazed
>   . . . .
> The boy expired. The father held the clay
>   And looked upon it long, and when at last
> Death left no doubt, and the dead burden lay
>   Stiff on his heart, and pulse and hope were past,
> He watched it wistfully, until away
>   'Twas borne by the rude wave wherein 'twas cast.'

Gericault pounces on the scene at once and treats it from the start as a central motif for his painting. In sketch after sketch he tries out different versions of the pose—the naked youth sprawled in the grieving old man's lap, face down, face up, tightly held, slipping away . . .

But that is no child, says Corréard, peering over his shoulder. That is a young man.

True, says Gericault. The helplessness of a small child may be pathetic, he says, but the helplessness of a grown man, a comrade brought down in his full strength . . . and that is his whole answer. Corréard is shocked but he holds his tongue.

In fact, the motif will not be seen as the death of a comrade. Denied the death of a small child, the picture's first viewers will be determined, like Lord Byron, to have at least the death of a son, and from the very start the pictorial group will be read as father and son. To be sure, Gericault does not speak of it in this way and he never will, but no one will ever have the slightest doubt: father and son. And while they are leaping to conclusions, the first viewers of the picture will go one leap further and call the old man Ugolino. That is to say, Dante's Count Ugolino, whom Archbishop Ruggieri had walled up in a tower along with his sons, leaving them to starve to death; Ugolino, who is usually pictured in a grief-stricken pose with his starving children clinging to his knees and pleading with him to consume them; Ugolino, who ended up blindly groping over the dead bodies of his children before *'fasting did more than grief had done.'* Dante meant to say, of course, that the poor fellow succumbed to starvation, but many have found it more thrilling to believe that Ugolino's stoic resolve finally collapsed and he ate his children—and didn't he end up, after all, in the ninth circle of Dante's hell, chewing on the skull of Archbishop Ruggieri?

In that way the figures of the grieving old man and the dead youth will come to be read both as father and son and as hidden references to cannibalism on the raft. It will do Gericault no good to protest.)

'We were now only twenty-seven remaining,' wrote Corréard and Savigny; *'of this number but fifteen seemed likely to live some days: all the rest, covered with large wounds, had almost entirely lost their reason; yet they had a share in the distribution of provisions, and might, before their death, consume thirty or forty bottles of wine, which were of inestimable value to us. We deliberated thus: to put the sick on half allowance would have been killing them by inches. So after a debate, at which the most dreadful despair presided, it was resolved to throw them into the sea. This measure, however repugnant it was to ourselves, procured the survivors wine for six days; but when the decision was made, who would dare to execute it? The habit of seeing death pounce upon us as his prey, the*

certainty of our infallible destruction without this fatal expedient, everything, in a word, had hardened our hearts, and rendered them callous to all feeling except that of self preservation. Three sailors and a soldier took on themselves this cruel execution; we turned our faces aside and wept tears of blood over the fate of these unhappy men.' So went the only woman on the raft—the expedition's *vivandière*—and her husband, both of them cursing and pleading and sobbing and struggling weakly.

(Against his will, an image of Alex flickers into Gericault's head: the stoic calm with which she refused to struggle against her incarceration at Chesnay; the way she accepted—the way she *embraced*—what was, in effect, the end of her life. His eyes fill with tears, which Corréard attributes to the pathos of their story and the power of their story telling.)

'This dreadful expedient,' they wrote, *'saved the fifteen who remained . . . the victims, we repeat it, had not above forty-eight hours to live, and by keeping them on the raft, we should absolutely have been destitute of the means of existence two days before we were found.'*

(So you see, says Corréard, under the circumstances it was not a crime.

On the contrary, says Savigny to Gericault, under the circumstances we were all, of necessity, criminals. There were many victims, he says, who were too insensible to know what was happening to them, but there were others . . . you cannot imagine . . . the begging, the pleading . . . half dead, after all, is still half alive . . .

But we needn't dwell on that, says Corréard.

Perhaps not, says Savigny.

They are afraid of each other, thinks Gericault. The survivors of that raft all know that their survival depended on a crime, and that only their fellow survivors know the depth of their guilt. They must all be afraid of each other.)

With only fifteen survivors the raft finally floated properly and it was possible to establish some order. By mutual agreement, all fifteen threw their weapons into the sea, being careful to save one saber to use as a cutting tool.

And then *'A new event, for everything was an event for wretches for whom the universe was reduced to a flooring of a few measures in extent, who were the sport of the winds and waves as they hung suspended over the abyss; an event then happened which happily diverted our attention from the horrors of our situation.'* A white butterfly—a common, ordinary butterfly of the sort that might be found among the pansies in any French garden—suddenly appeared fluttering over the raft. They must be close to land! Or had the butterfly been caught in some powerful air current and blown out to sea at enormous speed? Was it, like themselves, in great extremity, having seen its last flowering glade? *'It was the ninth day that we passed upon the raft; the torments of hunger consumed our entrails; already some of the soldiers and sailors devoured, with haggard eyes, this wretched prey, and seemed ready to dispute it with each other. Others considered this butterfly as a messenger of heaven, declared that they took the poor insect under their protection, and hindered any injury being done to it.'*

(Is that a moment for you? Asks Corréard.

But it was not a harbinger after all, says Gericault. A butterfly in distress? Men arguing over whether or not to eat the thing? He would not know how to paint that.)

The butterfly may not have been a harbinger but it did revive their spirits and their determination to *do* something. They started trying to catch fish again, though with very little success, and they invented a construction project for themselves: '*we loosened some planks on the front of the raft, and with some pretty long pieces of wood, raised in the center a kind of platform on which we reposed: all the effects which we had been able to collect were placed upon it and served to render it less hard; besides, they hindered the sea from passing with so much facility through the intervals between the different pieces of the raft; but the waves came across and sometimes covered us completely . . . every time a wave rolled over us it produced a very disagreeable sensation and made us utter plaintive cries.*'

Without actually speaking of it, each of the fifteen staked out his own territory on the platform they had built. '*It was on this new theatre that we resolved to await death in a manner worthy of Frenchmen, and with perfect resignation. The most adroit among us, to divert our thoughts, and to make the time pass with more rapidity, got their comrades to relate to us their passed triumphs, and sometimes, to draw comparisons between the hardships they had undergone in their glorious campaigns, and the distresses we endured upon our raft.*'

Meanwhile, '*a raging thirst, which was redoubled in the daytime by the beams of a burning sun, consumed us: it was such that we eagerly moistened our lips with urine, which we cooled in little tin cups. We put the cup in a place where there was a little water, that the urine might cool the sooner; it often happened that these cups were stolen from those who had thus prepared them. The cup was returned, indeed, but not till the liquid which it contained was drunk. Monsieur Savigny observed that the urine of some of us was more agreeable than that of others.*'

They grasped at small pleasures:

Someone found a single lemon among one of the dead men's possessions, and it would have come to violence if he had not shared sucks on the fruit with his comrades.

Someone found thirty cloves of garlic in a little bag, and that too nearly led to a violent dispute before everyone realized that there were enough cloves to go around.

Someone found two little phials of tooth cleaner—essence of cinnamon and cloves—which produced on the tongue a delightful if momentary sense of relief.

Someone found, and passed around for sniffing, a little empty phial that had once contained essence of roses.

Someone discovered that sucking on pewter produced a cool sensation in the mouth.

There were some who, desperate to cool themselves, bathed in the sea despite the sharks that followed the raft constantly—and oddly enough, the sharks let them alone, though they did suffer from attacks by man-of-war jellyfish.

There were some who conceived the idea that they should all drink up what remained of the wine and then destroy themselves, and had to be argued out of it.

There were some who, being certain that they were near land, built a smaller raft and proposed to paddle it to shore, but the thing capsized on being put into the water. *'It was then resolved that we should all await death in our present situation.'*

It was the twelfth day. *'There were not above twelve or fifteen bottles of wine left in our barrel. We began to feel an invincible disgust at the flesh which had till then scarcely supported us. In the morning, the sun appeared entirely free from clouds,'* and suddenly *'a captain of infantry looking towards the horizon, descried a ship, and announced it to us by an exclamation of joy; we perceived that it was a brig; but it was at a very great distance; we could distinguish only the tops of the masts. The sight of this vessel excited in us a transport of joy . . . yet fears mingled with our hopes; we straitened some hoops of casks, to the end of which we tied handkerchiefs of different colors. A man, assisted by us all together, mounted to the top of the mast and waved those little flags. For above half an hour, we were suspended between hope and fear . . .* '

(It is this moment, suspended between hope and fear, that Gericault recognizes as his moment, though the final painting shows not one but two flag wavers and they are on top of a barrel, not up the mast, which might have seemed awkward and slightly comical. One of the flag wavers is leaning on the barrel top, a shadowy figure with the light falling on the cloth that he is waving. The other flag waver is *standing* on the barrel, supported by a comrade, at the very pinnacle of the composition with the light falling on the muscles of his back—one of the most prominent and powerful black men in western art. As for the flick of paint that represents the ship on the horizon—the ship that might be coming to rescue them; the ship that might instead be about to disappear over the horizon—it is minuscule, a casual observer could miss it entirely. Not much for them to be pinning their hopes on . . . but still, a ship.)

'. . . *some thought they saw the ship become larger, and others confirmed that its course carried it from us; these latter were the only ones whose eyes were not fascinated by hope, for the brig disappeared. From the delirium of joy, we fell into profound despondency and grief. At last, to calm our despair, we wished to seek some consolation in the arms of sleep.*' That was the night of the twelfth day.

On the thirteenth day '*We proposed to inscribe upon a board an account of our adventures, to write all our names at the bottom of the narrative, and to fasten it to the upper part of the mast.*' While they were pondering this project someone at the front of the raft suddenly uttered a loud cry: '"*Saved! See the brig close upon us!*"

And in fact, it was, at the most, half a league distant, carrying a press of sail, and steering so as to come extremely close to us. We all embraced each other with transports that looked like delirium, and tears of joy rolled down our cheeks, shrunk by the most cruel privations. Everyone seized handkerchiefs, or pieces of linen to make signals to the brig. The crew, ranged on the deck and in the shrouds, shewed, by waving their hats and handkerchiefs, the pleasure they felt at coming to the assistance of their unhappy countrymen.'

Unhappy indeed: *'fifteen unfortunate men, almost naked; their bodies and faces disfigured by the scorching beams of the sun; ten of the fifteen were hardly able to move; our limbs were excoriated, our sufferings were deeply imprinted on our features, our eyes were hollow and almost wild, and our long beards rendered our appearance still more frightful; we were but the shadows of ourselves. We had scarcely escaped when some of us again became delirious: an officer of the army wanted to throw himself into the sea, to go and look for his pocket book; which he would have done had he not been prevented . . .*'

The commander of the *Argus*, the rescue ship, noted one other thing: *'Those that I saved had been living on human flesh for many days. When I found them the ropes that held up their mast were covered with strips of this meat, hung out to dry.*'

(Some of this—not the strips of flesh but the emaciation—is to be seen in a few of the preliminary sketches, but for the most part there is none of it in either the sketches or the finished painting. Even the figures that are clearly meant to be dead have robust bodies. The picturesque pathos of emaciation might do for genre lithographs, for newspaper illustrations, but a painting on this grand scale was aimed not at pathos but at tragedy, and tragedy called for perfectly robust bodies trapped in extremity and chaos.

For that entire voyage, Gericault thinks, was guided by the god of chaos—indeed, by Richefort. It was a story of disorder, a story of pandemonium let loose in the world, a story of dereliction working hand in hand with mindless fate to produce—what? A tragedy? A melodrama filled with dumb horror and heroes and villains? Or an ordinary disaster—simply the kind of arbitrary thing that can happen for no reason at all? Meaningless? Absurd? But while it was happening the pain was real enough, and it must have seemed that the pain would last forever. A living Hell, he thinks—the perpetually writhing bodies of the Last Judgment. Or perhaps only life itself, for the worst is never really over, he thinks, the worst is never behind us.

In this way he has come to see his own life as a kind of shipwreck—he and Alex cast adrift; he and Alex and the child that she will bear before long, cast into extremity by the god of chaos.

There are several preliminary sketches of a family group—a grief-stricken fellow supporting a dead or fainting woman with one arm while he holds a muscular and squirming child in the other.

But of course there was no such family, Corréard complains.

The artist's license? suggests Savigny, who rather likes the sketches.

Never mind, says Gericault, realizing perhaps that the family group is too tangled with his own emotions, his own pain. When it finally came to painting it on canvas he would never be able to see it through.

Again, tears come to his eyes, but Corréard and Savigny don't notice, they are coming to the part of their story that arouses their fiercest indignation).

At the port of St. Louis in Senegal *'we were received in the most brilliant manner; the governor, several officers, both English and French, came to meet us, and one of the officers in this numerous train held out to us a hand, which a fortnight before had, as it were, plunged us into the depth of despair by loosening the tow-rope which made our raft fast to the boat. We could not contain our indignation at the sight of some persons in this train.'*

Despite heavy seas and high winds, two boatloads of *Medusa* survivors had reached St. Louis in only a few days, so Captain Chaumareys and Governor Schmaltz were there to greet the survivors of the raft when they arrived. The raft people, in turn, were there to greet the rest of the boat people who had made it to land and now began to turn up in straggling groups with stories of their own ordeals, trekking through the Sahara desert, dependant on the mercy of the local 'Moors.' Corréard and Savigny could not deny that the boat people, the people who had sailed away and abandoned them on the raft, had also suffered:

'*. . . they were in distress, destitute of resources of every kind, without a guide, on a coast inhabited by barbarians; hunger and thirst cruelly tormented them; the beams of a scorching sun, reflected from the immense sandy plains, aggravated their suffering. In the day, oppressed by excessive heat, they could scarcely move a step; it was only in the cool of the morning and the evening that they could pursue their painful march.*

'*The women and young children inspired the greatest pity. These feeble beings could not put their delicate feet on the burning sands, and were besides incapable of walking for any length of time. The officers themselves assisted the children, and carried them in turn . . . but having met with some Moors, who never travel in these deserts without having their camels and their asses with them, all that were not able to walk mounted these animals; to obtain this indulgence, it was necessary to pay two gourds for a day; so that it was impossible for M. Picard, who had a numerous family, to bear so great an expense; his respectable young ladies were therefore obliged to walk.*

'*In the midst of these sandy plains it was absolutely impossible to shelter themselves from the rays of a burning sun. Scorched by insupportable heat . . . some of them partly lost their senses; a spirit of mutiny even showed itself for some moments. Many of those who crossed the desert have assured us that there were moments when they were quite beside themselves. An officer of the army, in particular, gave signs of the most violent despair; he rolled himself in the sand begging his comrades to kill him, because he could no longer bear up against so many sufferings.*

'*During their progress, they had to struggle with the most dreadful extremes of hunger and thirst; the latter was such that the first time that several of them discovered water in the desert, such selfishness was manifested that those who had found these beneficent springs knelt down four or five together near the hole which they had just dug, and there, with their eyes fixed on the water, made signs to their comrades not to approach them; that they had found the springs, and that they alone had a right to drink at them. It was not til after the most urgent supplications that they granted a little water to their wretched companions, who were consumed by a raging thirst.*

'*When they met with any Moors they obtained some assistance from them, but these barbarians carried their inhumanity so far as to refuse to show them the springs which were scattered along the shore. Sordid avarice made them act in this manner to these unhappy people; for when the latter had passed a well, the Moors drew water from it which they sold to them at a gourd for a glass; they exacted the same price for a small handful of millet.*'

At least they had the water and the millet. Still, one could not deny that they had suffered, though most of them had lived through it and had been spared the ultimate degradation of the raft people.

The boat people and the raft people were accounted for, but there was still the matter of the seventeen who had refused to abandon the *Medusa*. 'Very little was said about the men who had remained on board. Their companions had solemnly promised to send for them as soon as they should arrive at St. Louis, but these unfortunate men were already hardly thought of any more.' There was, however, much talk of the goods and money that might be salvaged from the abandoned ship, and Corréard protested: "'A more precious object, of which nothing is said, is the seventeen poor men who were left." "Pooh," answered somebody, "seventeen! There are not more than three left."' Corréard walked away in anger.

Two unsuccessful attempts were made to reach the *Medusa* in ships that were badly fitted out by a penny-pinching owner to whom Governor Schmaltz had granted a monopoly on the profitable salvage operation. Finally, 'they sailed for the third time and reached the *Medusa*, fifty-two days after she had been abandoned. What was the astonishment of those on board at still finding in the *Medusa* three unfortunate men at the point of expiring! But what had become of the fourteen others?

'Forty-two days had passed without their receiving the assistance which had been promised them, when twelve of the most resolute, seeing that they were on the point of being destitute of everything, formed a raft with pieces of timber which remained on board, the whole bound together, like the first, with strong ropes. They embarked upon it and directed their course towards the land, but how could they steer on a machine that was destitute of oars and sails? It is certain that these poor men, who had taken with them but a very small stock of provisions, could not hold out long. The remains of their raft were found on the coast of the Sahara desert by some Moors.

'A sailor who had refused to embark upon the raft attempted also to reach the shore. He put himself on a chicken coop, but he sank within a cable's length of the frigate.

'Four men resolved not to leave the *Medusa*. These unhappy men occupied each a separate place and never left it but to fetch provisions, which in the last days consisted only of a little brandy, tallow and salt pork. When they met they ran upon each other brandishing their knives. As soon as they had only brandy to drink they grew weaker every day. One of the four had just died when the schooner arrived.

'After having given the necessary succour to the three men, they proceeded to get out of the frigate everything that could be removed. M. Corréard had the simplicity to think that the shipwrecked people were going to recover a part, at least, of their effects, but far from it! Those who were on board declared themselves corsairs and pillaged all the effects which they could get at.

'When we asked if it had been possible to save any of our effects, we were answered yes, but that they were a fair prize. And the next day the town was transformed into a public market which lasted at least a week. There were sold effects belonging to the state, and those of the unhappy crew who had perished; here the clothes of those who were still living. Nothing was now seen in the town but Negroes dressed, some in jackets and pantaloons, some in large grey great coats; other had shirts, waistcoats, police bonnets—everything, in short, presented the image of disorder and confusion.'

At St. Louis they were all—boat people and raft people and the three from the Medusa—subjected to every kind of humiliation. Those who needed hospitalization—Corréard among them—'were laid upon truck-beds which, instead of mattresses, had only blankets doubled in four, with sheets disgustingly dirty.' Governor Schmaltz paid them a single visit and he promised them that their needs would be cared for and their condition improved, but nothing came of it and Schmaltz never visited them again.

One might think that the Governor's wife and daughter—they who had been hoisted off the *Medusa* in upholstered armchairs—would have paid visits of compassion, but no, *'these ladies carried indifference so far as to dispense themselves from the most common duties of humanity, by refraining from paying the smallest visit to the poor wretches placed in the hospital.'* Miss Schmaltz, in fact, wrote a letter to a friend in Paris *'justifying her relations with the shipwrecked persons . . . and trying to devote these unfortunate men to public hatred and contempt. In the singular letter, which has been circulated in Paris, she confessed that the sight of the shipwrecked persons inspired her with a degree of horror which she could not suppress. "It was really impossible for me," she said, "to endure the presence of these men without feeling a sentiment of indignation."*

'Left to themselves in the horrid abode which they inhabited, surrounded by men in whom their cruel situation inspired no pity, our countrymen, again abandoned, gave vent to their distress in useless complaints.'

More formal complaints to the authorities in Paris were equally useless. Dr. Savigny (requiring less medical attention than many of his comrades) had been able to return to France earlier than the others, and during his voyage home on the *Echo* he had composed a narrative of the entire disaster. Upon reaching Paris he had submitted this account to the Royal Minister of the Marine, le comte Du Bouchage, hoping that it might procure some recompense for the survivors and perhaps even advancement for himself. Du Bouchage, however, being an Ultra-Royalist with a reputation for granting commissions to incompetent ex-émigrés and political favorites, would have seen to it that the entire matter was forgotten if a copy of the account had not fallen into the hands of the Prefect of the Police, Élie Decazes. Decazes was a man with his own political ambitions, and it very much suited his purposes to discredit Du Bouchage, a potential rival for the King's favor. He passed Savigny's narrative along to the editor of the liberal *Journal des Débats*, where it was promptly published and created a great furor. Even in moderate anti-royalist circles the loss of the Medusa was spoken of not as a simple maritime disaster but as a political crime; in less moderate circles it was seen as a metaphor for the condition of France under Bourbon rule.

'This publicity, by means of the Journal drew upon M. Savigny the most serious remonstrances. For M. Savigny everything was changed; instead of the interest which his situation ought to inspire, he had called down upon himself the severity of the Minister, and was to justify himself for having dared to write that he had been very unfortunate by the fault of others.' Hoping to save Savigny from the wrath of Du Bouchage, the editor of the *Journal des Débats* printed a formal statement swearing that Savigny himself had not supplied the *Journal* with his manuscript, but the damage had been done. Savigny despaired of ever getting the recompense and advancement that he sought, and he resigned from His Majesty's service.

It wasn't long, though, before his accusations began to circulate in Senegal. *'The English translated the details contained in the Journal and inserted them in one of their own journals which reached Senegal. In this amplified translation there were some pretty strong passages which were far from pleasing the Governor, [who] perceived that there was but one means to combat the narrative; this was to endeavor to make it believed that it was false in many particulars. A report was therefore drawn up at St. Louis ; it was brought to M. Corréard to be signed, who, after perusing it, refused, because he found it contrary to the truth. The Governor's secretary came several times to the hospital to urge him for his signature; but he persisted in his refusal.'*

There were some, indeed, who did sign the Governor's whitewashing report, fearful, as one of them guiltily confessed afterwards, *'that the account which [Savigny] had drawn up of our misfortunes might render us odious to all our relations and friends.'* It might show them, that is, to have been guilty of cannibalism and the most brutal kind of triage. If nothing else, their ordeal had taught them to fear and distrust their comrades and to despise themselves.

There was an implied threat that if Corréard did not sign the report he would not be permitted to leave Senegal, but even a man like Governor Schmaltz would not dare to carry out such a threat. In the end *'M. Corréard's perseverance in withholding his signature triumphed over injustice, and his return to Europe was no longer retarded.'*

He sailed home on the Loire, and he was not at all pleased to find that Captain Chaumareys was sailing home on the same ship. He was even less pleased when Chaumareys insisted on treating him as a traveling companion, forcing him to endure an endless whine of complaint and self-justification: whatever had happened, it was the fault of the Bonapartist officers; or it was the fault of the Republican crew; or it was the fault of Governor Schmaltz. As for his own actions in losing his ship and abandoning it before it was fully evacuated: Mere bagatelles, said Chaumareys. Nothing would come of it.

In the end, very little does. Tried at a Courts Martial in February of 1817, Chaumareys is found guilty of abandoning his ship and losing it, but for what ought to be a hanging offense he is only reduced in rank, deprived of his medals and sentenced to three years of house arrest. As for sailing away from the convoy of ships that he was supposed to lead, and sailing away from the survivors on the raft, not a word is said, nor is a single word of the proceedings reported in the press.

Corréard, meanwhile, has reached Paris and applied at the Ministry of Marine for what he, like Savigny, feels is his due, and like Savigny, he has been repeatedly rebuffed. We owe you nothing, he has been told. We cannot lay this request before the King. So at last he too resigns from the service and he and Savigny set about expanding Savigny's manuscript, filling it with the most excruciating details, strengthening its accusatory tone and adding, for good measure, a plan for the gradual elimination of slavery—in short, ort of thing to create a scandalous best-seller.

They have no trouble in finding a publisher, and the book (*Narrative of a Voyage to Senegal*) is an immediate success in France and, in translation, throughout Europe. Such a success, in fact, that Corréard insists on publishing any future editions himself, and he is given the money to set up a press and bookshop (*Au Naufragé de la Méduse*) in the Palais-Royal. His sponsor is the banker, Jacques Lafitte—a leader of the liberal opposition and a supporter of the claims to the throne put forward by 'Monsieur Valmy,' Louis-Philippe, duc d'Orléans. The little shop quickly becomes a meeting place for the same liberal and Bonapartist crowd that one sees at Horace's. Corréard and Savigny have become celebrities.

Now you've put your foot in it, says Horace to Gericault. Lithographs for their book are all very well, but do you really intend to *paint* this scandal? I applaud your audacity, my dear, and I wish you luck, but you must understand that the Salon will see it as mere genre painting. You will get precious little support.

There is an awkward silence and then Horace goes on. Did you know, he asks, that my *Mameluke Massacre* is already as good as sold?

Gericault, of course, does not intend to make a genre painting, he does not intend to tell an anecdote or to paint a scandal. He wants only to make a painting anchored in physical reality, no classical rhetoric, no stylized generalization, and he has progressed in his sketches and studies to the point at which the circumstantial, the specific, the carefully observed become, by virtue of their very particularity, a universal statement: a realistic image of human flesh in extremity and at the same time an image of humanity suspended in a chaos of hope and despair; an image, he thinks, of life itself. By giving them form he will try to impose order on chaos and disorder, he will try to make sense of what seems to him to make no sense at all. And the form will be founded on close observation.

Close observation: being told that the Medusa's carpenter was among the survivors on the raft, he insists on meeting the fellow and commissioning him to build a little model of the raft. It will help me to *see*, he explains. It will help me to understand the experience.

And what good will it do? wonders Corréard. What can we expect from this spoiled charmer, from this dandy, this peacock? How can we ever expect him to understand the experience?

Close observation: I confess that I hardly know what death looks like, Gericault says to Brunet. I believe that you have friends at the Beaujon hospital . . . ?

* * *

11

SCÈNE DE NAUFRAGE

In the ghoulish spirit that seems endemic to medical students, Brunet's friends at the Beaujon hospital were happy to oblige. The hospital and the Bicêtre asylum and prison provided them with a steady supply of fresh cadavers and severed limbs and severed heads, and they were happy to wink at the regulations and let Gericault have access to whatever he wanted. Behind his back, of course, they joked about what they took to be a gentleman's morbid perversion. They hadn't a clue as to what he was up to.

Close observation: like the broken down carriage horse that he had brought to his studio while he painted his Chasseur—the horse whose smell, he claimed, fixed the idea of horse in his head—the body parts would force him to live with the sights and smells of death; they would fix the idea of death in his head.

There is a painting of two severed heads, a man and a woman—executed thieves from Bicêtre—arranged on pillows and bed linen as if lying together in some terrible marriage bed. The woman's eyes are closed—she might be sleeping peacefully. The man's eyes are opened as if he had just awakened with a start. It would all seem perfectly ordinary were it not for the bruised color that infuses their faces, the blood-stained bed linen and the stumps of the severed necks that the linen makes no effort to cover.

There are paintings of severed arms and legs in tangled

arrangements, embracing each other tenderly, arm and leg, hand and foot equal at last, as if in some amorous encounter. Here too the severed flesh is exposed, no effort is made to hide the bloody stumps, and the flesh is the color of a bruise.

Macabre? Overwrought? Graveyard horror meant to send a chill down one's spine? Not at all. In these paintings Gericault does not dramatize, he does not tell stories, he does not express attitudes or strike poses, he does not attempt to frighten us or disgust us. He simply *looks* and produces a cool, clear-sighted description of these fragments of nature, a description of what he sees. This is what it comes down to, he says, and it is stated as nothing more than a simple fact.

It is the most daring and defiant kind of realism. These are not sketches, they are finished paintings, though Gericault knew that they would never have the slightest prospect of being exhibited or sold in his lifetime. Still, they are finished with great care, and the painter Delacroix called them '*truly sublime. The best argument for beauty as it ought to be understood,*' adding that they proved that painting does not always need a subject. By 'subject' he meant anecdote, story, scene; he meant narrative significance and moral lesson and meaning—those things that have a life beyond what is actually shown on the canvas. He saw that, without those encumbrances, these paintings took a step toward abstraction, they struck one more blow against the classical *'beau idéal.'*

Close observation: Quite by chance he runs into Théodore Lebrun on the boulevard. They have not seen each other since Lebrun had found him in hair curlers and canceled plans to travel with him to Italy. Lebrun, who is just recovering from an attack of jaundice, does not expect a particularly warm greeting and he is startled when Gericault reaches out and touches his face, still a greenish yellow from the jaundice, and exclaims, Beautiful! Beautiful! Gericault brings his own face close to Lebrun's and examines the jaundiced complexion with his eyes and with his fingertips. My dear fellow, he exclaims, you must come and pose for me! Lebrun is puzzled and even a little frightened at first but he finally comes to understand that his complexion must indeed seem beautiful to this painter who is searching for the color of death.

Close observation: Gericault goes with his neighbor, Colonel Bro, to pay a condolence call on a certain General Letellier who has been grieving over the recent death of his young wife. They enter the General's bedroom only moments after he has shot himself in despair. They find him lying dead on his bed with his pistol lying, still smoking, on the bedclothes and his wife's scarf wrapped around his head. On the spot, Gericault brings out his sketch pad and records the scene with great clarity of detail and the most refined and elegant draftsmanship—no melodrama, no sentimentality, simply: this is what we saw. But it is shown with such delicacy and tenderness that the drawing has never been thought of as gruesome.

* * *

That was in July. In mid-August Alex came up to Paris and went directly to the clinic of the *accoucheur,* Dr. Danyau.

I must see her, said Gericault to Brunet (who had made all the arrangements) and Brunet had actually to stand in the studio doorway to keep his friend from rushing out. It is not what the family wants, he insisted, but that carried very little weight. He shifted to, It is not what *she* wants, and that gave Gericault pause. You wanted discretion for *her* sake, said Brunet, and there can be no discretion if you insist on running about . . . and in the end, Brunet prevailed.

When you consider the number of people who knew what was happening—Gericault's family knew, Brunet knew, Horace who adored gossip knew, Dorcy on his return from Italy in November would find out and have his suspicions confirmed—when you consider all those, the degree of discretion is surprising. There was so little gossip that subsequent generations of art historians knew only that there had been an affair with a married woman (not, after all, so uncommon) and knew none of the details. They speculated: Horace's wife? Caroline Allemande? And after the sculptor Etex revealed in 1885 that there had been an illegitimate son, there was speculation about the fatherhood; just possibly, it was thought, the *real* father was not Gericault at all but none other than the Citizen King, Louis-Philippe (and if the mother had in fact been Caroline Allemande, that might well have been the case).

It was not until 1976 that Michel Le Pesant of the French National Archives brought to light documents showing that Gericault's lover (and the mother of his son) had been his aunt. That revelation was followed by a great deal of scholarly tucking and squeezing meant to prove that the original speculations had not been so outlandish after all, but the facts were incontrovertible: on the 21st of August, 1818, Alexandrine-Modeste Caruel gave birth to Gericault's son. On the next day, however, when Dr. Danyau registered the child at the local town hall, the parents were listed as 'un-named.'

Brunet had been successful in keeping the parents apart, but Gericault had insisted on detailed daily reports and on hearing that Alex had gone into labor he had taken to his own bed, breathing heavily and complaining of cramps and fever,. Lying there distraught in the August heat, the bed sheets damp and twisted, his thoughts racing wildly this way and that, he found himself remembering the foaling mare that he had seen many years ago at Mortain, and he remembered Uncle Siméon's words: *This is how it goes. This is how one comes into the world.* Oh, my poor dear Alex! he thought, and he moaned loudly enough to frighten the servants.

A boy, Brunet finally announced. Small, they tell me, but a perfectly healthy boy, and his mother has asked that *you* name him.

Georges-Hyppolyte, he replied after only a moment's hesitation, as if he had known that he would be called upon and had rehearsed it. The *Georges* was for Papa, of course. And the *Hyppolyte*? Well, Hippolytus, the son of Theseus, was rejected by his father and sent into exile—but perhaps Gericault wasn't thinking of that. It was a common enough name, after all.

Yes, said Brunet. Hyppolite. That's *'of the running horses,'* isn't it?

Something like that, said Gericault. Don't look to me for proper Greek.

*   *   *

From the very start Brunet had been the go-between and the only one with whom Gericault could speak openly. Horace had avoided the subject for fear of provoking one of Gericault's fits of weeping and breast-beating—the sort of thing that Dorcy would have chastised sharply and stopped at once if he had only been in Paris and if he had only been told. Papa had avoided the subject not so much out of delicacy as from not knowing the proper form for such a conversation, but now the subject could no longer be avoided. Brunet would see to it that the child was brought to its foster family—the Dubois family of Mesnil-Durant in Normandy—but financial matters would have to be dealt with by Gericault and his father.

Papa broached the subject. Did you know, the value of number twenty-three has increased beyond one's wildest dreams? he asked, referring to the house in the rue des Martyrs.

I daresay, replied Gericault, who took no interest at all in such matters and had no sense of what Papa was driving at.

If one sold out, Papa continued, one would realize a considerable profit.

Papa, said Gericault in exasperation, I am going to a larger studio for the sake of one painting only, and then I'll be back. There's no need to dispossess ourselves.

No, Papa agreed. Not if we sell and stay on as tenants. You see, Colonel Bro has made a most generous offer . . .

But surely, said Gericault, we have enough as we are?

But we are not as we were, said Papa. I was thinking that if one sold out and put the proceeds into farmland, the revenues alone would more than cover our remittances to Monsieur Dubois, and the farms themselves would be a legacy for the boy . . .

A legacy. It was a new thought. Having allowed others to handle all the practical matters, Gericault had not, up to this point, thought in terms of provision for the future. It is kind of you, he said to Papa rather tentatively. It is kind of you to have worked this out.

Kind? asked Papa. To think of providing for my grandson? Gericault had also managed somehow not to think in terms of father and son, grandfather and grandson, until this moment. Now the thought of his son—not simply a child, you see, but his *son*—finally pierced his heart and he began to weep.

I understand, said Papa. It has been a strain. You must get some rest.

* * *

He tried repeatedly to see Alex and, repeatedly, she refused. She would not see him and she would not nurse the baby or even hold it. She turned away from anything that might create the illusion of a life in the future, and she went back to her prison, her little suite of rooms at Chesnay, unprotesting.

He tried repeatedly to see his son and, repeatedly, he was told that it would be unwise, that it would be indiscreet, that in any case Alex did not wish it. Then one day Brunet told him that the child's future had already begun, that he had already been taken to Normandy and that Gericault would do well now to put the entire unpleasant business out of his head. It was over.

His first thought was, I must talk to Dorcy. Dorcy would scold him, to be sure, but Dorcy would know that he was in pain and would know how to soothe him. Like Mama, he thought. Like Thunder. I must talk to Dorcy, he thought, and the thought itself reminded him with a start, as it had been doing repeatedly for some time now, that Dorcy was still in Rome.

He turned to Thunder, then, and threw himself into racing and jumping contests with the young officers who rode in the Champ-de-Mars. After a day of racing he hoped to return home drained and exhausted and able to sleep, but no, his nights were spent in a half-doze that was worse than wakefulness, tormented by vague thoughts of Alex, of his son—thoughts that faded and drifted away before he could catch them. On awakening, he remembered only that they were painful.

It was Horace who finally told him that he had better get to work. If you're thinking of the next Salon, he said, and if you still insist on making this picture, hadn't you better settle down and make it? And if you happen to be in need of studio assistants— it is a very *large* canvas, after all—you are welcome to any those young fellows who hang about at my place and call themselves students of Monsieur Vernet.

So several of those young men came instead to call themselves students of Monsieur Gericault: Pierre Lehoux, Antoine Montfort and, above all, Louis-Alexis Jamar, whose good nature and eagerness and unaffected admiration led Gericault to engage him as chief assistant. Jamar and Gericault both moved into the new studio on the rue du Faubourg du Roule, sharing the single bedroom and sharing the meals that were prepared for them by the concierge or, when they were feeling adventurous, by Mustapha, who quickly learned to make a variety of strange pilafs on the studio's heating stove.

* * *

When stories of an artist's quirks and peculiarities take on mythic proportions (Van Gogh's ear, for example) we are liable to become skeptical. Does the source have an ax to grind? Are the stories perhaps exaggerated? Are they even true?

Did Gericault, then, actually have his golden curls cut off? Did he really announce that he would not be seen in public until the painting was finished? Well, yes to the first question and a qualified yes to the second. He is sitting one day at his mirror combing out his curls—the curls that, in their *papillotes*, had put off Théodore Lebrun, the curls that Alex had fingered so lovingly, the curls that perfectly respectable young ladies often claimed to envy—and on a sudden impulse he simply takes up his scissors and cuts off a handful. For Alex, he thinks; it is the least I can do; and then he summons a hairdresser to finish the job. So yes, he does indeed have himself shorn, but the point is not to prevent his going out altogether, it is to prevent his going out into the fashionable world; it is to forestall invitations to afternoons and to evening parties and to balls—the sort of thing that might cloud his memory of Alex and tempt him to fritter away his time (and won't Dorcy be pleased!). So he cuts himself off from the world of distracting social events but, aside from that, he goes out frequently. That is how he comes to meet Nicolas Charlet.

He and Horace have ridden out of town to Meudon and there they are dining at the Three Crowns, hoping to meet Charlet who has been engaged to decorate the walls of the inn with painted ducks and hares and rabbits. Charlet is still obliged to do this sort of thing for a living though he is beginning to earn a reputation as a practitioner of the new art of lithography, publishing military subjects (with a heavy-handed Bonapartist slant), muck-raking cartoons exposing vice and folly in the government, and sentimental tributes to 'the French Working Man.' In time this work will lose its topicality and come to seem coarse and wooden, but at the moment it has a fresh, rough vigor that Gericault admires. Charlet seems to take physical pleasure in the deep, rich tones and dramatic contrasts made possible by the litho stone, and there isn't a trace of the School or the Academy in his work. He had, to be sure, studied with Gros, but after a while Gros had suggested very firmly that he leave his studio and follow his own impulses. There is nothing, Gros had said, for you to learn here.

Horace has told Gericault this story (he had it from the gossipy students in his studio), adding that Charlet was said to be coarse and vulgar and disagreeable, given to drunken sprees and cruel practical jokes on his friends, but Gericault only shrugged. You've seen his lithographs, he said. We have a lot to learn about this new method and he may have something to teach us. One must take one's profit wherever one can find it. I want to meet him.

So Horace has asked around and been told to try the Three Crowns at Meudon, and there they are.

The owner is delighted to have two distinguished Paris gentlemen as customers (his new decorations seem to have become an attraction before they are even completed!) and he is happy to convey their invitation to Monsieur Charlet: would he be kind enough to interrupt his work and join the two gentlemen at the far table . . . ?

So we must now deal with that peculiar man, Charlet. Shit,

gentlemen, he says, I'm in the midst of work, I'm trying to concentrate—but he accepts the seat that is offered him, he stretches his legs out under the table causing Horace and Gericault to draw theirs back, and he proceeds to scrutinize them, his hand on his chin, his eyebrows raised as if in surprise or alarm or perhaps just condescension.

He recognizes Horace, of course, who is a familiar figure on the boulevards of Paris. As for Gericault, Charlet has heard the story of the fellow's haircut, and the scarf tied around his head is a giveaway. He knows who they are, these two gentlemen in modish riding clothes, and he knows how to size them up:

Horace has taken an instant dislike to Charlet, and it shows; he is cool, distant, composed, and while it might be fun to take him down a peg, to upset his composure, it would not be easy. Horace floats smoothly along on his family name and his reputation and very little can upset him; he has a very secure sense of his own position. He was born, after all, in his father's apartments at the Louvre while Charlet was born in the city's worst working class slum—and both of them know it.

Gericault is another matter. He is fascinated by Charlet—by his very large, coarse presence, by his rude and bellowing manner, by his calculated reverse dandyism of unkempt hair and careless dressing, by the faint perfume of danger (positively an animal scent) that seems to hang in the air about him.

Charlet is equally fascinated, filled with a mischievous desire to find the flaws in this fellow's elegant and well cared for facade, to shatter that facade, to drag Gericault to the sort of tavern that he would never enter of his own accord and make him into a late night drinking companion, to go whoring with him, to make him a companion in the kind of thing that he has undoubtedly dreamed of but never dared to try—this rich young man who does not need to paint ducks for an innkeeper to earn his living.

And what fun it would be to see what he's like when he's had too much to drink!

One can only call it mutual infatuation at first sight. That much is immediately clear to Horace and he becomes more and more uncomfortable as the infatuation becomes more and more apparent.

Charlet makes the first move. My dear fellow, he says, you seem to have lost your hair.

Let us say, says Gericault, that I have disencumbered myself.

To avoid distraction from serious matters, Horace mumbles sourly.

And I intend to discuss serious matters with Monsieur Charlet, says Gericault. I should like to know what stones he prefers, and what crayons, and what ink . . . ?

Oh, whatever the printer has on hand, it doesn't matter, says Charlet, waving his hand dismissively and then raising it to signal *more wine* to the waiter.

He absolutely refuses to be drawn into a discussion of métier, but politics is another matter. He proposes a toast to Louis-Philippe, Duc d'Orléans—'Monsieur Valmy.' Valmy's day will come, he says. And did you know that he has acquired a copy of my latest album of prints?

Gericault congratulates him but Horace only stiffens a little. I understand that he's in your circle, Charlet says to Horace. (Indeed, the liberal opposition that gathers at Horace's studio pins its hopes on 'Monsieur Valmy.') I understand, says Charlet, that one can meet him quite often at your studio . . . ?

Horace will not bite. There is an awkward silence, and then

Charlet goes on: Can one just drop in, he asks, or must one have an invitation?

Horace is cornered. Any afternoon, he says. By all means.

Then it's more wine and more wine, and before long Charlet is on his feet singing a popular opposition song—*'Il n'y a plus d'argent en France . . . Vive le roi!'*—and urging Gericault to join him in dancing a little gavotte to the tune. To Horace's dismay, Gericault is not the least bit reluctant, he jumps up eagerly, and there they are, Gericault and Charlet, singing at the tops of their voices— *'Vive le Roi!'*—mocking the words and mimicking the dainty steps of the dance with exaggerated gestures, all elbows and knees and absurdly deep bows.

It is time to act, Horace decides, or they will end up drinking more wine and having to spend the night in Meudon.

They'll be waiting up for me at home, he says. Perhaps we'd better start back?

No one will be waiting up for me, says Gericault, but perhaps you're right. Will you ride back into Paris with us? he asks Charlet, and Charlet (who has been planning to stay at the Three Crowns) says, Yes, of course, it will be a pleasure, thinking: We shall see Vernet home, and then we shall see . . .

* * *

In fact, Jamar has been waiting up for Gericault in the studio on the rue de Faubourg du Roule, and he is beginning to worry.

Mustapha has curled up in his rug in his usual corner of the studio and gone to sleep. Jamar has been laying out the studio supplies, following Gericault's detailed instructions but certain that everything will have to be rearranged tomorrow. That is how it has gone for the last days, for the last weeks to be perfectly honest. They lay things out and then rearrange them, Monsieur Gericault delays and delays, he will not settle down to work.

For the most unlikely reason—because of Charlet—that is about to change.

Jamar hears a drunken warbling coming from the stairs outside— *'Vive le Roi! Vive le Roi!'*—and then Gericault bursts through the door in a state of quite visible exhilaration, though his clothes are spattered and his hair is matted with mud and God knows what else, and the seat of his trousers is ripped open from waist to knee.

He staggers toward Jamar, crying, Jamar! My dear little Jamar! and he puts out his arms—to embrace the little fellow? to hold on to him and steady himself? Instead, his arms encircle Jamar's waist, he lifts him off the floor, Jamar's feet are swinging in the air, he and Gericault are face to face, and Gericault kisses him full on the lips.

In unthinking panic and confusion, Jamar (who is half in love with Gericault anyway, though he has never dared to think physically) submits to the kiss, begins to return the embrace, oblivious to Mustapha's stare from his dark corner—not disapproval, just a stare—but the moment passes. Gericault swings him around and lowers him until his feet touch the floor again, and then Gericault sits down too abruptly on a little rush-bottomed chair that creaks in protest. We must be serious, he says to Jamar, slurring his words just a little. We must be sober. We must begin work in the morning.

Jamar is barely able to compose himself. Yes Monsieur, he says. In the morning, he says, and then he remembers. While you were out, he says, Monsieur Dedreux-Dorcy called.

Oh Lord! says Gericault, staring down at his spattered clothing. Dorcy has come back to scold me.

* * *

When two men go whoring together, the shared experience forges an erotic bond between them, and Gericault has just spent an hour in bed with Charlet and two whores.

He has been absolutely chaste since the day he learned that Alex was carrying his child, he has tried to present a cool and proper face to the world, he has tried to smother the peculiar mixture of grief and violent desire that keeps welling to the surface, and now at last Charlet has allowed him to erupt. Charlet lying in bed beside him, Charlet watching him intently and goading him, Charlet suggesting every kind of lasciviousness, encouraging every kind of wildness and risk, the abandonment of all decorum— Charlet has cracked the shell that he had formed around himself. He understands that Charlet is dangerous, he understands that there is violence lurking just beneath the man's surface, and he finds both the danger and the hint of violence exhilarating and liberating.

No longer feeling the need to restrain himself, he positively wallows in self-pity and self-contempt when he tells Dorcy the terrible news about Alex and young Georges-Hyppolyte: I am a monster, Dorcy . . . I have lost everything . . . I can do nothing . . . My heart is broken . . . I am helpless. The reddish beard that he's starting is soaked in tears.

Dorcy has never seen his friend so distraught. I might have been here to prevent this, he thinks. If I hadn't insisted on that fruitless year in Rome, I might have prevented this and I might have prevented Charlet. For Dorcy too sees the lurking violence and danger in Charlet. Like everyone else, he sees Charlet's rudeness, his coarseness, his vulgarity, his bad behavior, and, like everyone else, he is baffled by this new friendship.

We cannot all be born gentlemen, my dear, says Gericault, and a good thing too. Monsieur Valmy, he explains, *talks* of the French people; Charlet *is* of the people. The man is honest and direct, and I value that. And he has an eye. You mustn't see him as some kind of evil influence.

Well, if you must go about with him, at least you might protect yourself when you go to visit the ladies, says Dorcy, referring to a slight medical complaint that Gericault has mentioned rather boastfully.

Protect myself and insult those charming young ladies? Gericault asks.

It is hopeless. Dorcy, like Gericault's other friends, does indeed see Charlet as every kind of evil influence, a dark figure huddled and threatening in the background, a kind of Richefort who has smashed Gericault's compass and is steering him toward disaster. They cannot see—Gericault hardly understands it himself—that it is Charlet who, for all his wickedness and dark influence, has freed him to begin work on his painting. Charlet—Gericault's 'Richefort'—has released the energy that will be needed to paint the disaster that the Medusa's Richefort, 'the God of misrule,' helped to bring about. Gericault has allowed disorder to enter his life and, oddly, that very disorder has freed him to embark on this monumental effort to draw order out of chaos; for a painting, any painting, begins as a chaotic mess and order must be coaxed from it.

And how is that done? How does a painting get painted? It is a contest, a battle against chaos, a struggle full of false starts and changes of mind, mistakes and accidents, doubts and uncertainties and risks; there is a constant pushing and pulling, cutting and cropping, adjusting and readjusting and changing focus, something made to recede one day and brought forward the next, light cast here and then dimmed, shadow cast there and then brightened; there is a constant scraping away of yesterdays trials and stupid errors and a constant painting over and painting over. And when the painter can finally do no more he will, if he is wise, stop painting and he may, if he likes, call the painting finished.

And how did *this* painting, Gericault's painting, get painted? We cannot enter the act itself, we cannot trace the circuit of impulses flowing from eye to hand to brush to canvas and back again to eye that controlled even the slightest flick of the painter's brush. At best we can record the facts and ask questions and speculate.

* * *

To begin with there's the question of suffering. One cannot fail to notice that Gericault began work on the final painting only months after the birth of Georges-Hyppolite, and surely, the two events must be related? Oh, one must be cautious, one must allow for the possibility of simple coincidence; but surely even coincidence—co-incidence, simultaneity—is a kind of relationship? And surely, Gericault was still suffering, still seething with grief? And surely, that suffering and grief spilled over into his work? Why, right there in the painting, the only figure that faces us directly—right there is what we take to be a father grieving over the loss of what we take to be his son! And isn't intense personal emotion said to be one of the hallmarks of Romanticism in painting; and isn't this picture called the first great beacon of French Romanticism?

But does our knowledge of the artist's inner turmoil really throw light on the painting? Suppose that we knew nothing of that turmoil? Or suppose that we knew something to the contrary? Or grant that we know the facts and can't help knowing what we know—but is it perhaps more complicated than that? Does personal emotion have its limits? Can a painting that survives over time, a painting that one comes back to again and again, express nothing more than the artist's passions and torments of the moment, his passing sorrows? Doesn't it survive (if it does) precisely because the artist has transcended the personal emotions and the contingencies of his situation? Gericault's *Raft* is not simply the expression of a man succumbing to torment and disorder, but that of a man defying his torment and striving for order and surviving. We see not simply the artist's personal pain but pain transformed and transforming—humanity's pain. This is not about a man's loss of his son, it is about human loss. Oh, one must be very cautious indeed. The artist may suffer (though of course he needn't—one doesn't imagine that Rubens ever suffered much) but the suffering man is not the painter, he is the man whom the painter must overcome. We cannot look at a van Gogh painting through van Gogh's ear, we must look through his eye.

And then there's the question of size. Sixteen feet by twenty four. with figures twice life—size? How in the world did he arrive at that scale and those precise dimensions? The canvas, after all, was ordered in February, months before he had hit upon the final image and made the preliminary studies.

Years later, comparing Gericault's finished painting to certain large-scale works by Gros and Rubens, Delacroix would write: *They reach for the Sublime, which comes to some extent from the size of the figures. Proportion counts for everything in their power. If they were no more than life-size, they would not attain the Sublime.*

Is that it? A deliberate reach for a vague *sublime* that resides, at least in part, in a scale that elicits fear and trembling—*terribilità*?

Does size count, then, after all? Can size turn a private work into a public work (for this is clearly meant to be a public work)? Can size alone turn a genre scene—an event taken from the news—

into an image of the human condition? Can it alter the very substance of a painting?

Ever since his year in Rome, to be sure, Gericault had insisted on the superiority of mural to easel painting—*mere* easel painting, he would say. Michelangelo (who thought that easel painting was for women and children) had taught him that. After his time in Rome Gericault insisted that talented young painters should be given walls to decorate, not years of soft living at the Roman Academy. After all, he would joke, if the novice botched one wall of a room, he still had three more walls on which to make up for it. One wants great buckets of paint, he would exclaim on his deathbed, and brooms for brushes! A *bagatelle*, he would call the *Raft*, a *vignette*. But at sixteen feet by twenty four, where in the world did he imagine that this painting would hang, this mural without a wall? It was never going to decorate any connoisseur's salon and, given the subject, it could hardly be destined for the walls of any bureau or ministry of His Majesty's government. The Louvre, of course, could accommodate its size—but would His Majesty's government ever consider buying this testament to its own dereliction?

One might almost think that he painted with no thought to a possible audience, though he certainly intended to show the picture at the next Salon, and in fact the very act of painting the canvas was a kind of performance put on before an audience. A select few, we are told, were admitted to the Faubourg du Roule studio while he was at work, but when one adds them up it comes to quite a crowd. There was Dorcy, of course, and there was Horace (though he didn't come often, he was generally too busy playing to the audience at his own studio). There were Corréard and Savigny, when they could not be put off, and Brunet to shepherd them. There was Lebrun, who had recovered from his 'beautiful' jaundice but still looked so wan that Gericault was determined to have him pose for the grieving father's head. There was Cadamour, the popular model, to pose for the father's body (and retail the latest gossip from every other studio in Paris), and Joseph, the black model, to pose for the brave figure that teeters atop a barrel and waves a signal toward the horizon. There was Jamar, Gericault's assistant, who posed for the father's dead son, and there were the other youths (Horace called them Gericault's Kindergarten and Charlet, more cruelly, Gericault's Harem) who were invited into the studio to observe and to sketch and to pose for various figures on the raft: Montfort and Lehoux, the young hangers-on from Horace's studio, and Eugène Delacroix, a student whose work in Monsieur Guérin's studio had caught Gericault's eye. And there was always Mustapha hovering with trays of thick coffee and Turkish sweets. There was everyone, really, except for Charlet, because Gericault demanded absolute silence while he was working and with Charlet that was clearly out of the question; he could hardly be expected to keep his mouth shut for two minutes running, and he would certainly never submit to the carpet slippers that Gericault insisted on to muffle the footsteps of his visitors.

It sounds like a kind of social event, and indeed, in the days when the Salon ruled, the painting of a major work for the Salon did tend to become a social event. The great David's studio was always abuzz with students and hangers on who would throw off their clothes at a moment's notice to pose naked for the master's heroic *pompiers*. The constant hullabaloo in Horace's studio may have exaggerated the custom, but only slightly. The only thing unusual about the crowd that gathered in Gericault's studio was the enforced silence.

Young as I was, Antoine Montfort would remember, *(I was barely seventeen) it was often difficult for me to sit still for hours on end without getting up and accidentally scraping my chair. Sensing that this noise, in the midst of the general silence, must have bothered Monsieur Gericault, I would look toward the table that he stood on to reach the highest figures on his canvas, and he would smile back at me with an expression of benevolent reproach. The noise of a mouse, he would assure me, was enough to interrupt his work.*

Montfort was astonished by Gericault's gravity and his intense concentration—the concentration of a man using his painting to calm himself, to sort out the jumble in his head, to control chaos. (It's like riding Thunder, Gericault confided to Dorcy. *It just stops everything and lets me be.*

The way he proceeded, Montfort wrote, *was no less astonishing than his concentration.* He laid out the broad outlines of his composition on the canvas in a bold contour drawing and then, with no further preparation—no tonal under-painting, no sketched in details—he plunged directly into the final painting, filling in the contoured figures one at a time, not building them up slowly but skipping directly from outline to painted figure. One by one he arranged his models on the platform that had been set up to represent the raft, adjusting the pose with great precision to match the pre-determined contour on the canvas, and one by one he filled in sections of the contour outline, completing each section in a single day as if he were painting in fresco. As the work progressed the painted figures began to resemble enormous chunks of sculpture sprouting from the canvas, and years later Eugène Delacroix could still remember his excitement on seeing the painting in this state: *The impression was so overwhelming,* he would write, *that, on leaving the studio, I broke into a run and ran like a madman all the way . . . to the far end of the faubourg Saint-Germain.* He had been shaken by the immensity that he would call *sublime.*

Gericault may have seemed to paint his picture in fragments, but the final composition was always firmly in his head and bit by bit an organized, coherent image emerged. It can be argued that the image is in fact *too* organized, too tightly bound by its crisscrossed diagonals and interlocking pyramids, by the barriers that Gericault erected against disorder, but there are so many twisting and turning backs and shoulders here, there is so much writhing, there are so many thrusting arms and grasping hands, that the painting would be chaos if the figures weren't so tightly bound by the composition. As it is, the figures seem suspended between hope and despair, between one moment and the next, in a *tableau vivant*, as if they had seen the Medusa herself and were turning into stone. The painting is filled with violent movement, and at the same time it is frozen in stillness.

It is filled with contradictions. On the one hand, topical subject matter and concrete, circumstantial realism, the direct expression of real torment, every detail carefully researched and observed. Gericault interviewed Corréard and Savigny repeatedly, and the ship's carpenter as well. He worked out every single gesture and pose with his models. He researched the light itself, dragging Dorcy along on a trip to Le Havre to see how the sea and sky met and cast light upon each other. On the other hand, a kind of abstract, timeless essence embodied in somewhat idealized, monumental figures painted in the grand manner. No emaciated cannibals here, no strips of human flesh drying in the shrouds, no macabre horror, no sensational reporting. The pity and terror here are aroused by the vigor and energy of athletic, classical bodies. The painting is tragic not despite the vigor of these bodies but because of it. Their energy only emphasizes the extremity in which they are caught—struggling, athletic bodies entangled helplessly in their destiny, failed or failing and torn between hope and despair. What began as a shocking news item has been transformed into an image of the human condition.

An image filled, to be sure, with contradictions. On the one hand it looks back to a kind of Davidian classicism, on the other hand it looks forward to a kind of realism, and in addition it seems to herald romanticism with its intense emotion and its depiction of extremity—but those are really our terms, our labels, not Gericault's. He has been called a crypto-classicist, a proto-realist, a romantic, and then there are the more equivocal permutations: romantic realist, romantic classicist—it seems that we cannot understand what has happened, we cannot make history, without making categories and inventing sets of contrasts and opposites. Very few art historians have suggested that Gericault was, like most of us, simply trying to get by from day to day, trying to steer a course through opposing currents that carried him this way and that, not trying to break dramatically with any tradition, not consciously defying any canon, but using whatever came to hand if he found it useful and discarding whatever he couldn't use. He certainly never called himself a romantic or any of those things. The words, the concepts would have meant nothing to him, though we don't seem to be able to do without them. We think that they bring neatness and order to the general mess of history—how things happened. They make us think that we understand. They tell us what to see.

The label that you choose may very well determine the picture that you will see—a classical tableau or a realist genre scene or a romantic outburst of emotion—but every view contains its own contradictions. The realist view cannot accommodate the healthy, strapping bodies. The classical view cannot accommodate the unstoic emotion, the pathos that is imbedded in the details (all these life-size!): the helpless, sprawling legs of the two corpses in the foreground—legs that Delacroix would remember ten years later when he painted *Liberty Leading the People*; the beautifully painted stockings—so beautiful that they break your heart—that hang loosely around the ankles of the dead youth; his lovely opened left hand, his shriveled sex.

(So much exposed flesh, but only that one uncovered frontal view? Was there an unspoken convention? One sees the same thing in so many paintings of the time. Great masses of naked warriors, for example, but only one full frontal. As if to say, we must admire the naked figure, we must not be prudes, but let's not get carried away? Has anyone ever studied this?)

And why is the dead youth naked except for his stockings? Despite all the exposed flesh, everyone else does seem to be wearing *something.* Several of them are clearly wearing breeches, the kneeling fellow is wearing a shirt and some sort of tunic, the grieving old man seems to be wearing trousers, even the corpse that is sliding off the raft is clothed in some sort of shroud. Yet we have what is essentially an incongruous classical nude lying dead amid all these more realistically clothed figures . . . and of course it is the nakedness itself that can bring tears to our eyes.

As for the brooding, grief-stricken old man with the dead youth in his lap—the conventional pose that made everyone think *Ugolino* and so brought cannibalism into the picture—well, it *is* a conventional pose, the old man is the least convincing, most academic figure in the painting, though he is obliged to carry tremendous weight in the general scheme. He is the only figure, after all, who faces us, turning his back on the others who are struggling to rise in hope. He is surrounded by the dead, but unlike any other figure in the painting, he seems a bit detached. He does not share the desperate hopefulness of the others, but neither is he really overwhelmed by his grief. He doesn't seem to despair so much as to ponder despair. If he carries his intended weight it is only because the overall structure of the painting forces it on him.

For the meaning of this painting is embodied in the structure itself—the enormously complex arrangement of figures in multiple, interlocking, superimposed pyramids—the cat's cradle of diagonals that propel the picture's forces and counter-forces— the powerful surge upward toward hope, the equally powerful tug downward toward death and despair. This kind of pyramidal composition may have been a traditional device for organizing large-scale paintings, but few paintings had ever been as architecturally complex as this one. Delacroix seems to have studied it carefully and then simplified its scheme before painting his image of Liberty at the barricades. Picasso seems to have studied it and embraced its complexity before painting his *Guernica*.

A complex structure of conflicting forces, then—but the horizon clarifies everything. Gericault understood the importance of the horizon and he altered it constantly, raising it and lowering it (too high and the signaling sailors would seem to be engulfed by the sea, all hope lost; too low and the sea would hardly seem to pose a threat) and adjusting the scale of the rescue ship in the distance. If that ship stood too large on the horizon, the chances of rescue would seem too certain. Everyone knew, of course, that the survivors on the *Medusa's* raft were in fact rescued, but the picture refuses to acknowledge that. Gericault made the rescue ship smaller and smaller, and finally minuscule, as if to say, it is not about *they will be rescued* or *they won't be rescued*, it is about hope and despair and never knowing. The picture is about our permanent state of not knowing.

* * *

It is July and the studio in the rue du Faubourg du Roule, with the sun pouring in through the skylight, has become quite uncomfortable. The crowd of models and observers has begun to dwindle, though Jamar has remained faithful, and Montfort and of course Dorcy.

End of the Author's manuscript.

* * *

EDITOR'S AFTERWORD

Théodore Géricault's life after the completion of his masterpiece *The Raft of the Medusa* became a sequence of varying storms interrupted by periods of faint sunlight, but never clear skies. First of all, throughout the formidable and tumultuous world of Parisian artistic, political and social salons, negative comments took the lead: *Medusa* was mostly unwelcome. There was some praise from the Left, more condemnation from the Right. In-between was confusion: what was one to make of this fearsome canvas, without glory or heroism? Some perceptive approval came from painters such as David and Delacroix. Other artists objected to the painting's scale, its dark palette. To many critics it was unacceptable as to genre, a denial of every standard of the official Salon, of the Classical canon that had so long dominated painting in France.

Géricault, already deeply troubled in both his personal and professional life, could only be further disturbed by the general reaction to his masterpiece. Separation from those closest to him increased his anguish. Fears and feelings of madness became more persistent. Loss of confidence resulted in his turning down commissions. He was encouraged, however, to take *Raft of the Medusa* to England, where it toured with great success—indeed he became enthusiastic about English painting, painters, horses, and patrons—and he was intrigued by London's lowlife.

Back in France in 1820, he again turned down commissions. During a second visit to England he experienced a change of style, turning now to low-key, realistic scenes of life among the poor, and to production of numerous lithographic studies of daily life, including almost impressionistic views of the English horseracing scene. These provided needed income for his child's future. He also painted a remarkable series of portraits of the insane, compelling in their realism; these were not for sale; they amounted to a private experiment.

In 1822, a fall from a horse aggravated his already accelerating physical decline. Illness was accompanied by his increasing extravagance and imprudent investment. Riding accidents increased. About this time he again started to conceive large works on historical subjects but never went beyond sketches. Still in spurts of furiously aggressive riding, he further incapacitated himself, ultimately becoming an invalid. Bedridden in 1823, he came close to suicide. He was diagnosed as having a type of tubercular spinal decay. At this time his broker went bankrupt; his father's money helped to defray the loss. But life for Géricault had cost too much in every aspect: he died on January 26, 1824. He was 33 years old.

Thus may be summarized the final years of Géricault's life. Robert Hertzberg has left ample, often very condensed, notes concerning the ways in which he planned to treat the rest of the story he did not live to finish. He had planned the following chapters: *Salon de 1819; London-Paris-Brussels—London; Foundering; Portraits de Fous; Bedridden; Aftermath.* Perhaps the best way to outline his thoughts, especially about these last, unwritten chapters, is to quote from his outline of basic themes, defined at the outset of his work:

"Born in chaos—revolution and then mother's death—everything he does: his painting, cataloging studio [in obsessive detail]—retreat to torpor and to bed—even riding (controlling beast, sense of oneness) is an effort to control chaos, impose and create order, sense of unity. This begins to fall apart from London on . . .

"How, through art, he controls his inner violence and chaos. He has three modes: violent and self-destructive (Romantic—chaotic); energetic, diligent, and persevering in spurts—to control chaos. And then lethargic and idle, torpor. Alternate states of grandeur, recklessness, boundless energy, animality, violence—chaos—that he fights with seizures of compulsive drawing, fits of creativity—and then lassitude, lethargy, laziness . . . . depression, self-hatred. Riding, too, provides sense of unity.

"Vain man about town—Dandy—fashionable—flirt—musketeer, horseman, sportsman, debauchee—the outward image: come back to it over and over."

* * *

BIBLIOGRAPHY

Aimé-Azam. *La Passion de Géricault:* Paris, Fayard, 1970.

Aragon, Louis. *Holy Week.* New York: G.P.Putnam's Sons and Hamish Hamilton, Ltd. 1961.

Bazin, Germain. *Théodore Géricault: étude critique, documents et catalogue raisonné.* Paris: La Bibliothèque des arts, 1987-1997.

Berger, Klaus. *Géricault and his work.* Translated by Winslow Ames from *Géricault und sein Werk.* Lawrence, KS: University of Kansas Press, 1955.

Blot, Jean-Yves. *La Méduse: chronique d'un naufrage ordinaire.* Paris: Arthaud, 1982.

Bordonove, Geoges. *Le naufrage de la Méduse.* Paris : R.Laffont, 1973.

Borel, Richard. *Louis-Philippe et le romantisme.* Brochure, Collection "Les Grandes dates historique de France." Saint-Mandé (Seine): Éditions de la Tourelle, 1965.

Brookner, Anita. *Jacques-Louis David.* New York: Harper & Row, 1980.

Buisson, Gilles. *Géricault de Mortain à Paris ; Le Conventionnel Bonnesœur-Bourginière, oncle de Géricault.* Coutances : OCEP, 1976.

Byron, George Gordon Lord. *Don Juan.* Boston : Houghton Mifflin,1990.

___, *Prisoner of Chillon.* ***Mazeppa****, Lament of Tasso.* Oxford Plain Texts. Oxford: Clarendon Press, 1909.

Chedid, Andrée. *Géricault and Andrée Chedid, XIXe siècle. Collection Musées Secrets* (Paris). Charenton: Flohic, 1992.

Clément, Charles. *Géricault, étude biographique et critique avec le catalogue raisonné de l'oeuvre du maître.* Reprint of the definitive edition of 1879. Paris: L.Laget, 1973.

Corréard, Alexandre, and J.B.Henry Sauvigny. *Narrative of a Voyage to Senegal.* Marlboro, VT : Marlboro Press, 1986.

Courthion, Pierre, Introduction to *Géricault raconté par lui-même et par ses amis.* Vésenaz-Genève: P. Cailler, 1947.

Eitner, Lorenz, and Steven A. Nash. *Géricault, 1791-1824.* San Francisco: Fine Arts Museums of San Francisco, 1989.

_____. *An Outline of 19th Century European Painting—from David through Cézanne.* New York, Harper & Row, 1988.

_____. *Géricault—An Album of Drawings in the Art Institute of Chicago.* Text and Catalogue. Chicago: University of Chicago Press, 1960.

_____. *Géricault, his life and work.* London : Orbis Pub.,1983.

_____. *Géricault.* Catalog of an exhibition held at the Los Angeles County Museum of Art, Oct. 12-Dec. 12, 1971. Los Angeles: Los Angeles County Museum of Art, 1971.

_____. *Géricault's Raft of the Medusa.* London, 1972.

_____. *Neoclassicism and romanticism, 1750-1850 : an anthology of sources and documents.* 1st Icon ed. New York : Harper & Row, 1989.

Friedlaender, Walter. *David to Delacroix.* Cambridge, MA: Harvard University Press and London: 1952.

Géricault, Théodore. *Des Écoles de Peinture et de Sculpture et du Prix de Rome.* Pamphlet. Caen (France): L'Échoppe, 1986.

_____. *Géricault.* Numéro special de "Connaissance des Arts." Paris: 1991.

Goldwater, Robert, and Marco Treves. *Artists on Art from the XIV to the XX Century.* New York, Pantheon Books, 1945.

Grunchec, Philippe. *Tout l'oeuvre peint de Géricault.* Introduction par Jacques Thuillier; documentation et mise à jour par Philippe Grunchec. Paris : Flammarion, 1991.

_____. *Master Drawings by Géricault.* Washington, DC: International Exhibitions Foundation, 1985.

Honour, Hugh. *Romanticism.* New York: Harper & Row, 1979.

Laveissière, Sylvain, Regis Michel, and Bruno Chenique. *Gericault: [exposition] Galeries nationales du Gramd Palais.* Catalogue. Paris: Réunion des musées nationaux, 1991.

Mansel, Philip. *Louis XVIII*. London: Blond and Briggs, 1981.
Michel, Regis, ed. *Géricault / ouvrage collectif. Conférences et colloques.* Publ. par le Service culturel du musée du Louvre. Paris: la Documentation française, 1996.
Michelet, Jules. *Géricault*. Paris : l'Echappe, 1991.
Noel, Bernard. *Géricault*. Paris : Flammarion, 1991.
Office départemental d'action culturelle (Manche). *Autour de Géricault.* Catalogue, Exposition St. Lô. St. Lô: ODAC, 1990.
Rosen, Charles, and Henri Zerner. *Romanticism and realism : the mythology of nineteenth-century art.* New York : Viking Press, 1984.
Rosenthal, Léon. *Géricault*. Les maîtres d'art. Paris: Librairie de l'art ancient et moderne, 1905.
———. *La peinture romantique: essai sur l'évolution de la peinture française de 1815 à 1830.* Paris: L.H. May, 1906.
Sagne, Jean. *Géricault*. Paris] : Fayard, 1991.
Schneider, Michel. *Un rêve de pierre*: "le Radeau de la Méduse," Géricault. Paris : Gallimard, 1991.
Tinterow, Gary. *Géricault's Heroic Landscapes—The Times of Day.* New York: Metropolitan Museum of Art, 1990.
Vaughan, William. *Romantic Art.* New York : Oxford University Press, 1978.
Vigny, Alfred de. *Laurette, ou Le cachet rouge.* Edited, with an introduction and notes by Alcée Fortier. Boston: D.C.Heath & co., 1900.
Wind, Edgar. *Art and Anarchy.* New York: Alfred A. Knopf, 1963.
Zerner, Henry. "Mysteries of a Modern Painter," *New York Review of Books*, 5 March 1992.

Printed in the United Kingdom
by Lightning Source UK Ltd.
120089UK00001B/228